The Naked Tree

The Naked Tree

Pak Wan-so

Translated by
Yu Young-nan

East Asia Program
Cornell University
Ithaca, New York 14853

The Cornell East Asia Series is published by the Cornell University East Asia Program and is not affiliated with Cornell University Press. We are a small, non-profit press, publishing reasonably priced books on a wide variety of scholarly topics relating to East Asia as a service to the academic community and the general public. We accept standing orders which may be cancelled at any time and which provide for automatic billing and shipping of each title in the series upon publication.

If after review by internal and external readers a manuscript is accepted for publication, it is published on the basis of camera-ready copy provided by the volume author. Each author is thus responsible for any necessary copy-editing and for manuscript formatting. Submission inquiries should be addressed to Editorial Board, East Asia Program, Cornell University, Ithaca, New York 14853-7601.

About the Author

Pak Wan-so is the author of more than twenty novels, numerous short stories, and essays. She often deals with the themes of Korean War tragedies, middle class values, and women's issues. She is the recipient of highly acclaimed literary honors including the Korean Literature Award (1990), the Yi Sang Literature Award (1981), and the Korean Writers Award (1980).

About the Translator

Yu Young-nan has translated many English books into Korean and some Korean short stories and novels into English. She received the 1991 Korea Modern Literature Translation Award in the short story division with "Lesson One, Chapter One" written by Yi Mu-young and the same Award in 1992 in the novel division with *Farmers* by the same author.

Acknowledgments

The translation of *The Naked Tree* was undertaken with a grant from the Korean Culture and Arts Foundation in Seoul. After the promise of the grant, I contacted the author. Pak Wan-so didn't hesitate a moment when I asked which of her novels she wanted to see in translation. It was clear to me that she had a special attachment to her first book, written more than twenty years ago. A number of people helped me at various stages of translation. Laura Nelson read the very first draft and spent many hours with me, exchanging opinions and ideas, gently correcting me, and encouraging me all the way. Julie Pickering, a fellow translator and sometime collaborator, read both the original text and the translation. She had first-hand knowledge of the occupational hazard of our profession, namely frustration, and alleviated mine by sharing it. Maureen Karagueuzian and Diane Manuel edited the manuscript. More recently, Sally Gillis read it and provided me with valuable insights for improvement. My sister Young-mee Yu Cho spurred me along with her constant encouragement. Even after I had given up on the prospect of finding a publisher, she kept sending me information on publishers, including the Cornell East Asia Series. My husband Kim Seung-kyung, who was responsible for all the computer work in formatting, affably accepted my demands on his time. Finally, I am grateful to Cornell's Karen Smith for her help and flexibility.

One

A hand covered with tufts of thick brown hair thrust something in my face. It was a billfold, with a photo of a beaming young woman.

"Pretty," I said.

They expected lots of praise, but a languid response was all I could muster. Perhaps fatigue was getting to me this afternoon. After all, the GI seemed to be quite sensitive for someone so tall. Disappointed, he snatched the picture back and studied it carefully. His mouth spread into a grin, as if he felt reassured. I didn't want to miss a good chance for a sale, so I quickly turned on my professional charm.

"I've never seen anyone so pretty. You're lucky. Of course, you'll want a portrait for her. How about having it done on this silk scarf?"

I picked up a shimmery rayon scarf with a dragon silkscreened in one corner.

"No." He twisted his mouth and shook his head.

Then he walked to the showcase where a variety of silk fabrics, scarves, and handkerchiefs of different sizes were displayed. Without a moment's hesitation, he pointed to a handkerchief hardly bigger than my hand.

Cheapskate, I thought to myself. The handkerchief was the cheapest item we sold. The order would add up to only three dollars, including the cost of the portrait. I assumed a business-like manner, and asked the color of her hair, eyes, and dress; a must when dealing with black-and-white pictures.

"When do you want to pick this up?" I asked.

"As soon as possible. I've got to go back to the front the day after tomorrow."

Another headache for me. But I tried to put on a smile as I thought about the stack of order slips in my drawer, and changed the subject, trying to put a twinkle in my eyes.

"You must be enjoying your leave. Where are you stationed?"

"Goddamn Yanggu." He seemed to spit the words out, his face contorted in disgust.

"Too bad. How's the war going these days?" Another dumb question.

The corners of his mouth dropped, and he shrugged and lifted his arms, the typical Yankee know-nothing gesture. I was at a loss but decided to take a coquettish approach.

"Good paintings take a long time. For busy people like you, we have a special program. We can send it by mail, if you just give us her address and pay a nominal fee for the postage."

"No, you don't have to mail it. The painting is for me."

"Why don't you mail it to her? Everybody does that. Don't you want to make your girlfriend happy?"

Suddenly a peculiar lust exuded from his body.

"I just want to hug her picture. As soon as possible. Get it?"

He threw three crumpled one-dollar bills on the counter.

"See you the day after tomorrow," he said in a singsong voice before he left.

It had been cloudy and dark all day, and to make matters worse, the electricity was off. The four painters had been telling me they couldn't work well in the dim room. I dropped the order slip in the drawer set aside for quick deliveries and walked over to where the painters were sitting. With my hands loosely linked behind me, I urged them to get on with their work.

Then I threatened them. "I can't do it anymore. I can't stand the pressure every day. I'm going to tell President Choe we need more painters."

I could feel them all cringing, as if they were tiny fish squirming in my hand. It was understandable because the only time there was enough work to keep four painters busy was during the final week of every month when the American soldiers were paid. For the rest of the month orders only trickled in. Because the painters were paid by piece work, on slow days they all eyed me sadly, as if asking for the rare assignments.

Actually, I didn't think we needed more painters. Nor did I have anything against them personally. I just said nasty things to relieve my own irritation. My boss, President Choe, scolded me occasionally for referring to them as sign painters in such a condescending manner. He said it wasn't nice to look down on them. I wasn't contemptuous of them. I just couldn't find the right word for them, and it was easier to use a generic term.

If there was anybody I did look down on, it was Choe Man-gil, the one I called "President" Choe to his face, in a most respectful manner. About one-third of the first floor of the Eighth U.S. Army PX was reserved for Korean products, consigned to Korean merchants. According to President Choe, it was impossible to get the space without influence or shrewdness since it was wartime and everyone was so destitute and hungry. He bragged that others wished to set up shops selling embroidery, brassware, bamboo crafts, rubber shoes, leather and jewelry, but it had taken more than the ordinary business acumen on his part to come up with the idea of selling portrait paintings, which didn't require a particularly big investment of capital.

I called him "President Choe," or simply "President," often enough to keep him from becoming suspicious of my attitude. After all, he had opened the portrait shop in the middle of the first floor of the glittering PX. He'd hired signboard painters who worked for meals, he paid my wages, and he loved to be called "President." Every time I called him "President," the way he so greedily wanted to hear, I made a point of despising him all the more, as if that made us even. Suddenly the electricity came back on, and it was almost time to close the shutters.

"Shit! What a day!" Kim, one of the painters, rinsed his brush furiously in a murky liquid, and the others slowly began to straighten up their painting tools.

I gazed at the American products section on the opposite side of the PX, flooded with light. My heart ached with longing, as if I were watching a bright, exciting stage from the audience.

All those dazzling things, Made in USA, so lovely to look at. The salesgirls were making up their faces for the evening as the American goods sparkled behind them like a halo. I loved gazing at the glamorous scene.

After closing time the khaki uniforms that obstructed my view all day had ebbed away, and by the time the cleaning women had sprinkled water and mopped the tiled floor, the air had grown so transparent that I could distinguish the different colors of shiny lipsticks the salesgirls twisted up with such agility. Over time I learned that each of the girls, who had such exotic names as Diana Kim, Linda Cho, and Susan Chong, used a slightly different shade of lipstick. Still, I had not grown friendly with any of them.

I longed for a friend to walk home with, if only part way, but I couldn't seem to make friends, although at times it looked deceptively easy. When we lined up side by side in the narrow corridor, jostling as we waited our turn to be searched by the guards, we talked freely, our shoulders almost touching, drawn together by the sense that we were all victims of the unpleasant search. That bonding, however, was no different from the compressed air in a balloon. Once we were released through the gate, that was the end of it. Everyone dispersed without even saying goodbye.

The gloomy cold day was already wrapped in the darkness of early winter, dispensing with the formality of a sunset. The back alley, just past the gate, was unlit, and the dimly glowing glass door of the Japanese noodle shop opposite the gate accentuated the surrounding darkness. I walked briskly with short, quick steps until I reached the brightly lit market. A number of souvenir shops had sprouted up near the PX. I lingered as long as possible, trying to waste time looking at the things displayed in the shops, but they were hardly worth my interest. Red and yellow rayon scarves embroidered with the emblems of different divisions and companies, pipes, baskets, brassware.

When I reached the darkness at the end of the street, I began to run until I was gasping for breath.

Chungmu-ro, the busiest street in Seoul, was nothing more than a collection of unlit buildings and dark corners at this point in the war. Most of the monstrous buildings were unoccupied and some, like the Central Post Office building, stood with only their facades intact, the tops blown off by bombs and artillery. Fright swept over me at every dark corner, and the darkness brought home the reality that we were still in the middle of a war. I shuddered at the thought that "Goddamn Yanggu, Goddamn Chorwon and Munsan," as the Yankees were so fond of saying, were so close to where I stood. If only I could be far from those places. Somewhere like Taegu or Pusan, far from the war, where the houses still were brightly lit and the streets were thronged with crowds of people.

I walked in fits and starts until I broke into a sprint after Ulchi-ro, near the Hwashin Department Store. My heart constricted with fright, I ran through meandering alleys, lined with look-alike houses roofed in tile, alleys without lights, or corner stores to serve the neighborhood.

As I drew closer to my home, my eyes, which until then had taken in only the darkness, began to discern the dark sky studded with stars and my house, its corner distorted.

Then my fright peaked, as if my heart would stop at any moment.

"Mother! Mother!" I shook the gate so violently that the crossbar on the other side of the gate almost broke.

"I'm coming, coming. What's all the fuss? Tsk, tsk." My mother's voice called out in a slow, low tone as the heavy gate squeaked open.

"Mother, I told you to keep the lights on. Everywhere, the inner rooms, outer rooms, everywhere . . . "

"How will we pay the electricity bill, young lady?"

"I'm making money."

"All right, all right. I'll turn on the light in every room so the whole alley will be bright."

I knew better than to believe her, for she and I repeated the same conversation day after day. Holding her hand, I went through the middle gate and entered the yard where an old paulownia tree stood. The inner quarters remained out of sight, blocked by a stone wall. Entering the small gate in the middle of the stone wall put the spacious inner yard in full view. The area where the paulownia tree stood, which we called the "Middle Yard," was useless space. It was beyond me what beauty the ancestor who had designed our house saw in such space.

I glanced back at the collapsed servants' quarters before hurrying through the small gate in the middle of the wall. At this point, I let go of my mother's hand and rushed forward, like someone being chased, into the main room, the only lit place in the house. My mother clucked for no apparent reason and brought in the dinner tray even before my breathing settled back to normal. One whiff of her savory stew, and I suddenly felt safe.

"Why didn't you eat earlier?" I snapped irritably as my mother sat absently across from me while I dug into the rice.

Only then did she pick up her spoon with a slow motion. She moved slowly and noiselessly, chewing in her strange way, because she didn't have her false teeth in.

I lost my appetite before I had my fill, thinking that the act of eating was a cursed obligation. As I watched my mother chew, I placed my spoon on the tray and tried to swallow the waves of hatred that periodically welled up inside me. I didn't like my mother; in fact, I hated her.

I hated her mousy greyness. Her hair, streaked with white, looked grey, and her clothes were an exhausted grey, the color of a dirty dish towel.

But most of all, I couldn't stand her grey stubbornness. She never stopped thinking that she was alive only because she couldn't kill herself. Her obstinacy was terrifying.

My colorful ambitions, my desire to make life fun, swirled inside me but then withered when confronted by her obstinacy. My mother's stubborn shape, leaning against the grey wallpaper, and her toothless mouth set in an ugly line enraged me. I stood up and went into the other room, escaping.

The rectangular room, once used by my brothers Hyok and Wook, was too large to be lit adequately by a mere 30-watt bulb. Under its orange glow the corners of the room were still dark, and I shuddered violently. I could never get used to the depressing loneliness that surrounded me.

My mother told me that when I was small, from the time that I began to distinguish people's faces until I was four or five, I used to hide behind her skirt whenever I spotted a man clad in a dark Western suit. I couldn't remember how a dark suit appeared to my childish eyes but now, feeling as if I were no bigger than I was in those days, I wanted to hide from the dark giant of loneliness.

Some people are born with a penchant for loneliness, while others develop and then flaunt it, wearing loneliness like a badge or savoring it intermittently like a piece of candy. I didn't have that kind of flair. I liked many people and many things at the same time, and I constantly wanted to be swept away by one or the other of them. I was born that way and grew up that way.

"It was good in those days," I muttered like an old woman. I plucked the strings of the guitar hanging from the bedroom wall, but all I got was a low, depressing sound. So many things had sung in my brother Wook's hands, not just the guitar. Life back then seemed to have been filled with noisy, exciting sounds and countless, dangerous, dizzy colors.

So many things covered the walls; souvenir photos tacked straight or at angles, pictures of movie stars, awkward drawings, a few decent watercolors, postcards, baseball gloves stretched out like monsters, dirty Judo uniforms. Even the most clairvoyant shaman would have had a hard time divining the most cherished hobby of the room's former occupants. My brothers had always been busy, and how busy I had been along with them! There had been so many fascinating things scattered throughout Hyok's and Wook's world, and I had been so keen on taking part in whatever they were doing!

I had liked my brothers' merry friends who stopped by at all hours of the day, I had been engrossed in the same sports and popular music they indulged in, I had loved the movie stars they loved. And how we had all loved our mother who had such soft hands and who always cooked such delicious dishes for us!

After studying the disorderly display on the wall and plucking the guitar strings once more, I lay down on the floor on my stomach. Under my breasts I could feel a heavy sensation, like the pain of indigestion. I placed the pillow under the spot. I knew it was my heart, yearning to love someone or something, writhing within me. But what, how, and whom could I love? Who besides my brothers could help me find what was worthy of love, worthy of passion?

Even a worthless-looking friend used to inspire their praise. "He may not look like much but he's a national treasure when it comes to soccer," they'd say. Or "He looks like a jerk, but he's really brainy." As a result, I'd come to see their friends through their eyes and found that I could like them, too. I had accepted and understood things through my brothers' eyes. Without them both, how my mother had seemed to fade! If I had Hyok or Wook, I would have no problem finding Cezanne or van Gogh even in that painter Kim. I pressed my chest against the pillow under me, and lukewarm tears began to pool in my eyes.

The painters, President Choe, my mother, Diana Kim, Linda Cho. They all floated in dizzy confusion, as if I were looking at them with shortsighted eyes. Then, gradually, they became tiny dots, and I fell asleep.

Two

"Hi!"

"Hi!"

"Good Morning!"

"Good Morning!"

Crossing the arcade, which echoed with greetings, I spotted President Choe in front of the portrait shop as he raised his arm to me. Unnerved, I found it hard to hide my surprise.

I bowed and said, "You've come early. Is it Saturday already?"

"Do you think I only come in on payday? I should make a surprise inspection once in a while, shouldn't I?"

Choe usually appeared on Saturdays, grinning broadly. The dollars we'd earned for the week were exchanged for him in Korean won, in amazingly thick bunches, even after 20 percent was taken off for the use of the space.

Today certainly was not a Saturday, but Choe looked very happy and, as was always the case when he was happy, spoke in a boastful tone.

A tall, brawny middle-aged man stood next to Choe, smiling awkwardly, in stark contrast to our boss. He was wearing rather tight-fitting dyed army fatigues. An honest face revealed his good nature, and his tall, strong body and bright expression practically dwarfed Choe, whose well-cut Western suit and red tie suddenly looked vulgar. Amazed by the strange contrast, I returned the stranger's smile and pulled the order slips from my drawer, dividing them up roughly for the day among the four painters.

"Hold it, Miss Lee," said President Choe.

"Yes?"

"From now on, I've decided to use one more artist."

I looked back at the two men in surprise. Then this stranger is no more than a sign painter at his age, I thought.

"This is Mr. Ock Hui-do," said Choe, slapping the tall man's back, as if he were an old familiar friend. But perhaps because Choe was such a small man, the gesture looked inane and unbecoming.

Suddenly the threat I had made the day before had become a reality, and I could sense the other painters glaring at me.

"Well, we haven't had that much work recently," I said, "four was enough, and . . . "

7

I was about to protest in a voice loud enough to let the painters hear me, but Choe cut me off quickly.

"What talk! Am I not the owner of this portrait shop? From the beginning, my intention was to give a chance to unfortunate artists. More artists . . . "

"Ha!" I let a laugh slip at the words "unfortunate artists."

Whenever Choe took on someone new, he always lectured me gravely about "unfortunate artists," but by the time he let them go, he had derided them as "terrible painter bastards."

"What's so funny? Sooo, Miss Lee, you should try to understand my intentions and make an effort to increase the volume of business. The amount of work depends on your capability, right?"

It wouldn't have made any difference to him if we'd had ten painters. Sharing the same bowl of rice with still another painter was unfair, and because I felt sorry for them I was already doing everything I could to get additional orders. As a result, my skill in dealing with American soldiers had improved, and Choe Man-gil had steadily increased the number of painters. Business had grown little by little, and so had his income.

My favorable impression of the new painter evaporated. This well-built man was just another burden to me.

"Miss Lee," Choe whispered, "By now you should know how to make yourself attractive. How about working for a more sexy look, eh? If you had the right look, this shop could attract more customers, you know."

What did he want from me? Now that I'd had a chance to think about it, I could see that this puny boss of mine was no more than a persistent heavy weight on me.

"Well, Miss Lee, I'm busy, so I'll have to be going. Let's see. How about getting a new chair and asking the sergeant to issue a temporary pass? Take care, then."

From behind the screen where we hid mops, cans, basins, and the other inevitably messy paraphernalia of our work, I pulled out an old chair for the newcomer. When the chair squeaked and tottered under his weight, the man adjusted himself and found a more stable position.

"Shit!" groaned Kim, who was sitting next to the newcomer, dabbing the yellow hair in his portrait with a reddish-brown color.

Opposite them was "Cash." He was a Kim, too, but was differentiated from the former Kim by his nickname, since he was forever bringing up the subject of money. Cash mumbled as he shoved the memo I had attached to the back of a photo in front of my face.

"Miss Lee, what does this say? These mongrels have such grotesque hair colors!"

"Well, let me see." I tried to read what I'd scribbled down in one of my busier moments. "Yes, the hair is grey with a touch of silver, the eyes are blue with a touch of silver, and the clothes . . ."

"What mongrels!"

The painters clearly were out of sorts. All of them seemed angry at the newcomer and at me. Cash muttered "mongrels!" again, and Kim messed up the half-finished face in his portrait and fetched a new scarf, starting the sketch again.

"Shit! Nothing's going right today!" he complained.

If a painter ruined a scarf in anger, it was his loss because I made a point of recording the number of wasted scarves, canvases, and even handkerchiefs.

Ock Hui-do, whether or not he was aware of the painters' hostility, sat quietly with his back to us, gazing at the dingy curtain drawn over the empty display window. I pulled all the pictures out of my drawer to find some work for him, looking for something that would be easy to draw and didn't have to be delivered too quickly.

Faces, faces. All those foreign ladies' faces. Was it because they hadn't experienced a war raging about them that none of their faces betrayed a hint of worry? Their expressions didn't look human, nor did they look like animals. They looked more like gorgeous plants, or perhaps flowers in full bloom. Among them, I picked several who seemed to have notable characteristics and yet didn't have complicated hair or eye color.

"Will you start now?"

Ock turned his eyes from the window and answered quietly, "Thanks."

Then he took out of a brown bag all kinds of brushes. Thin, fat, flat, and round.

"My, did you bring your own brushes? We have brushes here. "

I explained the set-up as I glanced over at the useless-looking brushes we had sticking out of a can.

"We provide brushes and water colors. We provide cloth, too, but if you ruin any, you have to pay. If you ruin a scarf, that equals the cost of two paintings, so if you make a mistake, it's like working for nothing for a whole day. Still, we don't count the cost of watercolors for the ruined stuff, so maybe it's not such a bad deal. Oh, and if a customer isn't happy with the painting, we work on it until he's satisfied. Sometimes we have to do it all over again. Anyway, the most important thing is to draw as realistically as possible. Am I making myself clear?"

He nodded like a child, without answering. His eyes met mine momentarily. Shocked, I quickly shifted my eyes away. I felt like I had caught a glimpse of a wasted landscape.

As he settled down to sketch, he sometimes cocked his head to one side and said to himself, "Realistic, realistic," as if he were chanting. I could not trust him yet, so I went to stand next to him between customers, to take a look at his work and read my scribbles for him.

"You don't want to worry too much about making it exactly alike. If there's a little difference, say, if you could make a woman a little prettier than the photo, that's all right. You have to get the hang of it, you know."

"Well, you don't get the hang of it overnight. Some people had to work for years to get it," sneered Chin, who was usually quiet.

"Um . . . do you have any experience in this kind of painting?" I asked.

"Sure, I'm a painter."

"Oh, then you used to be . . . you must have been working for a movie theater."

"No. This is my first job. I was just a painter before."

Just a painter? Just a painter? I pondered his words, but soon was distracted by the busy routine as the Yankees began to stream in, one after another.

"Would you have a look at this?" The newcomer asked as he stood up, holding his first work, as shy and anxious as a well-behaved elementary school boy standing in front of his teacher.

His work was quite good. But instead of saying it looked all right, I smiled and told him I would ask the sergeant for his pass.

I went up to a group of American soldiers who were browsing at the display case and struck up a friendly conversation. I asked if they had girlfriends, and said, if so, there was no better way to show affection than to send a scarf with her portrait on it.

If any showed even a flicker of interest, I expressed my desire to see the handsome man's girlfriend. Once they took out their billfolds with their girlfriends' pictures in them, I was sure that I would get an order or two. Today I let not even one man slip away; I persisted until they placed an order, if only for a handkerchief portrait. The pressure of an extra mouth to feed made me more aggressive than ever.

Later I counted the dollars, considerably more than we'd taken in on other days, and made sure the sum was correct by examining the sign-up sheets. By the time I came back after depositing the money in the office and getting the temporary pass I had requested earlier from the sergeant, all the painters had gone except for Ock Hui-do, who was dabbing his well-washed brushes with cloth.

"Here's the pass," I said.

"Thank you for everything."

He took the pass, a type-written card no bigger than a business card adorned with a signature which looked like a crawling worm, and carefully buried it in his inside pocket.

"Shall we go?" he asked brightly, the fat brush bag under his arm.

"Why don't you leave the brushes here?"

I had begun to like him, I decided as I straightened up the items the other careless painters had left behind.

"My hand feels empty without them. Besides, they are precious to me." He said this without a hint of a smile.

Before leaving, he helped me line up the desks and chairs.

"Where do you live?" he asked.

"Kyae-dong."

"Then you can't take any public transportation, I guess."

"That's all right. I always walk."

"I live in Yonji-dong, but let me walk you to your neighborhood."

"I'm really all right. Don't worry about me. Just catch your ride and be on your way."

Without any more discussion, he walked beside me, his steps heavy from his army boots. In the depressingly cold weather, so typical of the winter *kimchi*-making season, the souvenir shops that catered to American soldiers were empty, even though it was still early in the evening. Gaudy embroidered pajamas fluttered about desolately, hanging from the eaves of a shop, and next to it a hawker, who had been busy calling out for Yankees earlier, stood hunched, dozing in the cold. I raised the collar of my raincoat and shrugged my shoulders. The smooth touch of the fabric on the nape of my neck gave me goose bumps.

Right in front of us a tall, gawky American soldier and a Korean woman strolled side by side, the woman leaning her upper body toward him. A man and woman together at least didn't look cold. Perhaps they had fallen in love because they were cold. I passed the dark alley without feeling scared, toying with the idea of falling in love with Ock Hui-do because I was so cold.

"You said you live in Kyae-dong. Where's your hometown?"

"Seoul."

"You're lucky. I'm from the north. Hwanghae-do Province. It was a good place." His voice suddenly sounded plaintive.

"Well, I have to go this way," I said, "I just remembered an errand I have to run."

I took the street leading to Myong-dong, although I didn't have a thing to do there. What he had been about to say was crystal clear. He was from the north, he lived a good life there. Of course, it couldn't have been like this. It was good then. How many times had I endured rambling talk of that kind? The monotonous words my mother chanted, the bragging of the painters babbling with spit foaming at the corners of their mouths, the empty words of longing people uttered, whether they were cleaning women or day laborers. Of course, it wasn't like this back then. It was good then. I didn't have the patience to hear them out because I thought delusions about the past were more miserable, in worse taste, than delusions about the future.

Myong-dong was bright and crowded. Every store had a display window. I stared longingly at the warm, soft winter coat a slender mannequin was wearing and stopped in front of a toy stall to see a playful chimpanzee that poured whisky into a cup before bringing it to his mouth.

I stood in the darkness once more. A black cathedral towered against the skyline. I longed to pray for something but I couldn't think of anything that I wanted to pray for.

Maria, who would know it but you.

Something surged up from inside of me.

Maria, only you would know.

A sense of innocent longing shrouded my frozen body.

Maria, who would know it but you.
Maria, only you would know.

What came next? I found myself trying to remember the words of the poem I used to recite. When I realized that I was just mimicking the poet and borrowing his feelings, the fun disappeared. Only the things that were mine, without any pretention, were left. Feelings of fright and coldness. They were the only feelings I had, incredibly vivid and strong. I broke into a run down the dark street. Repeating "I'm scared, I'm scared," I fled as if pursued.

Three

The box lunch, cold hardened rice in a small rectangular aluminum container, could be finished in several mouthfuls after dividing it into bite-size pieces with my chopsticks. Even this quick lunch was not welcome at the PX. There were no restrictions on employees having lunch there, but most people ate out. The employees at the Korean products section, who couldn't generate any extra income, were the ones who had to endure the embarrassment of cold box lunches. We all did similar work in the same building, but our lives were as different as the origins of our products. I wolfed down my lunch in a corner of the employees' rest area, a makeshift nook shielded by thin boards on four sides, and rinsed my mouth carefully with cold water to get rid of the embarrassing *kimchi* smell.

The rest area was a rest area in name only. It had a lone bench and a mirror and was mainly used when the girls reapplied their makeup or when the cleaning women changed their clothes.

"Have some gum."

Diana Kim entered the rest area with a large purse slung from her shoulder and offered me a piece of gum. She began to chew a piece herself.

"You look like you've already finished your lunch. I was thinking of buying something good for you today, Miss Lee."

"What?" was all I could come up with.

I didn't want to look too humble in these humiliating situations, but not being a sociable person, I only managed to look disappointed.

"Do you have something to tell me?" I asked.

She's going to talk about that again, I thought, feeling a surge of boredom. I assumed a look of nonchalance, spat the gum onto a tissue and rolled it up.

"It's come again. Well, I need to answer this time. What should I do?"

She tore off a multicolored wrapper and poked a ring-like candy into my mouth. I liked the tart candy that made my tongue contract, but I felt crabby.

We had gotten to know each other because of our similar shortcomings. She could speak English like an American woman (at least to my ears) but she couldn't read or write, while I knew only the phrases that were needed at the portrait shop.

A few days earlier, an American soldier who had come to pick up a portrait had started to complain. When he said the picture didn't even remotely resemble his sweetheart, I apologized, making clear that we would do it again. However, he kept talking a mile a minute in his excitement, and I couldn't understand anything he said. I tried to save face in front of the painters by pretending to understand him, inserting a word or two here and there. He finally exploded, after realizing that we were talking about two completely different things. He shouted, and I was almost in tears when Diana Kim materialized, almost miraculously.

She approached, her high-heeled shoes clicking on the cement floor, and with only a few words, dismissed him. Then she looked down at me with contemptuous but, nevertheless, sympathetic eyes. I thanked her in the confusion of the moment, and trying to minimize my embarrassment, I said I sometimes had difficulty because the English I had learned at school was so different from spoken English. I wanted to show that I was not really an ignorant girl. When I sensed that she was interested in my excuse, I boldly lied that I had been an English literature major at E College before the war, but then the war broke out, et cetera, et cetera.

She sounded very surprised when she said, "Oh, my goodness, we have a lot in common."

"What do you mean?"

"You're half-dumb, although your eyes can catch the writing, and I can speak, but unfortunately I'm blind as a bat when it comes to reading English. Interesting, isn't it?"

I didn't understand why it was interesting, but I took on the job of reading and answering the letters she received from her boyfriend back in America. That's how I ended up paying for my lie.

Diana said she knew lots of girls who could read and write, but they were all so gossipy and sly, having been exposed to that kind of thing for so long. For that reason I was perfect for the job, she said.

While I was reading the letters which began with "My darling Diana" and going on about how heartbroken he was without her and how he missed her so, Diana kept filing her long, beautiful fingernails, cracking gum loudly. Blocked by her thick eyelashes, the expression in her eyes couldn't be seen. She had to concentrate on her nails, but the bags under her eyes revealed her age.

My darling Diana, we won't be separated for long. I will think of a way to bring you to America, whatever it takes. I love you. I need you.
Your faithful Bob.

She didn't betray any reaction but simply admired her nails, gorgeous as a cactus flower, and yawned widely, saying, "Is that all? Christmas is almost here, but he hasn't mentioned a present."

The opening of her round throat was revealed, as desolate as a doorway to an empty room, a bleak room devoid of both suffering and ecstacy.

"Write a letter for me. Don't act so prim, eh?"

"I don't know how to write that kind of letter."

"You mean you don't have experience? Don't pretend to be so innocent. Just write something. Hot and passionate, how's that? And how can we drop a subtle hint about the present?"

The cleaning women entered, pushing a large trash box in front of them. They hitched up their skirts, pulled down their underwear, took out endless tubes of toothpaste and bars of soap from the trash box, and stacked them up on their calves, tying each row tightly with an elastic band. They heaped up the goods tier after tier, pulled up their underwear, and in no time they were fat with a layer of goods reaching from their calves, over their buttocks, to their waists.

They pulled their skirts back down, put on their coats, and swaggered out. They were on their way to make an illegal transaction during the lunch hour. They were experts at the smuggling act but managed to look as clumsy and dense as before. Another group of women, who had already finished their transactions, came in as if they were simply returning from lunch, walking slowly with humdrum expressions. Diana Kim and the other salesgirls flocked around them, sharing dollars and a fat wad of Korean won in a brisk, efficient manner. Diana seemed to be out of sorts over the distribution. She had a brief quarrel before stuffing a wad of money into her large bag.

"If you behave like this, I'll see you don't get another taste of it. If you don't do it my way, I'll do it myself."

"Don't be silly. How can you put anything over this waist?" A woman circled an arm around Diana's slender waist, but Diana's eyes glistened coldly under her stiff eyelashes.

During the confusion, I put down the letter from Bob and ran from the rest area, galloping down the stairs. The rattle of the container inside my empty lunch box echoed gloomily. I shook the box at Misuk, who was at the brassware section in front of my shop, and sat down in my chair.

In the Korean products section, the larger stalls for jewelry and embroidery had several employees, but the brassware and the portrait sections had only one salesgirl each. Misuk and I always watched each other's shop during lunch break.

"What kept you so long? I couldn't wait until you came down, so I just gobbled up my lunch crouched behind the display box."

I suddenly felt curious about this girl who was two years younger than me, with her shiny hair braided into two pigtails and those healthy cheeks. Would she be bleak inside?

"Will you yawn for me?" I asked.

"Can you yawn on demand? I've yawned enough today, though, because there wasn't much business."

"Then open your mouth. Say ahhh."

Without asking why, she opened her mouth widely. I could see the vivid pink of its inside and the hanging uvula. She immediately closed her mouth and went back to her shop, where an American soldier was browsing. I sat without knowing what to do, disgust rising up in my throat as I thought of Diana's empty room and Bob's love letter that was like a telephone ringing there.

I wasn't sure if it was myself that I hated, or the others, or both. Whatever it was, I wanted to crumple the dingy scenery around me, myself included, and toss it away like rubbish.

"Shit!" His short, fat brush oozing with red, Kim was about to ruin the picture he had just finished, but then thought better of it. He swallowed his fury and threw the brush aside instead. He lit a cigarette.

"What grotesque mongrels!" Cash said as he felt about in his pockets for a cigarette. Then he made a clicking sound with his tongue. "What mongrels! Do you happen to have a butt?"

"If they're such mongrels, why do you keep painting their damn faces?"

"I'm just asking you for a butt. Besides, can't you figure it out? I do it for money. For money. Do you paint as a hobby? Do you do it because it's art?"

"Yes, it's art for me. A houseboy can play the role of a boss, so why can't a sign painter be an artist?"

"So you have a mouth to talk, all right. Don't act so dim. I'm just asking if you have a butt."

"If I had one, I'd have given it to you instead of teasing you. Hey, Miss Lee, why don't you grab yourself a Yankee and ask him to buy a carton of Lucky Strikes? It would be easy if you just put your mind to it."

"Miss Lee always acts so high and mighty."

They had shifted the target of their attack in my direction. But I smiled without answering them, for I could guess that they, too, wanted to crumple up everything around them. Ock Hui-do put down his brush, slapped each of his shoulders several times, and turned toward the window in an exhausted way. The window was nothing but a space; once a display window, the wood had been removed to enlarge the space, and it was covered with a grey curtain, so no one could look in from outside. Nothing could be seen, but he sat facing that grey curtain as if he were enjoying an unfamiliar view.

I was thinking of raising the curtain a little for him when Diana Kim patted my shoulder, smiling. "I just came up with a great idea. It hit me when I was looking into this direction."

"What is it?"

"If I want to milk a present from him, I might as well give him a present first. Something inexpensive but wonderful. How's that sound? What if I send him my portrait?"

"Well, I don't know."

"I'm sure it will work. It's a perfect idea. Which of them is the best?"

She shoved her face closer to my ear, lowering her voice, and a strange smell, a mixture of fragrances, overwhelmed me. I pulled away hastily and, without thinking, pointed to Ock Hui-do.

I instantly regretted it. With loud clicks of her spike heels, she was marching towards him.

She said, "You've got to draw my portrait as fast as you can. You'd better do a good job because it's for my sweetheart in America."

I couldn't hear what he said.

"Oh, my! You don't have to be so high and mighty. I'll pay as much as the Yankees. I'll give you six dollars directly instead of paying the cashier. In dollars. It's all yours. Still, you won't do it?"

Ock didn't answer.

"Why are you hesitating? Just sketch me quickly. What? Bring a picture in? Gosh! What nonsense! You simply can't deal with these sign painters. You want a photo when the real person is standing right in front of you? Don't you know what a model is, huh? Let me see your samples, anyway."

She flicked through the portraits Ock Hui-do had drawn, comparing them with the photos, chattering nonstop and tilting her head this way and that.

"You should have played up this feature, but you simply ruined it. And in this one, you made the woman look ten years younger than the photo and it's probably already ten years old! One of these days you'll get it for painting these pictures. Do you think the Yankees are that stupid?"

I couldn't see Ock Hui-do because she was blocking my view, and I couldn't hear what he was saying. But I was so embarrassed by my mistake that I didn't dare to get closer.

"If you really want a photo, that's just as well. I don't have time to be your model, anyway. I'll bring in a photo tomorrow. You make it really sexy so that my sweetheart will go crazy for me."

She walked away, winking at me. My eyes met Ock's and stayed there for a long time. Exhaustion and depression were reflected in his eyes, momentarily overwhelming his good nature, and I felt his depression stab me. I recovered from the momentary pain but felt sorry for him for a long time.

On the way home I followed him quickly because he had left a little earlier than I did. I wanted to do something for him, like listen to his tale of the good old times that I had interrupted several days before.

"You must have been angry because of that woman. I'm sorry."

"No, not really."

"I didn't mean to do that. It was an accident," I stammered, "I had no idea she would behave so rudely."

"What's the problem? She promised a good price for a picture. You're acting a little strange today."

Come to think of it, perhaps I was the one who was strange. If Diana Kim had talked that way to Kim or Cash, would I have given it a second thought? I tried to be indifferent to Ock Hui-do's feelings, but a strange sense of loss remained in my heart.

Under a tacked-up proclamation issued by the Marshal Law Enforcement Headquarters, a newspaper boy was hawking tomorrow morning's newspaper in a drawling tone. Next to the boy an old woman was counting money, smoothing the crumpled bills in front of her piles of American cigarettes. Ock Hui-do bought a newspaper from the boy and glanced at the headlines by the light that streamed out of a shop, but he soon folded it up roughly and shoved it into his pocket.

Puppet Army Ready for Major Attack, the headline read.

"I hope this winter passes without trouble," Ock Hui-do mumbled.

I was about to say something but decided not to. I sensed that his mood belonged to him alone tonight.

The sound of artillery reverberated in the northern sky. My heart fluttered with fright. I didn't believe peace would come as either a victory or a cease-fire. I expected the war to continue, sweeping repeatedly up and down the peninsula. Everyone was foolishly hoping for peace, but it wouldn't work that way. The war would end only after disaster had engulfed everyone. The war wouldn't wrong only me and my brothers Hyok and Wook. A crazed, shrill longing and at the same time a fear of the war; I was always unbalanced and exhausted because of the conflict that raged within me.

Four

An electrician who had been changing light bulbs here and there had finally come to the one that had been off for several days on the ceiling above my desk. I retrieved my chair which was right under his ladder, placed it at one corner of my desk, and started taking care of the things I had to do.

Choosing the photos to be distributed to the painters, picking a few decent portraits to be placed in the display case, separating the ones to be sent up to the wrapping department on the second floor, copying the addresses the customers had left and attaching them to the bundles sent down from the wrapping department to be taken back to the second floor where the post office was located. I knew my routine well.

"Miss, excuse me," the electrician called from the top of his ladder with a sheepish smile. "I'm sorry, but could you hold the ladder?"

I held one leg of the upside-down V and looked up at him. The ladder was sturdy and stood firmly on the tiled floor. It wouldn't have wobbled a bit if I hadn't held it for him, but he kept worrying. He turned the screwdriver, removing the milky bulb cover and sticking it under his arm. He looked down again and said, "Hold it tight, okay?" He looked apprehensive.

"Don't worry," I said, spreading out my arms to hold the two legs firmly.

He was so frightened of falling that he might have tumbled down on his own accord if I had taken my hands away. It was clear that he had not been an electrician very long. This isn't the right job for him, I thought. He unscrewed the old bulb, put it in the pocket of his work clothes, took a new one from another pocket, put it in, and started to replace the cover. He must have screwed the bolts in crooked because the cover didn't fit. He kept working on it, and his posture grew more stable as he lost his self-consciousness.

He didn't look down again, but I looked up at him, while he was totally absorbed in his work. It was a new experience for me to observe someone standing directly above me.

His Adam's apple, that unique male feature, and his firm square jaw with its shadow of beard sent sweet vibrations through me unexpectedly. While he was fretting over the work he couldn't do well, the feelings I was experiencing for the first time were transformed into a more concrete desire. I wanted to lean my forehead on that shadowy chin. The image brought a tickling sensation to my forehead, and a refreshing pleasure spread throughout my body.

"Well, I'm coming down. Hold on tight, please."

He was steadier coming down than he had been climbing up.

"Thank you. It will take me a while to get used to the work," he said, scratching his head in mortification.

To my great surprise, his face was quite ordinary from the front. I felt as if I had somehow been duped.

"Why are you looking at me like that?" he asked, stopping in the midst of folding his ladder.

I rubbed my tingling forehead and said, "You looked totally different from below. You looked like a real fool, but face to face you don't look like one at all."

I was making it up, but he flushed like a boy and said, "I was shaky because today's my first day at work. I'll get used to it."

He folded the ladder and walked toward the shop across the way.

Ock Hui-do had been drawing Diana's six-dollar portrait since early that morning. He had the airbrushed photo in front of him, but the portrait he was drawing was much closer to the real Diana.

"Why don't you make it more like the photo?" I muttered as I hovered over him.

Kim ridiculed him. "Do you think you'll get anything out of it? If you are paid five times more, you'll have to work ten times harder."

Cash butted in as if he were afraid of losing a chance for a wisecrack, "It's always easier to draw mongrels than a full-blooded Korean."

"Full-blooded Korean? How can you call a Yankee slut a full-blood?"

"What an ignorant man! What's full-blood got to do with what happens between man and woman? All that matters is the parents' blood."

They're at it again, I thought.

Cash launched into a tirade about the purity of Korean blood and the mixed-blood of the Yankees, foaming at the mouth and sprinkling in obscenities.

By and by Ock finished Diana's portrait and pounded his shoulders on each side, much longer than usual, his eyes fixed on the grey curtain. Cash's theory of Korean superiority grew cruder and more obscene, and the other painters, who enjoyed it more than his other half-baked theories, helped him along by joking and agreeing with him. Ock's back remained a rock, devoid of emotions.

Suddenly, I hoped Ock Hui-do would be different from the others. He's not like the others. He's not like the others. I clung to the idea like an insect's sensitive feeler that has found a source of honey.

"It was nice of you to help me out this morning. I'd like to invite you to a tea room. Would that be all right?"

The electrician, whom I met on my way home, said it so sweetly that I agreed. "Of course."

As we walked side by side, I studied his profile from his jawline to the neck. I wanted to experience the same tingling sensation that I had felt in the morning but couldn't. He was a little taller than me, medium height for a man, so I was not looking up at him. His face, from the front, was thoroughly ordinary.

As soon as we sat down at a corner table in the Utopia tea room, he said, "My name is Hwang Tae-su." Then he added in English, "And You?"

"I'm Lee Kyong. My given name has only one syllable, so people call me Kyong-a."

We smiled and I thought we had become instant friends.

"When you look down from the top, do you see anything out of the ordinary?" I asked.

"The top?"

"The top of a ladder."

"Well, it was my first time, so my legs wobbled and I couldn't enjoy the scenery below. But what's the big deal about the top of a ladder? If you think of looking down at the world, there's always the second floor, the third floor, a highrise building, and of course high positions in the government."

"Still, I think it would look different from the top of a ladder."

"Why do you keep talking about the ladder? It's unlucky, you know."

"Then why did you choose working on a ladder as your job?"

"Choose? I hardly chose it. To choose means being picky. Who's lucky enough to be picky about a job these days? I just squeezed in when there was an opening."

"Well, you didn't mind trembling on top of a ladder, so you managed to squeeze into this PX."

"Oh, well." He scratched his head.

"Are you a draft dodger?" I asked sharply.

PX workers, of course, didn't enjoy the privilege of military exemption but they wore military uniforms and rode American commuter buses to work, so I had heard that draft dodgers flocked to the PX for jobs.

"Far from it. I may not look like it, but I was given an honorable discharge because I was wounded."

"I don't believe it. How could you get an honorable discharge with four strong limbs?"

"I look all right on the outside, but I have a horrible wound on my thigh. It still hurts sometimes."

He drew his eyebrows together and pressed his thigh as if it really hurt. "Really? Does it hurt right now?"

"Nooo," he grinned and straightened out his eyebrows. Then he slurped the barley tea and called the waitress to ask for a match, winking at her. He looked frivolous, and I wasn't sure whether or not he had told the truth.

He lit a cigarette, exhaled the smoke expertly, and said, "Well, I did what I could for my country and I didn't want to think about saving face, so I ran around trying to find a job. I ended up as an electrician at the PX, but that doesn't matter. I've seen lots of money changing hands. I want to be part of it. I have no other ambitions. I just want to save enough to continue school after the war, like all the others, without worrying about money. I've struggled. I came down from the north. I have only two more years of college to go, so after the war I'll graduate and get a job at a good place. I'll gain trust in a few years and then respect in a few more. What do you think?"

"It seems a bit boring."

"I knew you'd say that. One needs to brag in front of women. I just spill out a bunch of ordinary ideas."

He smacked his lips a couple of times and stretched his arms as he leaned his head against the back of his chair. The firm, square jaw, the shadow of beard, and his sturdy neck came into view, and I was again stirred by a refreshing emotion.

I flushed, drank up my barley tea to squash my shame, and rubbed my forehead briskly as it began to tickle. He straightened his head, his face returning to its ordinary state again, and asked, "How about you, Miss Lee? How's the portrait shop? Isn't it dull?"

"I don't work as a hobby, either. I am serious about making a living."

"You're still a student, aren't you? Last year of high school? A college student?"

I didn't want to go into the story about how I had failed the college entrance examination and spent several months in despair before the war broke out.

"The war has broken down the order of things so people experience strange things," he said, "People meet in strange places. Isn't that more natural? It seems like a tragedy to cling to an old sense of self in wartime."

"What do you mean?"

"Like Ock Hui-do. I'd heard he was working at the portrait shop but when I saw him, I felt strange. Of course, he only knows painting, but . . ."

"Do you know him then?"

I was astonished. Thinking back, though, I recalled that he had exchanged greetings with Ock when he passed through our shop with his folded ladder.

"He's more than an acquaintance, I should say. We're from the same hometown, and he was very close to my eldest brother. They still meet sometimes."

"What did he do?"

"I just told you. He only knows painting. He came to the south during the latest evacuation, so maybe he's not well-known here yet, but informed people should know about him. He won the national prize several times during the Japanese occupation. Maybe he even got one of the grand prizes, too."

"Then you mean he's a real artist?"

I had never dreamed Choe's "unfortunate artists" would include a real artist.

"I've always thought he was a born artist. He couldn't be anything else. I crossed the 38th parallel right after the liberation, but he remained until recently because he has a big family. I sometimes wonder what he had to do up there in order to survive. Maybe he had to draw a portrait of Kim Il-Sung or something. If that's the case, then knowing nothing but painting is a tragedy, isn't it?"

I thought back to when I had asked Ock Hui-do what he used to do. He had simply said, "I am just a painter."

"I heard he has five children. He should have thought of something else to do. Instead he's still painting."

He's different and he's not like you, I thought.

"Luckily his wife is competent, so she's managing somehow."

He's not like the others, but nobody knows it, and a competent wife would only nag him competently, I thought.

"My brother says his wife was a real beauty once."

"Let's go."

I stood up and left the tea room ahead of him. A cold gust of wind swept through my hair. I stopped to wrap it in a scarf.

"Why are you upset?"

Tae-su hurried to catch up with me, put his face closer to mine, and straightened my hastily wrapped scarf and pulled my bangs in a friendly way.

"You don't know how to wrap your hair properly."

I felt he was being too friendly too quickly, but I ignored it and said, "Goodbye. See you tomorrow."

"I'd like to walk you home."

"That's all right. I want to go alone."

Alone, I calmly accepted the pity and affection I felt for Ock Hui-do and his stubbornness. Both feelings crept into me like the darkness.

At home my uncle was waiting for me.

"Why would any girl want to roam about until this hour? Why did you have to get a job? What a shameful thing to do! Why can't you just stay home before getting married like a good girl?"

He started scolding me before I had time to greet him properly. I knew my uncle was not worried about me at all. He just thought he was supposed to behave that way. He thought it was an elder's obligation to find fault with the younger generation, especially when there was no male in the house. As the head of the clan, he thought it was his duty to be more particular and meddling, a role well-suited to someone who was concerned with the well-being of his flock.

"When did you arrive in Seoul?" I asked.

"Today. I should come up more often, but it's not easy with the documents they require for crossing the river and things like that."

I simply smiled, not feeling particularly sorry for him. I knew that he had just dropped in at my house after checking on his own house.

"I was about to discuss this with your mother, but why would two women want to live in a haunted house like this? When you wanted to come up to Seoul, I consented without much thought because I wasn't settled in myself, but I can't sit back and watch you live like this. This house isn't fit for sane people! Why don't you come down to Pusan with me? If not your mother, at least, you, Kyong-a."

He stopped and looked at my mother, but when she didn't react, he went on, "If you don't like that idea, how about going to my house and staying there? I'm sure we can't find a buyer for this house, but we could just lock it up. My house is much cozier."

He must be having a problem with the people watching his house, I decided. They probably used things from his storeroom, helped themselves to the quilts he had tied and put up in a high place, and sold soy sauce and red bean paste from his jars. I could imagine all that without being told.

"My heart aches when I see the way your servants' quarters have been destroyed. It must be hard for you. But Sister-In-Law, how can you live in this haunted house? In the house where that horrible tragedy . . ."

"But where can I go? I'm going to die in this house, too."

"Why are you talking about death already? What about Kyong-a? You should live long and share Kyong-a's happiness."

My mother smiled but didn't answer. It was an empty smile in which I could see something like wisdom. I realized that she wouldn't be an obstacle to her daughter's happiness.

"Well, I don't know, I'm just suggesting it for your sake."

"Why? Don't you like the people who are looking after your house?" I couldn't resist saying it.

"Well, they stole the most valuable things, and whenever I come, they behave as if I were a charity case. What a shameless . . ."

"You shouldn't worry about it. Isn't there something wrong when some people flee, while others are left behind to look after their belongings?"

"Did I ask them to watch over our things? They volunteered. They should feel grateful and behave like decent people. I didn't mean to ask you to come to my house to watch over it. This haunted house . . . "

"Are my cousins all well?"

"Yes, Jin received a medal and was promoted to the rank of lieutenant colonel. He's been sent to a very good post, but Min is performing his military duty in name only. Thanks to his brother, he's got it easy. Nan and Mal go to school. Their main complaint is not having a piano at home, but who doesn't experience some hardship as a refugee?"

His children hadn't been hurt in the slightest during the war. He looked happy at that moment. His happiness seemed to be perfect compared to my family. Perhaps happiness was tastier when sprinkled with others' misfortunes.

"They talk about you a lot. They ask why you can't live with them, instead of living here like this. Mal misses you the most."

"I miss her, too," I said just to be polite.

In my heart, however, a nasty thought swirled. The war isn't finished yet. It will continue many, many years, and disaster will strike everybody equally. I just happened to receive my share earlier than others.

"You must be tired. Why don't you go to bed?" I said to my uncle.

After spreading out a mat for him in my room, I lay down beside my mother for the first time in a long while. Still, we had little to talk about. My mother let out a low sigh.

"Did Uncle give you any money?" I asked.

"Yes. He said it was for our living expenses."

"How much?"

"I don't know. It's over there. You can count it later."

"Did he eat here?"

"Yes."

"What did you cook for him?"

"Nothing special. I just served what we usually eat."

Had my mother, once such an expert hostess, become demented?

"What did he say about my job?"

"He complained that we'll have a hard time marrying you off now that you're working there."

"Do you think so, too?"

"No."

I turned my back to her. My uncle's cough filtered through the walls intermittently from the other room, as if he couldn't fall asleep either. I couldn't tell whether my mother was asleep or not as I couldn't sense even her breathing.

The bleak wind set the shutters clattering, and the sliding door hummed. The wind swished through the house, making grotesque sounds here and there.

I pulled the quilt over my head.

Still, I could hear the wind, the wind that shook the haunted house, that rushed through the hole on top of the roof of the servants' quarters, that trampled the broken tiles, that shuffled through the broken pieces of the rafters, that dislodged the clay underneath, that shook the loose wallpaper and spider webs, that stirred the piles of dirt. The sound of the wind rattled my eardrums mercilessly, even when I put my hands over my ears.

I couldn't help but think of Ock Hui-do. He's different from the others, he's different from the others, I chanted. Perhaps I was attempting to knock on the door to a new life by repeating it.

Five

A Christmas tree stood in the center of the arcade, and colored lights flashed on the Santa Claus and the four reindeer that pulled his sleigh. The arcade was bustling more than ever, packed with shoppers, and the Korean products section was in utter confusion. Housecoats and pajamas with embroidered dragons and peacocks on them sold like hotcakes, and the small flower baskets were gone in no time. The owners of the Korean products section enjoyed the unprecedented business, and the salesgirls in the American products section were indiscreet in their restlessness, making dates with GIs, talking about the coming parties, and bragging about the presents they would receive from America.

Outside the PX, the streets were as desolate as ever, weighed down by the dark, anxious atmosphere of a city so close to the front line. Nobody was stupid enough to be caught up in the spirit of a foreign holiday.

The portrait shop was doing a good business as well, and I kept busy with my work the whole day, but I made some stupid mistakes because my heart fluttered at intervals. I was fraught with anxiety. Mine was not like the others' Christmas-season excitement, however, and my anxiety wasn't solely due to the war or the darkness in the streets.

I had begun to think I was in love with Ock Hui-do. The thought was painful at times, sweet at others, and frightening once in a while. I couldn't figure out exactly what my feelings were, but I couldn't drive the idea out of my mind.

Tae-su bustled around on the heels of the sergeant who was installing the Christmas decorations. He would call out "Hi!" to me in English from unexpected places like the top of a ladder or the frame of a display window. Sometimes he winked at me, and he liked talking about silly things, his overall-clad behind perched on my desk in a friendly manner.

"How do I look now? Like a born electrician, eh?"

"Does that make you proud?"

"Sure, I'm proud of it. Now I don't tremble at the top of a ladder any more. Instead I can enjoy the scenery below me."

"Scenery?"

"Yes, it's really something."

Playing with a screwdriver and a pair of pincers, clattering them one against another, he explained what he meant by the scenery. So-and-so had double whirls of hair at the top of her head, and so-and-so's bra-less "things" were visible inside her loose neckline.

When I got angry, he said, "I tried so hard to come up with those lines to make you laugh. How do you think I feel when you get angry? Laugh, for my sake. Besides, laughing is good for your beauty and health."

I had to smile and say, "That's enough. Now go. Otherwise, the sergeant will catch you, and you'll get fired."

He buried his chin in an exaggerated way and said, "That won't do. No, sir. If he is fired, this young man will be ruined, pining for you."

Today, out of the blue, he asked, "Can you dance?"

"No. Why do you ask?"

"In a few days there's going to be a party for the employees in the basement snack bar."

"A party?"

"Yes, the Yankees are throwing it for the Korean employees. They said there's going to be unlimited popcorn and Coke."

"That sounds awfully cheap. Just popcorn and Coke?"

"What did you expect, steaks?"

"Steaks or popcorn, it's still cheap."

Suddenly I was infuriated. I crumpled up every piece of paper in my reach and said, "I really hate Coke and popcorn, and things like that. It's like eating leftover food at a mansion. Surely, you don't mean you want to go to the party for your share like some starving beggar, do you?"

"No, I don't want to go to eat, but I just want to see what a 'party' is like. I just hoped I could dance, holding you in my arms."

"What? I said I can't dance."

"I can't, either. What's the difference? Still, I want to try. Hm? Won't you go with me, please?"

I had to laugh again. Was it because he was still young? He spoke so spontaneously that I couldn't think of him as lewd or sneaky. His face was so ordinary, yet it lit up with his simple wish, like that of a boy; a face that didn't have any hidden intentions. For a minute it seemed so attractive, so fresh that it dispelled my hatred of popcorn and Coke. I shook my head violently, trying to push the attraction away.

"What a stubborn girl! I'll get to you one of these days," he winked and walked away, as if he weren't hurt at all.

Diana Kim stopped by during the lunch break for the first time in a long while. She was very excited.

"You won't believe what happened. I need your help. Let's go outside."

"You can tell me here," I said firmly.

"I asked you to go outside because I can't talk here. You must still be angry. I just don't understand. Why do you have to be so persistent when it's none of your business? You're more meddlesome than you look."

She seemed to have forgotten what I could do to help her, for she spat out her mind, her eyes filled with contempt, as they usually were. I shuddered with hatred for her. When she came to pick up the painted scarf from Ock, she had teased him with the same eyes.

"Incredible. You call this a portrait? You don't expect to earn six dollars for this trash, do you? How can you call yourself a painter?"

"How can you say something like that? This man is . . . He is . . ."

I was about to tell her who Ock Hui-do was, but I couldn't bring myself to do it. If I did, it would be a joke to Diana and the other painters. Only I knew he was not like the others. The only thing left for me to do, the one thing I could do for him, was to get the money for the portrait.

"Just tell me which part you don't like. I'll ask him to give it a touch-up. Or, if you prefer, he can do it all over again," I pleaded with her.

Ock Hui-do said quietly, "I won't do it. Ask somebody else."

He snatched the scarf out of Diana's hand and crumpled it up. The blue veins on his hand stood out, revealing his anger, but his face was as calm as ever.

"Oh, my, how can you do that? How can you do that to my face? Give it to me. How dare you crumple up my face! It might be all right if I iron it. If you're going to throw it away, I'll just take it."

She took the scarf without paying. I kept after her about paying, like a devil, just as she had described me. I tried to persuade her, saying that it was quite a good picture, that the GIs did it for fun anyway. Nobody expected a real portrait, and even if she didn't like it much, she could grab Bob's heart if she sent it along with a fantastic letter.

Frequently consulting a Korean-English dictionary, I spent a whole night composing a letter that was crammed with expressions of love and longing. The letter finally satisfied her, and she said she would only pay for the portrait later if she got some results.

"I never pay up front. Even when I was selling my damned pussy, I always got the dollars first and stashed them deep in my pocket. So if I get a present from Bob, and if it's worth more than six dollars, I will see what I can do. Don't pester me any more."

I gave up on getting her to pay, but after that I didn't bother concealing my hostility. I felt free, as though I'd thrown away some miserable old clothes. I could ignore her when I ran into her, and it was wonderful to know that I was completely beyond her manipulation.

But today she suddenly seemed to be trying to draw me into her orbit, to use me once again. I ignored her cajoling tone and made my fingers fly over the abacus. It was Saturday, and I was recording the five painters' work for the week, the money they were due, and their total income for the week, so as to make it clear at one glance. The portrait shop's income was on the rise thanks to the Christmas rush, but Ock Hui-do's share was the smallest. I let out a low sigh and shut the book. She still hadn't gone away. She stood there playing with her large red purse, opening and closing it repeatedly. The metal clasp clicked loudly, and my eyes caught sight of a fat roll of one thousand won inside.

When she saw that my eyes had brushed over them, she smiled teasingly and said, "Stop acting like that. I've had a plan all along. I wanted to have a talk with you today and give you the money for the picture."

She fiddled with her purse again, opening and shutting it once more.

"Come on, let's go. I'm so happy, I'll go crazy." Her voice rose when she sensed that I was coming with her.

I followed her, dispirited. I thought I could get the money this time. Five children, a nagging wife. The thought that I could do something for Ock Hui-do prompted me to follow.

When I sat down opposite her in the tea room, I was amazed. Her eyes twinkled beautifully, perhaps from pleasure, and she spoke in short breaths, perhaps from utter happiness.

"You stubborn girl! Aren't you going to ask what this is all about?"

"I think I know. Maybe Bob said to start the wedding procedures."

"Don't be silly. Do you think I'd be excited about something like that?"

"What is it then?"

"It's this."

She peeled her shiny black gloves carefully. A diamond, the size of a tiny pea, glittered on her ring finger. Suddenly her well-manicured hands had become more gorgeous and radiant.

"Bob sent this to me. I was tearing open his letter when something dropped out, something wrapped tightly in tissue paper. I picked the paper up and looked inside and found this. It is a diamond, and a real one at that, and it got to me, despite the careless way he sent it! Isn't it amazing that it didn't get lost in the mail? Yankees are admirable, really. There's no way it would have gotten here if we damned Koreans were handling it. I can't even send money to my mother in the countryside because I can't trust anyone. How can I trust the damned Korean post office? No Korean would have ever left that diamond get through, right?

"My, what was I thinking?" Diana chattered on, "Read this to me, will you? We've got to answer the letter. The last letter was great. That's why he sent this. Go ahead and read it."

"I'd rather have the fee for the portrait first."

"My, you're getting really slick lately. All right. How much was it?"

"Six dollars."

"Oh, was it? I'll give it to you in won since you'll have to convert it, anyway. Six dollars' worth? Then how much is it by the official exchange rate?"

"If you want to pay in won, shouldn't you pay the black-market rate? The difference is considerable."

"You really are getting cheeky. I don't care if you don't read this letter. You're not the only person who can read it for me, you know."

Her excitement had cooled and her eyes glistened with a metallic gleam. I was terrified, thinking that I had blown another chance to make Ock Hui-do happy. I wanted him to know that I was helping him, so that he would think of me as a grown-up and his equal. I wanted him to know that I was mature.

"All right, calculate it any way you wish, then."

She dropped one corner of her mouth in a crooked smirk that showed how sorry she felt for me and counted the bills deftly. I fixed my gaze on the diamond, and when she handed me the bills, I shoved them into my pocket without counting them and began reading Bob's letter.

As usual, he had made a list of exaggerated expressions of love, but there was no specific plan. All he said about the diamond was that it was a symbol of his undying love. While I was reading the letter, she blew a puff of steam on the stone and gave it an earnest rub with her handkerchief. She didn't show any particular emotion even after I finished reading.

"That's nothing special. No mention of an engagement or a wedding." I was free to be cynical, now that I had buried the money in my pocket.

"What? Did you say wedding? I'm well past the Yankee slut stage where everyone is dying for an international marriage. Do you think I want to go and live in America where everyone will look down on me? No way. I want to live right here. I'll make lots of money and look down on others. All I want is money."

"So, is the diamond real?"

"I had it appraised at the jewelry shop before I came to see you."

"So what will happen with you and Bob?"

"Nothing. Do you think just because the diamond is real, the 'I love you' is real, too?"

"I can't believe he sent a real diamond just for fun."

"People from a rich country like to show off that way, I guess. The Yankees are so impulsive, aren't they? I heard at the PX they are going to feed the Koreans popcorn and Coke in a couple of days. They call it a party. They are so cheap, you know. Bob's like that, I guess."

I didn't get it. If American prosperity represented nothing more than a flood of popcorn and Coke, I could treat their vulgarity and frivolity with contempt. But for the life of me I couldn't believe that the diamond was in the same league as Coke as a measure of wealth. If their affluence didn't suffer from a lack of tradition and a spiritual poverty, wasn't the wealth itself terribly frightening?

I handed the fee for the portrait to Ock Hui-do as he carefully straightened out his tools after the other painters left.

"What's this?"

"I got it from Diana. Today."

"I just gave it to her."

"Just gave it to her? Do you know how much she profited from the picture? You don't need to waste your efforts so frivolously. So I . . ."

"All right. But I can't believe that terrible woman parted with her money willingly. Why did you do it?"

His wise eyes were sad and embarrassed. I felt worse than if he had been furious.

"Why? Was it a mistake? I just wanted to help you out."

"Kyong-a, do I look so incompetent that a young person like you needs to help me?"

I wanted to cry. Everything had turned out wrong. He seemed more heartbroken than when Diana had treated him with contempt, and I appeared like nothing more than a young person circling around his despair. He hung his head for a long time, as if he were suppressing something. By the time he looked up at me, he had regained his calm.

"I'm sorry. You tried so hard to help me."

His eyes were so gentle that they seemed to caress me. We walked out to the street together.

"I want to spend this windfall."

He peeped into the display window of a clothing shop but continued to stride down the street.

"Now what shall I do? It wouldn't be right if I bought something for you with this money. How about having dinner together?"

"You don't have to. Why don't you go home?"

"I'd like to have a drink," he muttered as if to himself, though he didn't seem to be searching for a bar. He walked on, weaving through the waves of people crowding the streets of Myong-dong. Their excitement didn't seem like wartime. I was thinking of saying goodbye, but I couldn't find the right moment, so I walked along next to him.

"I'd like to have a drink," he said finally.

"Then have a drink. I'll just say goodbye."

"Don't go. Please stay with me."

I was about to turn and run, but he pressed my shoulder with his hand and held me in place with his heavy eyes.

"Don't go. I won't take you to a bar. How about going somewhere cozy, so you can have a meal and I can drink just a little? We have money. It's free money. It's nice to have a little free money to spend. Ha, ha, ha."

He laughed in an exaggerated way, trying to look cheerful, but I sensed a desperation hidden deep inside.

We ended up in a Japanese restaurant. It was a tidy place with *tatami*-floored rooms and braziers, decorated with bunches of camellias and chrysanthemums in the entrance and the corridor. The room was pleasantly warm, thanks to the high-necked Japanese porcelain brazier filled with glowing lumps of pine charcoal. The *sukiyaki* kettle, brought in on top of a small portable range, began to sizzle with the aroma of cooking meat. I stirred the *sukiyaki*, ladled out a well-cooked portion into a bowl, and placed it in front of Ock Hui-do. He poured the yellowish *sake* into a white cup and drank it. He looked at me as if he were about to say something, but he just smiled. His eyes were warm again. I was about to say something myself but instead stirred the kettle intently. I savored the moment, as if it were as fragile as glass: the calming atmosphere, the perfect room temperature, the delicious aroma, and the act of serving someone whom I wanted to love. He was already on his fourth cup of *sake.*

"Why are you drinking so quickly? As if you were drinking spring water."

"Spring water? Right. When I'm thirsty, I long for alcohol more than spring water. Sometimes that's the way my thirst feels."

"Like today. I'm sorry. I had no idea you would be so upset."

"Don't be silly. Why would I be upset? I'm having this delicious meal, thanks to you."

He gulped down his drink.

"I think you're drinking too much."

"No problem. I can't even feel it. You're afraid of drinkers. That's why you're looking at me that way."

"I'm not afraid, only worried. Wine enhances certain emotions."

"What do you mean?"

"It enhances merriment when people drink in a happy mood, but it can increase fury at other times."

"You know a lot about alcohol."

"My father enjoyed drinking. I often served him when he was drinking."

"Then he must have vented his anger at you."

"No, not really. He was always happy when he came home, and he loved drinking with his meal as I helped serve him. When he was pleasantly drunk, I played the spoiled girl and made him promise lots of things."

"What kind of promises?"

"I made him promise to raise my pocket money or to take me to a nice restaurant for a Western meal. Things like that."

I was flushed by the warm memories.

"Were the promises kept?"

"Of course. My father never drank too much because he always drank with his meal. Still, in the morning he pretended that he didn't remember. But I think he actually wanted me to remind him of his promises."

He smiled as if my story were really interesting, resting his cup on the table.

"A very good father you have."

I was about to agree with him, but I was jolted from my recollections. I felt as if something inside me was about to lose balance. I tried to prevent it from happening by shaking my head repeatedly. Then I picked up a bite of the cooled *sukiyaki* from my bowl and tossed it into my mouth. The slippery noodles were too sweet, almost nauseatingly sweet.

He picked up his cup again and said, "A good father," and grinned.

"Not any more. He died."

"Oh, is that so? I'm sorry. You must have loved him very much."

"Loved him? Now I hate my father."

Now I had completely lost my balance. Everything was messed up inside my head; my deep love for my father and the resentment I felt because of him. I grew fierce in order not to cry.

"What do you mean? You're so abrupt."

"My father died. One month before the war, on a very peaceful and bright day. He died with his sons and daughter beside him. Comfortably and irresponsibly, he left us behind. He left us behind," I shouted.

At first, he seemed to be taken aback, but his face took on a warm and sympathetic expression.

Encouraged, I blubbered, "That was it. How could he . . . I've experienced so many terrible things alone. I asked my father to help me. I prayed so earnestly. Even the devil's heart would have been moved. When my father died, I thought he had become a god. Well, if not a god, a superman or something. But he ignored us. He didn't do anything for us. How could he? I was so tired of hating him that I decided not to think about him any more."

I sobbed violently, hoping he would feel more sympathy for me.

"Now, now, that's enough. Let's wipe away our tears."

When I felt his two arms embrace my shoulders, I cried more furiously, indulging myself in the pleasure of weeping. The handkerchief he handed me had a faint smell of tobacco and oil paint. I wanted more, and I flung my body into his arms. His chest was so broad, as comfortable as a cradle. A deep feeling of contentment came over me. I didn't want to lose it.

"I like you. That's all right, isn't it?" My heart pounded a bit, but I asked without hesitation or any sense of shame.

"Of course it is."

"Really? Promise?"

I couldn't believe I had gotten his approval so easily. I wrapped my baby finger around his and gave it a determined shake before releasing it. I stayed in his arms, with a feeling of restful bliss and contentment.

"Now, let's go."

He lifted me up, supporting me with his arms. We went out to the street.

"Let's walk a little. Is that all right?" I asked.

I wanted to confirm my happiness and savor it for a long time. The streets were quite empty and some of the stores were already closing. A boy who was selling roasted chestnuts from a torch-lit cart yawned broadly and began to gather his goods.

"You still have some money left, don't you? Buy me some roasted chestnuts," I pleaded, leaning on his arm.

When we stopped in front of the boy, he began to shout as if he had been awakened from his slumber, "Warm roasted chestnuts! Soft, tender roasted chestnuts!"

He stopped to grin with a confused expression. The chestnuts were cold.

"These aren't all that warm," Ock said as he handed over the money.

"Wait a moment. I'll warm them up until they sizzle. It'll take only a minute."

The boy smiled, showing two rows of white teeth, dumped the chestnuts into the wire basket, and stirred the fire pot. The fire flickered weakly in the white ashes.

"We'll take them as they are," I said.

I stuffed the chestnuts into the pocket of Ock's baggy jacket of dyed military fatigue and began husking them one by one before tossing them in my mouth.

"I know an interesting place," I said, "Let's go and look."

"It's already late. Won't your family worry about you?"

I thought of the chimpanzee that I had watched a few days before at the toy vendor's. I had giggled at it, but looking back, I felt sorry for that me; I had been so miserable. I wanted to show off my happiness to the chimpanzee as it poured whisky and drank it over and over again.

At the makeshift toy stall under the eaves of a house the vendor was dozing. The chimpanzee, with a bored expression on his comic face, stood holding a whisky bottle in one hand.

"Excuse me. Would you wind him up, please?" I asked in a friendly voice, pointing to the chimpanzee.

The vendor opened his eyes widely, surprised, but he didn't seem to mind. He wound the spring at the bottom of the chimpanzee, and it began to move its body rhythmically, pouring the whisky and drinking it over and over again. People gathered one by one. I chewed the chestnuts, laughing to my heart's content and moving my shoulders to the rhythm of the chimpanzee's movement. The spring was almost unwound, the whiskey-lover's movements grew slower and slower, and finally his frenzied drinking ceased. People went away one by one. The exciting time had gone by so quickly. The chimpanzee stood lonely once more, having finished pleasing people. His loneliness, his isolation from human beings and animals alike, brought a lump of thick loneliness and frustration to my heart.

I looked at Ock Hui-do. He was staring at the chimpanzee the way he stared at the grey curtain after putting down his brush in the middle of his work. Suddenly it occurred to me that he was suffering from the same loneliness as the chimpanzee. And I couldn't help him at all. The contentment I had felt evaporated like bubbles. Silently I was pushed away from him. The chimpanzee, Ock Hui-do, me . . . I realized in my bones that all of us suffered our own loneliness which others couldn't share or relieve.

We walked to the edge of Kyae-dong without speaking.

"I'm almost there now. Why don't you go home? It's so late," I said.

"I'll walk you to your house."

"I can go by myself."

I removed my hand from his pocket, fled down the alley, and turned the corner. I dashed toward my house, my eyes fixed on the distorted roof in the distance. Just as he had his loneliness he didn't want to share with anyone, I had my own which couldn't be relieved by anyone else. It was my job to walk down that long alley, feeling frightened, no less than the day before, and with pain that had almost become physical, a pain that I couldn't share with anyone.

I told my mother I had already eaten and went directly to my room. She followed me and sat absently for a long time.

"Why don't you go to bed?" I asked in an irritated voice when I couldn't stand her any more.

"I got a letter from your uncle."

"And?"

"He said to send you down to Pusan. As a big uncle, the only way he can save face is by sending you to college. His tone was unpleasant, as if I were keeping you in this house."

My mother hadn't uttered so many words without a stutter for a long time.

"Do you think I should go?"

"Do as you wish."

"Will you go with me?"

"If I intended to live in Pusan, why would I have fought so hard to come here in the first place?"

"Same here."

We had said everything we had to say. Still, my mother sat there dumbly. I changed into my pajamas and yawned loudly.

"I'm so sleepy. Wake me up early tomorrow."

"Well . . . If you aren't going because of me, give it another thought."

"What? Do you mean you'll go with me?"

I hated my mother, but sometimes I was curious about the strength and hope I provided in her life.

"No. I can't go. I'm comfortable here."

She stood up as if she were afraid that I would ask her more questions.

I didn't want to go to Pusan at all. It had nothing to do with my mother. Living in this vast old house, just the two of us, we were not bound by any affection or obligation. We must have been caught by the spirit of the old house. I couldn't leave it, but it wasn't because of anyone else.

Six

The next morning, even before I opened my eyes, the first thing that came to me was Ock Hui-do's embrace. It had given me complete trust and peace like a cradle. As I lay under my quilt, the recollection of his warm chest was refreshing and sweet. However, a faint clatter coming from the kitchen and the tick-tock of the clock's second hand broke my reverie, and I grew as restless as the red hand raced around the dial.

I wanted to believe that my relationship with Ock Hui-do had changed since yesterday, but I couldn't be sure. In my memory there was the residue of the feeling that he had pushed me away. My thoughts grew more tangled as I washed my face, straightened up my room, and ate breakfast. The only clear thing was that I needed him.

I love him. I need him. Repeating these words over and over in my mind, I calmed down and gained courage and confidence. When I saw him, I might be able to see that something had changed between us. If it hadn't, I would have to be clever and smart enough to make our relationship different.

But Ock Hui-do didn't come to work that day or the next. As I went through my daily routine, I sometimes made mistakes and snapped at the painters, not knowing what to do with my restlessness.

Another Christmas tree was erected right in front me, its bulbs flashing in turn, as if they were winking at me. My eyes grew tired and my head throbbed.

"Good morning," Tae-su said in English, all smiles, as he walked up holding loops of electrical cords.

"Don't you know what time it is? Why are you being so silly?" I retorted sharply. I was not in the mood to joke around with him.

"My mornings begin when I see you."

"Cut it out."

"Why are you so low today? You'll get wrinkles if you frown too much."

"Well, if I were you, I wouldn't worry about other people."

"I don't want a wife who ages faster than me."

"Really, I'm not in the mood for jokes. Just leave me alone."

"Come to think of it, you look pale. What's wrong?"

He sobered up and looked at me as if he were really worried about me.

"It must be that tree. All that ragged gold paper and those flashing lights make me dizzy. I think I'm going crazy. Can you move it away from here?" I was just trying to be contrary.

"Well, the sergeant told me to put it right here. He's very particular. What can I do?"

Tae-su scratched his head and flared his nostrils, looking distressed. I couldn't hate him when he looked so artless.

"I've got a good idea." He grinned suddenly, and slapped his palm with his fist. "Wait a minute."

"What is it?"

"I'll go to the power room and cross the wires or something. I can make all the lights go out."

I had to laugh at his farfetched idea.

"Don't be ridiculous. You know who'll have the worst time of all if the electricity goes out!"

With a snap of my chin, I pointed to the painters whose faces pinched with concentration. Ock Hui-do's empty seat stabbed at my heart.

"Uh, Mr. Ock Hui-do isn't in today?"

Suddenly a bright idea struck me.

"Do you know where Mr. Ock lives?" I asked.

"No."

"Perhaps your brother knows."

"He might. Why?"

"I have to go and see him. Please find out for me. Will you, please?"

"Maybe he'll be in tomorrow."

"If he isn't, I'll go see him. We have so many orders coming in right now."

"Boy, I didn't know this business was so lucrative."

"It's the busy season. You'll find out for me, won't you?"

"That won't be difficult, but . . ."

"If you like, we can go together. I'm easily scared, so if you could, come along with me."

"It would be a great honor. Going along with you at night . . . All right."

"Really?"

"I want to ask you a favor, too, and you have to agree." He stressed "have to," mimicking me with his lips pouting.

"What is it?"

"Will you go to the party with me tonight?"

"What? That trashy party again? Who would want to go there?"

"I do, with you, really."

"I'm not going."

"All right. Then I won't find out where Ock lives. You don't care, right?"

"You're being disagreeable. All right. I will go with you."

I was angry at him, but I couldn't dislike him for his pleading. Besides, I was a little curious about the party.

Twisting the cords in his hands, he said, "So Mr. Ock's absence helped me?"

"I don't know what's the matter with him. Perhaps he doesn't want to work here any more."

"Well, I don't think it will be easy for him to find a better job. He's not aggressive, you know. Maybe he's sick. By the way, what are you going to wear tonight?"

All he could think of was the party.

"Will you be ashamed if I go in this outfit?" I pretended to be offended, lifting the corner of my old navy blue jacket.

"No, I like you as you are." His voice was low and hoarse, and his eyes took on a strange gleam. He suddenly looked mature.

I was about to laugh off his comment as usual, twisting down my mouth, but I was strangely flustered and didn't know what to say.

Closing time had been moved up one hour, and people were giggling, excited about the party. In the rest area on the second floor the cleaning women had already changed into velvet skirts and gaudy silk blouses. They sat in a row, making up their faces and arguing earnestly over whose fabric was more expensive, whose was from a better maker.

In a corner I pretended to comb my hair but immediately returned downstairs and self-consciously waited for Tae-su. First, the fat buttocks swathed in velvet skirts swaggered down the stairs leading to the basement, followed by the laborers transformed by their neat suits. Then the salesgirls, clad in flashy dresses, jammed the stairway.

I felt more stupid by the minute, and I hated the idea of going to the party so much that I wanted to flee.

"Have you been waiting long?" Tae-su asked bashfully, fumbling with his shirt collar, as if the red necktie made him uncomfortable. His shyness was as fresh as a tender green shoot that I couldn't bring myself to trample on.

"Do we really have to go?" I asked, pouting.

But when he offered his hand, I held it without hesitation. Together we went down to the snack bar, already swarming with people. The din of their voices, mixed with music, deafened me and the layers upon layers of people blocked my view. Holding hands, we were carried to the center of the room until we reached the spot where the activity was crazed. The music came from a portable turntable and the din that drowned out the music originated from the food area where boxes of Coke were stacked and popcorn was being made.

"Let's behave ourselves. Let's save face as Koreans."

Wherever you went, you met a patriot or two of this type.

"What's the use of saving face? Where can you use it? Does it feed you?"

"Let's wait in line for the food."

"That's right. Everyone line up."

"What do you mean? Then there won't be anything left for us except air."

"Bastards! Do they call this a party? Shit! Didn't they say they'd let us eat as much as we wanted?"

"Don't be so impatient. It takes time for the machine to make the popcorn."

No matter how fast the popcorn maker spewed out popcorn, it couldn't meet the demand. Tae-su and I were pushed about. A few people who did not care particularly about food danced, brushing against each other, a little distance away from the food. The cleaning women flopped down on the tiled floor, crunching the popcorn and gulping down the Coke in earnest, their velvet skirts hitched high up around their waists, revealing their dirty rayon slips.

"Shit! What can you expect from these damned Koreans? Shit!"

A tall man spat phlegm to the floor, after being pushed away from the battle for food. He glared at the mass of people. He appeared to gather his resolve again. He flung himself into the fierce activity once more.

Pressing his hand against mine, Tae-su looked totally dejected.

"You said you wanted to dance," I said sweetly to encourage him, but he kept getting pushed away to the edge, still holding my hand.

"They invited people without thinking about the size of the hall. Of course, it wasn't really a formal invitation. How could there be so many people?" He wanted to explain the frenzy in a logical fashion, but he couldn't finish.

In a place like this nothing looked more backward than behaving in a reserved and rational manner. I wanted to expose my ugly side like other people, who were frenetically having fun.

I pulled Tae-su to where people were dancing. Diana's white face floated among them, next to the head of a black man, rough and dark. She looked like a woeful lily beside him.

"Let's dance or go get a Coke. Come on." I grabbed one of his hands helpfully, placing it around my waist, but he let it drop and said, "Wait a moment. Those SOBs."

Looking in the direction in which he was glaring, I saw several GIs jamming the doorway between the kitchen and the hall, watching our struggles in fascination. The sergeant who was in charge of the first floor was among them. They were smiling triumphantly, as if they were satisfied with the play they had put on, as if it were a success beyond their wildest expectations.

Tae-su's neck reddened and he looked like he couldn't bear the disgrace.

"Come on, let's dance, or at least get some popcorn."

"No. Aren't you ashamed?"

"Ashamed? Why? Everyone is doing it. I can be like everyone else. It's exhausting and useless to pretend we're different from the rest."

"But the Yankees are watching us. They think it's funny."

"I want to have a good time, so why are you upset over nothing? Let them have fun in their own way. We don't have to think about our different nationalities. The difference is between those who have empty stomachs and those whose stomachs are full. If they had suffered a war and had been hungry for entertainment and food for as long as we have, they'd behave worse than we do. And if we were in a position to dole out things, we would be more arrogant and showy."

"So what do you want me to do?" he blurted out rudely.

I whispered into his ear more sweetly. "Well, let's dance and behave like ugly people. Please don't try to be different from the others, all right?"

I led him into the whirl of dancers. Diana's lily-like face floated around me for a while and was gone. I swaggered about, brushing against the others, feeling a sense of pleasure as if I were rolling in mud.

But before I knew it, Tae-su was leading me, and with his strong arm around me, he took me up the stairs and soon we were outside. I felt the cool, pleasant night air on my flushed cheeks. A policeman and an MP, standing at the entrance, eyed us up and down, but let us pass without a search.

"Today we can pass freely, even here. We could have smuggled out a Coke bottle or something," I joked.

Tae-su didn't answer, but strode on furiously, his arm still around my waist. He looked sullen. I hummed to myself, oblivious to his mood. Suddenly, he stopped and embraced me impulsively.

His cold lips brushed over my flushed cheeks in several spots, but then they parted my lips, urgently going between them, as if he were looking for a place to warm his frozen mouth.

I shook my head to avoid his lips. All I experienced from my first kiss was that it was cold.

"I'm sorry," he apologized in a low voice, but he still held me tightly and wouldn't release me.

I could hear the pounding of his heart. It was not that I didn't like it, but I felt so confined that I wriggled out of his embrace.

"Why are you doing this now? You could have done it as much as you wanted over there. You acted so high and mighty."

"I don't want to talk about what happened there."

"But everyone was doing it."

"Why are you playing dumb? You must know that what they were doing in there and what I did just now are two different things. I love you."

"Do you mean that it's better for lovers to be in a secluded place? You're the one who badgered me into going to the party, you know."

"That party stinks like a sewer. Stop talking about it. A man dreams of going to a party in a suit, with his sweetheart. I went, thinking that my dream had finally come true, but all I saw was ugliness. I'm sorry, anyway."

"It was fun. Everyone was having fun."

He twisted my arm suddenly and said, "Why do you keep teasing me? Do you think I could watch you among those whores and let the Yankees look at you with contempt? You should be different from other women."

He almost sounded threatening. Still, I had never seen his eyes so filled with longing. I didn't know what he wanted from me. If he wanted a longer kiss or a longer embrace, I could go along with it, but if he wanted me to be different from other women, that was a problem. Just as much as each person looks different and has a different personality, I was different from other women, but Tae-su seemed to expect me to be different in other ways as well. He seemed to want to think of me as a rose blooming from a sewer pipe. Perhaps I could pretend I was one, taking his fervent wish into account, but it was embarrassing and bothersome for me. After all, there was no reason why I should perform like a clumsy actress just to make him like me. I didn't love him and I didn't want to give up the freedom in our relationship, which was not restricted by anything like love.

He nervously lit a cigarette but threw it down and trampled on it after only a couple of draws. Surely he was about to say something.

In an attempt to alleviate his nervousness, I said, "Look at the sky. Aren't there a lot of stars?"

It was too obvious a trick. He exploded.

"Don't tease me. I'm not in the mood to look up at the sky. I have more important things to discuss with you."

If he kept trying to discuss important matters with me, I was certain my arm would suffer a few painful twists.

"Bye, I'm sorry," I said, dashing into the darkness.

Seven

The next day and the day after, Ock Hui-do's seat remained empty. The days without him dragged on endlessly, and I suffered from the despair that I might never again have the painful joy of meeting his uniquely good-natured eyes, eyes without a tinge of stupidity.

I had come across Tae-su that morning.

"Have you found out where Mr. Ock lives?"

To my relief, he nodded his head vaguely without launching into his usual chatter.

Every American soldier who came that day seemed to find some fault, big or small, with their portraits. I sent each portrait back to the painters, even the ones I could have talked the soldiers into accepting if I had put in a little effort.

"Miss Lee, what's wrong with you today? Do you want to see me and my family in a row, smothered by these rayon cloths with mongrel faces on them because we can't afford to buy the ingredients for rice cake soup for the holiday?"

Of course, it was Cash, the one with the dirtiest mouth, who had the most rejected portraits. He raised his voice, looping one of the rejected scarves around his neck and pretending to yank it. The other painters began to grumble along with him. Ignoring their protests, I lifted up a corner of the grey curtain that was drawn over the display window.

It was snowing outside. The fluttering snowflakes sometimes hit the window, but they didn't touch the cheek that I pressed against it. It was only natural because between me and the snow flurries was the window, albeit thin, but for a while I was anxiously hoping that the flakes would touch my cheek, hoping to be swept away by the joy of snowy days.

"Miss Lee, a customer!" Chin called out.

I returned to my desk and took the photo, asking the color of the eyes, hair and the clothes, and recording the delivery date. I stifled a cry, a cry for help. I was afraid I would go crazy because of this boring work.

The painters were whispering with one another.

"She was crying behind the curtain."

"What did you expect? Pushing a girl around like that? Tsk, tsk."

"As if you were not part of it."

Why were they so nice, so terribly nice at times? I couldn't put up with anything today.

Tae-su stood waiting for me, shoulders hunched as the large snowflakes fell around him. I ran toward him. My empty lunch box clattered in the shapeless postman-like bag I carried, slung from my shoulder. I dashed up to him and caught his arm with my hand. He tottered a little and smiled gloomily. I slid, hanging from his arm, giggling for no apparent reason.

I knew I couldn't subdue the tickling ecstasy that I felt right now, just as I had not been able to free myself from the depression I had felt all day.

"Did anything interesting happen today?" he asked, brightening a little. I shrugged and licked the flakes with my stretched-out tongue.

"You were frowning all day."

"Was I?"

"What a fickle girl!"

Instead of answering, I clung to him more closely. What blessing it was to have someone waiting in the snow! I gazed at the dazzling dance of the snow caught in the headlights of the passing military trucks.

I could see glittering slices of past moments, twirling around. Just slices, unconnected, with no emotional strings attached, so I could enjoy them freely. The mysterious harmony of the bright sunlight on the lush green leaves I spotted when I accidentally tilted my head back on the way to school. . . . My father in his traditional black serge overcoat, and my elegant mother, clad brightly in a pale blue silk overcoat, walking a few steps behind him whenever they went out together. . . . A tray full of row after row of fat dumplings prepared on the last day of the year. Hyok and Wook in their first custom-made Western suits, so handsome I barely recognized them. . . . My mother's belongings that she and I had both loved dearly. The white otter-skin collar, the thick gold ring she always kept on her finger. . . . The purple paulownia flowers dropping into the middle yard on a bright day. . . .

I was puzzled by the thickness of the stack of postcards hidden inside me, but I was joyous. I looked at them like a child looking at pictures. I was not so stupid as to try to piece them together to make a story.

"We should get something for the patient, shouldn't we?"

I was jolted back to reality when Tae-su stopped in front of a vendor. The woman was polishing small, firm red apples with a cloth. I picked the prettiest ones and dropped them into what had once been an old cement bag. I kept finding pretty ones, and the bag grew heavy before Tae-su paid for them. As we walked, I felt such a strong desire to bite into the firm red flesh of an apple that the roots of my teeth tickled. I handed one to Tae-su and bit into one myself. Crunch, crunch. That tart flavor, the pleasure of biting into the crisp flesh. I ate several in a row.

"You eat too many cold foods," Tae-su remarked as he took the bag from me and shifted it into his other hand. He wrapped his arm around my waist and said, "Don't you want to have a little boy who crunches apples, a boy who has red cheeks?"

"Who do you think that boy will look like?" I realized it was the most preposterous response.

"You and me, of course." His face came closer to mine until I could feel his breath.

"What are you talking about?"

I pretended to be genuinely surprised, but I felt sorry for Tae-su. Nothing was wrong with a red-cheeked boy, but it would take so long to have a baby. It was so far in the future. Five, ten years. With a war raging just over the hill, how absurd it was to stand in the middle of a bleak street dreaming of a future five or ten years away!

I wouldn't be able to lead such a slow-paced life. I wanted to jump the tracks of everyday life and live a bold life in the fast lane.

Tae-su removed his arm from my waist as if he were snubbed and walked in silence. After passing several streetcar stations, he asked, "Shall we take a trolley or shall we walk?"

"Where does Mr. Ock live?"

"Some place called Yonji-dong, I think."

"Are you good at finding houses?"

"I've been to that house several times. It turns out he's staying in the house of a friend who took refuge in the south."

When we arrived at the next station, an empty trolley came to a halt, and we stepped aboard. We got off at Chongno 4-ga and Tae-su walked briskly ahead. As we turned into an alley, he stopped, looking around. It seemed we were almost there.

I was gradually enveloped by some kind of heat. It was an urgent longing, so urgent that I couldn't wait five or ten years for the red-cheeked boy. I was being chased by a longing, a longing like self-abandonment.

Finally Tae-su stopped at a low tile-roofed house and held his flashlight up to read the nameplate. It didn't say Ock Hui-do.

"This is the house. I've come several times before, but never at night."

We shook the gate a couple of times, and a girl, who was almost the same height as me, removed the bolt and peeped out. Smaller children spilled out after her, making a fuss. By the way the children behaved, it seemed they rarely had visitors. The inner quarters were closed off with shutters. Only the outer quarters were lit and not very brightly.

"It's Tae-su. Is Mr. Ock in?"

"Oh, Tae-su? What brings you here?"

"I came with Kyong-a. Are you very ill?"

"No, only a little. Come in. It's cold outside."

We spoke through the sliding paper door, removing our coats and shaking off the snow. After a rustling sound of straightening-up in the room, the door opened quietly. A woman I thought must be Ock's wife looked out. The children surrounded us with curious eyes, talking and giggling among themselves.

"Come in, please," said the wife.

"Come in, although it's messy," said Ock. He was leaning against the wall on a mat spread out on the warmest part of the floor. His wife took our coats politely and hung them on the wall.

"It's just a cold. And you came all the way in this snow. Thank you, anyway."

Ock burst into a fit of coughing before he could finish. His wife placed her hand on his back, and as soon as he stopped, she brought a porcelain ashtray to his mouth so that he could spit out the phlegm. He seemed to have the flu that was going around.

"How's your brother these days?"

"Well, he keeps busy."

"We're so preoccupied with our own lives that we can't seem to find time to have a drink together."

"My brother says the same thing."

While they exchanged dull pleasantries, Ock's wife handed each of the children an apple and sent them to the other room. Then she peeled some apples, cut them up, and arranged them on a plate. I studied every move she made.

She was wearing a dark pleated skirt and a man's khaki winter jacket, which somehow seemed to accentuate her delicate neck and face. Her neck was long and slender, and I caught a glimpse of her freshly washed undershirt inside her baggy jacket. I kicked myself for being drawn to her, but her white, slender neck didn't look as if it could bear anyone's hatred.

For a long time I chewed the piece of apple she handed me. She hadn't spoken a word. She had sent her children to the other room and offered me the apple with her eyes alone. Her eyes and her gestures were rich with expression. I began to grow angry. I couldn't imagine her nagging her husband.

The pristine undershirt, peeking out from the drab, loose winter jacket. Why did her long neck and delicate face have to resemble the Modigliani women I liked so much? Frustrated and anxious, I shifted my sitting position, biting my lips nervously, for I couldn't define my feelings toward her.

"The floor must be too cold. Oh, dear." Embarrassed, she put her hand under my knee to check the temperature of the floor.

"Ah, come over here," said Ock Hui-do, lifting one side of his mat.

I moved next to him, put my hand under his mat, and looked at him. He smiled slightly when our eyes met. I smiled good-naturedly, copying him.

"Kyong-a has been worried because you haven't been coming to work. Today she fretted so much about coming to see you that I showed her the way to your house."

"Thank you."

"It is the busy season now. I had no idea business was so good. They hassle her all the time and she's grown quite irritable. I hope you get better soon."

"I'm almost completely recovered. I need a few more days at most."

"Were you very sick?" I addressed him for the first time that night.

"I think it was the cold and exhaustion. I hadn't been sick for a long time. I'm almost recovered. I hope the cough stops, though."

He stopped to cough again. Without thinking, I was about to put the porcelain ashtray up his mouth and rub his back, but of course his wife was already doing it.

How I wished I could do that for him! When his coughing fit subsided, Ock leaned against the wall in exhaustion, and the children opened the sliding door and took turns peeking in. It must have been time for us to leave.

At last the youngest child flung open the sliding door and entered. He felt the apple bag with his hand. He was a friendly-looking boy. I pulled the boy gently to my lap and gave him an apple, then lightly pressed my nose onto his clean, soft hair. He had a nice smell. The child chomped the apple vigorously. I grew glum. The nice smell and the chomping sounds were refreshing, and yet depressing at the same time. I embraced him tightly in order not to show my tears. The healthy boy finished the skin first and began working on the flesh. When the seeds were revealed, I felt like bursting into a wail.

"We should go," I pushed the boy aside roughly and got to my knees.

"Why, can't you stay longer?"

"My mother is waiting for me," I blurted, surprising myself.

"What a baby! Do you miss your mother already?"

Tae-su teased, winking at me, and playfully stabbed my cheek with his finger. He helped me into my coat and wrapped my scarf securely around my head. He didn't forget to arrange my bangs, as before.

I had to endure the generous smiles of Ock and his wife, for they seemed to find us really cute. An insult would have been easier to put up with. I stamped my feet as I put on my shoes at the stone entryway, but I was still furious. Even when the children spilled out from the other room, saying goodbye loudly, I remained silent.

At the dark middle gate, the wife's rough but warm hand grabbed mine. "Thank you for coming. You've been so helpful to our children's father."

I shook off her hand, jumped over the threshold, and grabbed hold of Tae-su's arm.

The snow had stopped, and the clear sky was lit by cold stars. A brusque gust of wind tossed the snow on the ground into the sky. Snowflakes crept into my sleeves and skirt. I was cold. As we walked, my teeth chattered.

The trees along the street, towering like huge skeletons, trembled, wailing in the blast. The wind grew stronger, howling like a fierce animal. Tae-su took off his jacket and placed it over my coat. Still, I shook uncontrollably. I was afraid that I might be blown away like the snow, so I held tight to his waist. Still, I trembled.

"Let's share your jacket," I said.

"I'm all right. It's not that cold."

"Let's share it. I need your warmth."

"What's the matter? Maybe you're getting sick?"

We clung to each other, the jacket over our heads. There was nobody and no light in the street, as if we were left all alone after the end of the world, and only the snow churned skyward in the desolate street. Tae-su massaged me, as if he truly expected to thaw me out. The light of a police box spilled out to the street in the distance. We let go of each other near the police box and grabbed hold of each other as we walked on.

"Please walk me home. I don't think I can make it by myself."

"Don't worry. Pull yourself together."

He kept rubbing my body, as if I were freezing to death, and said, "Don't be so quiet. Say something."

"Are you afraid that I might lose consciousness?"

"No, of course not. But perhaps you can forget about how cold you are."

"Mr. Ock's wife is a beauty."

"She's all right."

Our conversation stopped again. The old palace wall on one side was endless, and the trees inside howled like hungry animals. After a long while, Tae-su started again.

"Say something."

It was funny that he seemed so anxious.

"Shall I sing?"

"If you want."

Three-brother-stars in the darkening evening sky

The song seemed so pathetic because of my hoarse voice that I stopped singing. Not only the three brothers but numerous other stars, densely spaced, shone from the moon-less sky.

"Do you know what a light year is?" I asked.

"Who wouldn't know?"

"Tell me about it."

"Well, uh, the light year sounds like a time unit but it is a unit of distance. Light can circle the earth seven and a half times a second, and one light year means the distance the light travels in a year, not a day or two, mind you."

"I know that much."

"Then why did you ask?"

"I meant, can you understand that kind of distance? Can you grasp what it means? Millions, billions of light years. Can you even imagine that?"

"What are you talking about?"

"You asked me to say something. I'm just overwhelmed by the fact that the three-brother-stars are so far away."

"You could call it infinity, I guess."

I caught sight of my house with its disfigured corner. We had already arrived at my alley. I stopped walking and took in a deep breath. I withdrew my body from the warm jacket and stood straight.

"We're here? Which is your house?"

"Go now," I ordered firmly.

"Which house is it? Don't I deserve some hot tea?"

"My house is a long way from here. Now go."

"You asked me to walk you home. Are you shooing away the person who accompanied you in this cold? This is too much."

"Please go now," I demanded more loudly now.

I was cold, but not cold enough to make my teeth chatter, and my grave determination to be alone from that point on made me strong.

Tae-su was about to turn to go, but said dull-wittedly, "I'll stand here to watch you go."

"I said go now," I shouted, stomping my feet.

Puzzled, he muttered, "Damn," and turned away. He disappeared around the corner without looking back. When I could no longer hear his footsteps, I boldly faced my house. The large Korean-style structure, with its missing eave, looked like a great legendary bird that had lost a wing. Having given up flying, it lay like a useless monster. I was so frightened that my hair stood on end, but I felt I was right not to share my fright with other people yet. I dashed up the long alley as if I were charging toward something. Only when my body bumped into the gate did I stop. I shook the gate with my whole body until it hurt.

"Mother, Mother," I cried.

"I'm coming, I'm coming. What's the fuss?" My mother's low voice answered, a voice without longing or welcome, and as always her dragging footsteps approached and the gate squeaked open. I grabbed my mother's hand. Her rough hand, neither cold nor warm, never returned my squeeze, yet I still hoped.

The gusts of wind had swept the snow from the middle yard to the bottom of the stone wall, making a large mound. The paulownia tree swayed as if exhausted, its limbs drooping to the ground. The snow must have fallen here also. It was almost midnight, but my mother must have forgotten all about me.

"I'm late today. What time is it?"

"I don't know."

"It was a terrible wind. I was almost swept away by it."

My mother didn't respond, but trudged to the kitchen like a shadow and began to set out food on a tray. Standing at the stepping stone by the entrance, I stood awkwardly, looking up at the sky and at the snow-covered yard.

'My mother is waiting for me. My mother is waiting for me.'

'What a baby.'

My mother came out with a tray. It was only then, as I was taking off my snow-covered shoes, that I noticed the light was on in my room. Taken aback, I rushed inside, not bothering to shake off the snow from my clothes, and flung open the door.

The guitar lay on the floor. Several photo albums were scattered around open, with photos spilling out to the floor, and in one corner a judo uniform lay in a pile. I instinctively sensed body heat radiating from the uniform.

So this was why my mother didn't have to wait for her daughter. Clutching the judo uniform to her bosom, looking at the pictures, plucking the guitar . . . I couldn't suppress the feeling that surged in my throat. Was it pity or rage?

My mother slowly entered the room, shoulders bent, holding the tray in her hand.

"You were in here before, weren't you?" My voice was shrill. "I've told you a million times. Don't come into this room. I told you never come in here by yourself."

My mother smiled strangely.

"Why were you in here? I told you not to enter. I told you never to come into this room by yourself."

"I was sitting in my room and I heard the guitar. It sounded like Wook playing."

"That was the wind. I walked home through that storm and nearly froze to death. It was not the guitar."

I stressed each word in the sentence. I had to suppress the impulse to pick up the guitar and smash it to pieces on the floor.

"It was not this damned guitar."

I swung the guitar over my head.

"No, no," my mother's voice rang with metallic urgency, suddenly twenty years younger.

She charged toward me to win back the guitar. I shivered with the impulse to smash it, turning round and round and holding it high above my head. My mother attacked me. She was not a shadow any more. She was a healthy, passionate woman with a strong throbbing pulse once more.

Finally my mother grabbed hold of the neck of the guitar, scratching my arm. I desperately pulled it away, holding one side, and when she yanked it, I was thrown to the floor. Still, I didn't let go.

It was a desperate fight, the guitar wedged between us, as we rolled around like lunatics, panting like a pair of winded animals. I finally lost hold of the guitar and stood up, panting and gasping. My mother had won. The long-awaited attempt to sever our ties with the past went up in smoke.

When the guitar and judo uniform were returned to their proper places and the photo albums occupied their corner of the bookshelf once more, the room was no different from other times. We sat down to the dinner tray as if nothing had happened and began to slurp the *kimchi* soup, now cool.

"There was a letter," my mother said, with a grotesque movement of her mouth, in a tone as dull as usual.

"From who?"

"I think it's from your uncle's family in Pusan."

My mother took the letter from the wardrobe drawer after she finished her slow, unappetizing meal. It was from Mal. Mal was the only cousin who was younger than me. How proud I had felt when she first called me "Older Sister."

My Dear Older Sister Kyong-a

It is almost four months since you left Pusan. How are you? I miss you. You are so far away and so close to the front line that I'm afraid for you. Aren't you afraid of the war? Oh, I hope your mother is well, too. Did she make her delicious winter kimchi this year? Our kimchi is terrible this year. My brothers say it is because our aunt didn't help make it. If her hand had swished through the spice mixture, it would have been different, they say. I agree. But my mother blames the weather. She says kimchi *can't possibly stay tangy in this warm weather.*

I'm not writing to talk about kimchi. *I hesitated several times, but I had to write. Remember when my father went to Seoul? I heard my parents whispering late into the night. My father thought he should take your mother to a doctor, and my mother said it would take a shaman to exorcise her, not doctors. He mentioned something about a mental hospital. I was so shocked. Then they talked about you. That you're leading a tainted life, so it will be impossible to marry you off to a good family.*

Older Sister, I'm afraid. Why do these things happen to a happy family? I can't believe it. My brother Jin will go to Seoul soon. Please come back with him. Even if you have led a tainted life, I understand. I realize it's because you didn't want any help from my family. Older Sister, don't worry. Take our help. We are family. My mother and father also feel it is their duty to help your family. We're doing very well economically. They say everything is going really well.

Older Sister, I miss you. Please come back to Pusan. And let us be happy like before.

I wanted to talk to somebody, so I answered the letter promptly.

Mal, we had an amazing storm tonight. I saw the spectacle of snow twirling up from the ground into the sky. On a night like this I'll bet the kimchi *wouldn't spoil even in Pusan.*

My darling Mal, I just can't understand why you worry about us. My mother is very healthy. She looks ten years older because she refuses to put in her dentures but she's as strong as a person twenty years younger than her age.

I stopped to massage my aching shoulder and back, and continued.

This evening I arm wrestled with my mother, but I lost. I was so bored, that's why I asked her to do it for fun, but I lost. I'll bet you can't believe it, but it's true. As I said before, your aunt is stronger than many young people. If anything has changed, it is that she won't put in her dentures. As you remember, my mother was very particular about her appearance. She tried very hard to look pretty and young for her husband and sons, but she won't do it for me. But what can I do? My father's three-year mourning period hasn't come to an end, so it's only normal.

Am I tainted? I think your father is going senile. I've just become a little more careful about my appearance, that's all. Your father doesn't seem to understand the fact that girls grow up to be women.

Mal, I haven't even thought of independence or anything like that, even vaguely. I guess I'm shameless. It's simply that I like Seoul and I find my own house comfortable. That's all. So whatever Cousin Jin says, I'll stay here. I know he's busy, so tell him he doesn't have to visit us.

I'll close now. Goodbye.

I stopped writing. It was late. The night would usher in an empty tomorrow, so empty that nothing could fill it. I wished there were no tomorrow.

The wind continued shaking the weak spots in the old house, the corrugated iron shutters, the doors, and windows. My mother finished with cleaning up and slammed the sliding door shut.

"It sounds like an attack, tsk, tsk," she muttered as she went to her room.

Tonight's storm really did sound like a war. I wished the angry waves of war would surge over us, cutting today from tomorrow, rampaging mercilessly, reducing people to misery. A violent pleasure swept through me, and I laughed like a witch. I also trembled with the fright that the war would rush over me. If only I could avoid that blind devil again.

The two wishes, forever contradictory, lived in me always, plunging me into a frenzy every once in a while. Soon I would be cut in two. I felt a physical pain that really seemed to sever me into two. I paced around the room to forget the pain, taking my memory back to the time when the pain had begun.

Our refugee life, quite comfortable at my uncle's house . . . No, it was before then. The bleak moments as we fled Seoul . . . No, it was not then, either. Back at Christmas time, when I packed my bundles, unpacked, and packed again without telling my mother, not knowing whether we should flee . . . No, it was not then. Further back, after Seoul was re-taken by the UN forces, the empty house and the yellow ginkgo leaves in the back yard, the vivid blinding yellow, the yellow against the cobalt blue sky, the yellow streaming down endlessly, my eyes still hurt with the yellow . . . No, it was not then, either. Then it was before then, before, before . . .

But I stopped my memory from running further back. Why had those old ginkgo trees been so miserably yellow? Why had I looked up at those leaves, thinking that I wanted to die and then, that I wanted to live? I was still uncertain about that when my memory stopped and melted into the yellow.

Eight

With the dawn of the year 1952, I turned 21 years old. On New Year's morning I sat down to a breakfast tray that held only *kimchi* soup and rice. I had pleaded with my mother to make some dumplings for New Year's for several days, but she had only answered vaguely. In the end, she failed me.

I dumped the rice into the sour *kimchi* soup and tried to spoon some into my mouth, but it was not easy. An unappeased desire was lodged in my throat.

"You could have made some dumplings. White rice cake may have been too much, but . . ."

My mother chewed slowly, finishing the same amount of food as usual and then muttered as if to herself, "What's so important about New Year's? What nonsense! You're not a baby any more!"

The hot lump in my throat lurched up. I tugged at the end of my mother's skirt as she rose slowly with the tray in her hand.

"Mother, we're still alive. Living things change. We can prove that we're alive by changing."

"Why? We're still alive this way."

"Change gives life. Mother, I'm starving for life. If only you had changed the rice into dumplings . . . It would have been easy for you to do. Can't you understand that such simple, easy things might give your daughter life?"

Mother's dull eyes were unfocused, and I couldn't tell if they were gazing down at me or at the wardrobe behind me. It occurred to me that she was simply waiting for me to let go of her skirt. I also realized how obstinately my wish had been rejected and how powerless I was in the face of that rejection.

I let go of her skirt, muttering weakly, "I am not asking you to do it all the time. Just sometimes, Mother, just sometimes . . ."

But my mother had already gone down to the kitchen with the tray. The sound of the aluminum bowls clattering and water running drifted out of the kitchen.

It was my first day off in a long while. I mopped the floor and polished the mother-of-pearl wardrobe with a rag. I paid special attention to the long-life herb, the deer, and the cranes inlaid on the wardrobe. These symbols of longevity glistened mysteriously when I was finished.

However hard I polished my ancestors' dreams, my own desires could not be satisfied. On the grey wall I hung a cola company's calendar that I'd gotten from some Yankee. Having just slid down a ski slope, a healthy-looking couple was quenching their thirst with a cola. The vivid colors of their skiwear caught my eye. I began to feel an uncontrollable longing for the colors. My longing had been suppressed, dormant for a long time, but now it flared up like an inflammable material meeting a flame.

I flung open the wardrobe door and began rummaging through the clothes. White, grey, at best, jade; that's all there was. Finally I found the Korean dress I had worn for New Year's two years before. The deep orange skirt and the rainbow-striped blouse with the deep orange cuffs seemed so new that if I just ironed out the folds, they could be transformed into a dazzling New Year's dress. The rainbow-striped sleeves excited me.

My heart raced, and I took out a white rayon slip and a pair of my mother's thick cotton socks before going into the room across the hall. Having plugged in the electric iron, I carefully ironed the brocade skirt as if caressing it. I took a long time to do the skirt and blouse, enjoying the elegant sheen so typical of the silk fabric, appreciating its soft, light texture.

I took off my navy blue pants and grey sweater and kicked them across the room before I put on the white slip, the skirt, and the blouse. Perhaps I could have used a bit of makeup, but except for that, everything was perfect. I stood in front of the large mirror that reflected the whole length of my body.

I lowered myself to the floor gently in a deep dignified bow.

My father had grinned broadly and said, "Now she looks like a lady, dear. It's about time for us to look for a son-in-law, don't you agree?"

"Daddy, don't tease. Please," I spread out my hands in front of me, playing the baby.

My father looked at me and then at my mother, who sat elegantly next to him, and said in feigned ignorance, "Dear, why is she behaving this way? Do you know why?"

My brothers grinned and teased, "I'll bet she will dance around to get the New Year's bow money from her father-in-law even after she's married. Tsk, tsk. Father, it won't work. Let's not be too hasty about marrying her off. Look how she gets when she hears she's not ready to be married yet. So she wants to get married, eh?"

After I had gotten enough bow money, I had come back to my room, taken off the confining Korean dress, and changed into comfortable clothes more fitting a tomboy.

I had forgotten all about that pretty outfit. The me I saw in the mirror didn't look like my contemporary self. It was the "me" from two years before. I felt distant, and because I had been so pretty then, I was even a little jealous.

I stole out of the house. The wind on those days before Small Cold, the 23rd division of the 24 part lunar calendar, was so bitterly cold it hurt. However, the skirt of my Korean outfit billowed in the wind like a winged dress. I floated along lightly, almost unconscious of my weight.

The Utopia tea room was not busy. Johann Strauss's "Waltz of Spring" was playing at just the right volume. In the far corner I saw Tae-su raise his hand. I felt like a butterfly as I approached him.

"How could you keep me waiting for so long? My eyes nearly popped out looking for you."

Nevertheless, he was grinning. I sat down cautiously, pulling the back flap of my skirt carefully to the front. He kept smiling and looking at my gorgeous dress, but he didn't tease or praise me as I had expected.

"I've been waiting for two hours. Even a cat can pretend to be embarrassed, so how about pretending to be sorry? You're one shameless girl."

I was not sorry at all, so I smiled just a little, looking up at the familiar landscape on the wall. It had been Tae-su's idea to meet today, and I had never said yes, so there was no reason for me to feel sorry. I hadn't come of my own free will. Perhaps the winged New Year's dress had flown me there.

The day before Tae-su had been excited about the coming year.

"How about meeting somewhere tomorrow?"

"Why?"

"What do you mean why? Tomorrow is 1952. Tomorrow is next year. It's a holiday, too. Let's meet somewhere. We can figure out something fun to do then. All right? Come to that place, Utopia. Ten o'clock. The earlier we meet, the better."

I hadn't thought about whether I would be seeing him or not. The next year he was talking about seemed so far away. It didn't seem like the next day but like some time in the future that had nothing to do with me.

"I was all dressed in my New Year's dress, but I didn't have anywhere to go."

"What? I asked for an apology and this is what I get?"

Tae-su snatched my frozen hand but released it gently. The waitress came with the coffee, then opened the cast iron stove, and gave the red coal briquette a poke or two before closing the damper and walking away. The stove sizzled and the surface turned a rosy red.

My body gradually thawed. My flesh, covered with goose bumps under my clothes, grew warm as my blood began to circulate, and the coffee warmed my lips and throat. The coffee was very flavorful. I didn't dislike sitting opposite Tae-su.

"Hey, waitress, can I have some matches?" He called to the counter, snapping his fingers and forefinger. He pulled the thin tape from the new Lucky Strikes.

"Why can't you buy a lighter? They're everywhere."

"You don't know what you're talking about. I go around without a lighter or matches, with only cigarettes, so I'm dying for a smoke, I'm a nervous wreck. Then, if I find someone lighting a cigarette, I bow and ask for a light. That first drag is the best in the world. Besides, it's an excuse for flirting with the waitresses in tea rooms."

"Have you ever been slapped on the cheek when you asked an old man for a light?"

"Not yet."

He breathed out smoke rings into the air. He was one year older today, but he was as frivolous as ever. He still had the air of a naughty boy who had sneaked into a closet to smoke his father's cigarettes. I doubted if he could really appreciate the taste of a cigarette. I probably knew more than he did about different brands. I recalled my father's elegant smoking. I had yet to meet anyone who smoked with the dignity of my father.

In the summer, he used to lean back in the wicker chair with the north window wide open, smoking his pipe, as if he didn't have a thought or a worry in his mind. Actually, it was difficult to tell whether he was deep in thought or simply worry-free.

Ock Hui-do smoked elegantly enough, although not nearly as nicely as my father. When Ock smoked, one could get a glimpse of a heartache too deep for words. The painters loved smoking as much as anybody, but they clung to it desperately, creating an impression of poverty. Because of this unexpected image of my father, I began to dislike Tae-su. Dressed in a grown-up outfit, I wanted to sit across from a man of more experience.

"Where shall we go? Do you have any interesting ideas?" he asked.

"I don't care where we go."

"Let's go to the movies, have lunch, then wander around. That's all I can come up with."

He yawned widely. I wanted to yawn along with him.

"Isn't there something more intimate we could do?" he added.

"Intimate?"

"I don't mean anything particular. I just want to feel contented. I miss the feeling of loving someone and being loved by someone. We don't have that between us."

"That's only natural. We're not in love, you know."

"Don't tease me, please."

His silly expression was transformed into the innocence of a boy. I gazed at him in silence. Perhaps he was more sensitive than he looked. The anxiety and anguish on his brow grew. Perhaps it was because of my gaze. I couldn't look away, however, and his discontent was infectious. My heart ached terribly. But my pain was not for Tae-su.

I was thinking of Ock Hui-do. His wife with the white slender neck and their five children. The youngest one, with the nice smell, so healthy. I couldn't endure the passionate longing and frustration I felt. I played with the long tie on the front of my silky dress, rolling and unrolling it over and over again.

"Let's go somewhere, anywhere." I stood up, making an effort to relax my contorted face.

"Already?"

He hastily picked up his cigarettes and gloves, looking a little regretful. From the way he didn't even bother to wink at the waitress, I could tell he must have been quite serious.

We went to see "Homecoming" at the Sudo Theater. I didn't care for the movie much, but I felt as if we had been driven out of the theater when it ended. The street was filled with a sense of bleakness. We peered into several eateries, trying to find a place to have lunch. My feet were numb from the cold floor of the unheated theater.

"How about some Western food?"

"No, I'd like to sit comfortably on a heated *ondol* floor."

"Because your majesty is wearing a *hanbok*, eh?"

"Right. Imagine me sitting on a chair, taking off my rubber shoes and lifting up my feet in their cotton stockings to warm them at the stove. You wouldn't like that."

"Well, I don't think I would dislike it."

My feet were frozen, almost to the point of total numbness. At times they slipped out of my rubber shoes, touching the asphalt. Not many restaurants were open on New Year's Day.

After a lot of wandering, we finally found a place with a warm *ondol* floor, although it was not very clean. A waitress brought in the tea, which looked like murky dishwater. I tucked my feet under the floor cushion and massaged them.

"What would you like?"

"As it's New Year's, I think I'll have the rice cake and dumpling soup," I said.

"Me, too."

The skins of the dumplings were thick, with the corners still uncooked, so that I could taste the raw wheat flour. I pushed them to one corner and ate a few slices of rice cake, then stopped altogether.

Tae-su ate voraciously. He looked miserable eating the bad food with such relish. It made me sad. Was it because I knew so well what it meant to eat solely to fill one's stomach? I gazed at him eating, wondering if he knew the food tasted terrible.

"How was it?"

"Fine, I was hungry. Why didn't you finish yours?"

"I wasn't that hungry. Do you always eat with such an appetite?"

"Sure. What would you do with a man who's picky?"

"I heard the dumplings Hwanghae-do people make are as big as a person's foot." I laughed, surprised at my own words.

"It is true that our sticky rice cakes or crescent rice cakes are bigger than those in Seoul, but that's because we are simple and down-to-earth. You know, it's the people who make the food, the same way the slick Seoul people spread out an array of side dishes just to please the eye when there's not much to eat. But why do you have to compare my hometown's food to a person's foot?"

He pretended to be offended, but he made sense. And what about the women of Kaesong, so neat and charming? I wanted to brag. About Kaesong women, about my mother.

"Have you ever tried Kaesong food, real Kaesong food?"

"Well, I'm not a connoisseur. I just eat to fill my stomach. I never thought about where certain dishes originated. Are you from Kaesong?"

"No, but my mother's family is. My mother is an expert at cooking the most delicious food." I pushed my remaining dumplings around my bowl with a spoon and continued. "Kaesong dumplings look kind of funny. They have thin, chewy skins, made with dough worked long and hard. The filling, rich with the flavor of sesame oil, is stuffed to make fat, round dumplings. First, you make a crescent shape, then you bring the two ends together, and it looks like a person with a fat belly, holding his hands together behind his back. The rice cake soup is even better. It is called *chorang-ttok*. You roll the well-pounded rice powder into a thin log and then rub it with sesame oil. It is much thinner than the Seoul variety. It's pressed with a bamboo knife once, then cut further down, so it looks like a small silkworm cocoon or a figure 8. . . ."

I gestured, pretending to cut the rice cake. I felt like an art lover discussing an exquisite work of art. Tae-su didn't show much reaction, however, despite my enthusiasm. From the way he had devoured the terrible food, I would have expected his mouth to water, but he looked rather bored, even though he wore a grin on his face.

"When will I have the honor to be invited to such a delicious feast? That's what I'm wondering."

My enthusiasm dampened immediately. I pictured my grey mother and her sour *kimchi* soup. Would there ever be an invitation to the feast, and if so, when? I was the one who wondered more about that than Tae-su.

"By the way you talk, my future mother-in-law must be an amazing cook. I expect I will enjoy fine food. And they say a mother-in-law loves her son-in-law the most."

"Don't be silly. Crescent rice cakes that look like human feet are more your style."

Tae-su's silly joke brought me back to reality and I felt nauseous at the sight of the cold dumpling soup in front of me. The girl cleared away the bowls and wiped the table clean. We stepped out onto the street again and wandered about in the bleak winter alley.

There was nothing wondrous there, only the invisible cold, dry wind whipping black soot up from the grey sidewalk. Clark Gable's smirk on a movie poster, which flapped about with one corner unglued, was nothing new as we had just seen the movie. The unexpressive grey buildings had their windows shut tight, looking like so many match boxes, their only distinguishing features being whether they were horizontal or vertical.

I should have stopped at some corner to say goodbye, but I hesitated. It was too light to go back. I couldn't envision myself walking home, gazing at my house in the daylight. One side of the roof gone, the gap on the ridge yawning like a hole leading to hell, the shattered roof tiles. Looking at them seemed as sacrilegious as picturing Confucius without a stitch of clothing on his body.

My house must stand under the black sky in the dark. I would feel scared, almost awed, standing in front of it. The climax of my day was embedded in that very moment, and I couldn't change it.

"How about going to my house? We can warm up there."

Tae-su's low voice rescued me. I nodded deeply and followed him without speaking. His arms encircled my waist intimately.

"Aren't you cold in this thin, pretty dress? You were shivering so much the other night."

Perhaps he was waiting for me to shake again. But I didn't.

"Do you want my jacket?"

He wanted me to shiver. I shook my head, pulled away from him, and walked along, leaving a little distance between us.

In a Hoehyon-dong alley, dotted with restaurants, Tae-su's room was in an old two-story Japanese building. It stood out because of the urologist's sign on the ground floor. He said he rented a room on the second floor.

A narrow staircase led from a glass door on the street to the second floor, so Tae-su could reach his room without going into the clinic on the first floor. While he was opening the large lock, I gazed at the sign, "Hoehyon Urology Clinic."

The four-and-a half *tatami* room was chilly. Tae-su hurriedly ignited the wood in the stove. I assumed he didn't need my help, so I sat on the window sill. Tae-su lit some paper and dropped it onto the thin pieces of wood, building a large fire. Then he began adding logs, warming up the room in no time.

He whistled as if building a fire was his favorite pastime, and with a clang of the lid, it was done. He brushed the dirt off his hands and grinned.

"Do you live here by yourself? I thought you lived with your brother's family."

"I lived with his family before I went into the military, but after I was discharged and began working, I found this place for myself. I have nephews and nieces and I felt bad about taking up space in the home of my brother and his wife."

"How many nephews and nieces do you have?"

"Five."

"Is that so? The same as the Ocks. Maybe Hwanghae-do people like having big families."

"Five isn't so many. My sister-in-law's work is still in progress."

"In what?"

"The species preservation project. She's not even forty yet."

"Do you think Mr. Ock is still in progress, too?"

"Could be."

I suppressed a deep sigh. My body adequately warmed now, I looked around the room. It was a simple room without personality. The grey walls displayed a single picture, the kind one would expect in a country barber shop; the rest was empty. Imagining Tae-su buying the landscape from a frame shop, I couldn't help but smile and the tension disappeared.

"How do you like it? Cleaner than you expected?"

"No."

"You must be disappointed, then. I cleaned up and even decorated in preparation for your visit."

I smiled broadly, thinking that by decoration he must mean the picture.

"Did you think I was living in a decent place?"

"No. To be frank, I hadn't thought about where you lived." I told the truth.

"Really? I thought women daydreamed about their boyfriends all the time. Don't you?"

"Well, maybe you do."

"What else can a young bachelor do when he's alone except think about women? If I say women, you might feel offended, but sometimes I picture the bedroom of a pure woman like you, and other times I imagine Diana Kim rolling around with a nigger."

I gazed out the window at the approaching dusk. As the lights in the shops came on one by one, the passersby looked even colder. The torch on a peddler's cart began a pale dance, and a woman next to it began to collect the chewing gum that she had laid out for sale.

It will get even darker soon. The distorted dark roof and the sharp thrill. I was measuring the darkness with the delicate sensitivity of an artist.

"Are you angry because of what I've said? But believe me, I think of you all the time."

As always, I didn't know what to say when Tae-su got serious. The conversation died and everything felt awkward.

At the small desk next to the window, arranged in a pile according to size was a dictionary, an English magazine, and a photo album. I picked up the album and flipped through it quickly. He immediately came to sit next to me on the window sill. Undoubtedly he wanted to explain the photos to me. I would get to know him better. Know about his past, his friends, his family, all the unnecessary details of his history. I didn't want to bother to learn about any of that, so I turned the pages quickly, never giving him a chance to butt in.

The cast iron stove glowed red from the heat, and the small room was stifling. I pressed a flushed cheek against the pane to cool it. One by one the lights were coming on.

The darkness thickened visibly like water colors spreading across paper.

"Kyong-a, You're so pretty today."

He slowly turned my face toward his. He was trembling. He pulled me into his arms. I could feel the pounding of his heart against my cheek, but my eyes were glued to the outside, measuring the density of the darkness. His hot lips brushed my cheek, cool from the glass, and moved down to my mouth. He seemed anxious, as if he were searching for me in an almost rough way. My eyes remained fixed on the window, still measuring the density of the darkness outside.

Nothing in my body opened to him. My heart beat quietly, never breaking its normal rhythm and my temperature didn't rise more than the stove had already raised it.

He caressed earnestly, with growing impatience. I let him touch my body, but my eyes were glued to the outside. Without feeling anything particular, I could see everything clearly. He finally knelt down on the floor and buried his face in my skirt.

"How can . . . Kyong-a, how can you . . . ," he wailed.

He seemed to have finally begun to realize how meaningless and miserable a one-sided passion between a man and woman could be.

I pulled my silk skirt toward me little by little from where it lay crumpled mercilessly in his arms. He looked even more pathetic with his face in my white rayon slip. After a while he turned on the light and lit a cigarette.

"Do you dislike me?"

I was so shocked by his forlorn expression that I said emphatically, "No, no," even shaking my head.

It was not a lie, but I was distressed because I knew I would have answered the same way if he asked the opposite question. He moved his lips as if trying to say something more, but he ended up simply taking a long draw on his cigarette.

"Shall I make us dinner? You'll help me, won't you?" He asked, having regained his composure.

He slid open the closet door. A folded mattress and bedding were stuffed on the shelf, and on the bottom shelf was a shabby array of cooking utensils and ingredients including a bottle of soy sauce.

"I have to go."

It was completely dark out now. The world was engulfed in a thick darkness.

"Because your mother is waiting for you. Right?" he responded wearily as he shut the closet door.

He didn't attempt to make me stay. I picked my way down the steep stairs, and when I stepped out into the street, illuminated only by the light of the red cross over the entrance, I took a deep breath of the cold night air.

"Goodbye. I had a nice time today," I said, as he followed me down. Then I walked away fast without waiting for a response. After a while, I looked back to make sure that he was not following me and began enjoying a slow walk, looking around.

I passed a street permeated with cooking odors, not unpleasant. Then I came out to a brighter, more exciting street, lined with Western dressmaking shops and haberdasheries. I would have liked to linger to enjoy the sights, but I kept smelling something.

It was the smell of *kimchi* soup. I could smell the sour stench even when I pinched my nose with my fingers. My anger at my mother and the misery I had felt that morning flared up inside me.

Was my yearning for dumplings simply a matter of appetite? No, it was more urgent than appetite, like a thirsty tree's craving for sweet rain, or a burning desire for affection and tender love. How could she be so blind? My own mother?

My hatred for her, suppressed so far because she was my own flesh and blood, surpassed the limit of my patience. Her unbelievable stinginess, her frightening obstinacy. No one had the right to hurt another human being that much. How could she be so tightfisted with her affection and tender love?

I took several deep breaths to cool my seething fury. Suddenly a realization stopped me in my tracks. I remembered Tae-su's expression when he was kneeling on the floor. He must have been as miserable as I was when I didn't get dumplings on New Year's morning.

Was that possible? What if he were as hurt as I had been? What difference could there be between his desperate sigh, "How can . . . Kyong-a, how can you . . ." and my plea, "Sometimes, just sometimes . . ." as I clung to my mother's skirt?

I pressed my head against a display window where a mannequin in a pink spring coat was spinning. The pink coat rotated round and round. The mannequin kept turning without feeling dizzy, wearing a permanent smile. I was dizzy, my thoughts turning this way and that. I felt that the rotation of the pink coat must be preventing me from thinking. I closed my eyes. I saw that grey mother of mine and breathed in the odor of *kimchi* soup.

The decision came easily. I retraced my steps. I felt like sobbing because of the sympathy I had for Tae-su. I wanted to give him everything I could. Why hadn't I realized it before? I told myself nobody should be as miserable as I was when I couldn't have those dumplings. I raced down the street lined with the Western dressmaking shops and haberdasheries, and turned into the alley filled with eateries.

While running, I tried to think of ways I could avoid another failure. How could I open myself to him? I recalled the moments he had looked attractive. I liked the recollection of his firm, manly jaw with its shadow of a beard. If I pressed my forehead against it, a miracle would happen to me, like a bud opening up in a warm breeze. Hadn't I once wished to press my forehead against his chin and listen to his heartbeat? That's what I would do first. I wouldn't worry about what came next. Tae-su would take care of the rest.

I finally came to a halt at the urologist's sign. Tae-su's room was dark, and a large padlock hung on the glass door leading to the second floor.

Nine

The first thing I saw as I stepped in the PX was Ock Hui-do. I bounced across the arcade. Good things are so much better when you don't expect them.

"Happy New Year!"

"Happy New Year!"

I greeted everyone I met as I crossed the PX, including the cleaning women and laborers. The painters were shaking hands with Ock Hui-do, as if they were meeting him for the first time.

"I'm sorry. We didn't even go to see you while you were ill. Are you feeling better?" said Chin politely, who was usually quiet and gentle.

"You must have been really sick. For the poor, getting sick is worst."

"You've grown thin. You used to look so good. Tsk, tsk, have a cigarette."

Kim and Cash were being very kind. They had ignored Ock until then. I wanted to be part of it, too.

"Happy New Year!" I greeted each painter happily, for I really wanted to bless them. I turned to Ock Hui-do and repeated the greeting. Afterwards I added in a small voice. "Are you all right now?"

"Yes, thanks to you," he answered, also in a low voice. And that satisfied me.

"Miss Lee, you're much prettier now that you're a year older."

"Miss Lee, you should get married this year. It's not good for a girl to work here too long."

"Why? Are you afraid that Miss Lee will be whisked away by a mongrel?"

Now, like Cash, all the painters called the Yankees mongrels.

"Damn this miserable world! Korean boys get dragged off to war and the mongrels get all the pretty girls."

"Hey, don't worry about them. If you don't want to lose your woman, you'd better draw those mongrels' pictures as fast as you can."

"That's for sure. You finally said something right for a change."

They smoked, joked around, then began to get their tools ready. I started sorting the photos. I had taken only one day off, but my hands didn't move as fast as before. It was satisfying to realize that Ock Hui-do was behind me, but I was queasy because I wasn't used to that kind of feeling.

70

The Christmas tree, still clothed in its strips of gold and silver paper, sent out an endless display of red and blue winks. The transistor radios that the Yankees carried over their shoulders emitted "Puppy Love" in a hoarse voice. I didn't dislike the mood but wanted to believe I couldn't calm down because of it.

At the candy counter in front of us, Diana's diamond glittered on her ring finger as she sold cookies to American soldiers and counted the dollars. Her hands were delicate and beautiful, as if they were meant for diamonds.

Suddenly she placed her elbows on top of the display case and rested for a while, with her hands clutching her hair and covering part of her forehead. The red fingernails and the diamond, in the midst of her black hair, looked indescribably beautiful. I thought how beautiful she could be if only she thought of something besides money.

Tae-su passed, carrying a screwdriver, a pair of pliers, and some other tools. He didn't greet me or wink; he acted as if nothing had happened. I didn't feel anything particular toward him, either. The time that I wanted to be more generous and charitable to him had already passed. He may have looked somewhat tired, but it seemed to have nothing to do with me.

Ock coughed from time to time. His cough was not as bad as I had heard at his home, but sometimes he coughed for a long time.

"For a cough, radish juice steeped in honey is the best. That is, if you can find real honey," Chin muttered out of pity for Ock.

"Don't you know how expensive honey is? Why don't you drink water boiled with green onions and apricot pits?"

"What a foolish thing to say! Where can you get apricot pits at this time of year? Where I'm from, people steep eggs in vinegar and drink it."

The painters offered their remedies one by one.

Cash, who had been quiet, stretched and said, "What strange cures! If they all worked, doctors would starve to death. At least you didn't recommend anything like a combination of dog shit and cow dung. Don't you agree, Mr. Ock? The best thing to do after an illness is to eat well. When there's no fat in your stomach, you get weak and the cough won't go away. At night you have cold sweats, you feel dizzy, and something in your belly seems to suck your voice in so you can't speak sometimes. Isn't that so, Mr. Ock?"

"So now you're into fortune telling, eh?"

"Fortune telling? It's simply a good examination, sir."

"If you perform an examination, you are supposed to offer a prescription."

"All right. Then in order to help Mr. Ock build his strength up and since we're all hungry, how about going out for some *sollongtang* soup with lots of delicious fat floating on top? How does that sound? We may have fallen on bad times and have no choice but to paint mongrels to make ends meet, but our hearts haven't dried up, have they?"

"Hear, hear."

They were all very kind today.

"What about me? Can I go along too?" I asked, smiling.

"Sure, but somebody has to watch the store. Miss Lee, can we bring some sweet rolls for you?"

"All right. I'll watch the store, but be sure to bring lots of rolls."

They scrambled out the door together. A group of Yankees passed by, sipping Cokes and chomping on hamburgers. I hated their glistening obesity.

I called out to Misuk in the brassware section. "Doesn't it seem like something good is going to happen this year?"

"Why?" she asked as she ran toward me. "Where did all the painters go?"

"For lunch. They said they would bring back some rolls, so don't eat your lunch."

"Really! How nice!"

She sat right next to me. I put my arms around her shoulders and pressed my face into the nape of her neck. Several strands of her hair tickled my nose, and a pure human smell, not clouded by cosmetics, reached me.

Breathing in the milky fragrance, kind of a combination of wild flowers and newborn animals, I was filled with a longing for people, a longing so urgent that I grew sad. Inhaling her odor, I caressed the end of her long braids.

"What kind of good things will happen, do you think?" she asked.

"It's just a vague feeling."

"I think everyone feels that way on New Year's." She sounded very grown-up. "If a woman marries an American legally, do people still call her a Yankee slut?" The direction of her conversation shifted suddenly. "I think I'll marry an American."

Instead of giving her a response I snorted.

"I mean it."

She looked as if she were confessing a grave secret, when I simply wanted to relieve the fatigue of a long afternoon, breathing in her comforting smell of puppies and wild flowers.

"You must have seen him. The PFC who comes to my shop every day for an hour or so. He wants me to marry him and go to America."

"Do you like him?"

"I'm not sure whether I like him or the idea of going to America."

"Do you want to go to America that badly?" I was taken aback.

"It doesn't have to be America. I simply want to leave this country. I'm sick and tired of war, evacuation, and starvation. I wish I never had to see these miserable things again."

She pierced a piece of paper with the point of a pencil as she spoke, repeating the motion on ever-shrinking spaces.

"It's so dirty, like sewage. Real sewage. So dirty and miserable," she murmured, wetting her dry lips with a flick of her tongue.

"What is?" I asked, simply because it seemed rude to remain silent.

"My house. It's a sewer. You probably couldn't even imagine it."

I chuckled to myself behind her back, without asking why her house was a sewer. I couldn't resist laughing since she herself was fragrant, since she was fragrant in the midst of sewage, and because she only knew the smell of sewage, not her own fragrance.

"Why are you laughing? I'm not joking. I'm trying to have a serious conversation."

She had yet to discover that I was not the right person to talk to about serious things.

"What's an international marriage like?"

"You mean the process?"

"No, the forms can take care of themselves. I mean what's it like in practice?"

She stammered, but her piercing pencil grew swifter and surer. Her flushed cheeks looked so fresh it seemed they might emit a fruity fragrance at any time.

"You'll find out after you get married."

"Well, I want to know in advance. I can't figure out what the future with him will be like. I was just attracted to the idea of going to America, but I can't figure the rest out. I wish someone would guarantee our future together."

It seemed like I was supposed to be that "someone," but I didn't have the slightest desire to be.

"Everyone has some fears before marriage. That's why they made up the Four Pillars of Fortune and why they check people's horoscopes before they get married."

I had been leaning comfortably on her shoulder, but now she yanked her head up and spoke in an uncharacteristically hysterical voice. "I don't mean that. This is totally different."

At that moment the painters piled in, picking their teeth. Kim threw me a large bag of rolls, and Cash winked and said, "Miss Lee, we all pitched in for those rolls."

"Now that our bellies are full, it's time we started drawing those damn mongrels again, right?"

I handed a roll over to Misuk and stammered, "What can I say? The only thing I can guarantee is that if you marry him and have his child, it will be a mongrel. That's one thing for sure, I guess."

I blurted that out, having heard the painters mentioning "mongrels" so often, but Misuk shuddered as if pierced by a sharp skewer.

"How could you use such a word? That word is used for animals. I'm surprised at you."

She dropped the roll she was eating and fled to her shop, her eyes brimming with tears. I followed her with some rolls, but she was so furious that she refused to look at them.

The painters started working, but Ock Hui-do was staring at the grey curtain. I approached him. I couldn't tell whether his tired eyes were gazing at the curtain or at something behind it. He was engrossed in something anyway, something that had nothing to do with me.

I paced around him and cleared my throat. He was immovable, like a rock. If only I could shift his focus toward me. Pacing around him, I straightened the painting tools and spread out scarves. Still, he didn't awaken from his reverie. Perhaps I would have to stand on my head on the tiled floor to get his attention. If I walked on my hands, sweeping the floor with my black hair, everyone, including Ock, would look at me. I could do that. You bet I could. I wished I could, but I simply sighed deeply, standing on my two feet.

Misuk sat slouched forward, her forehead almost touching the display case. The part in the middle of her black hair was straight and neat. I sighed again for Misuk. I was so distant from Ock Hui-do and from Misuk. They were not absorbed by distress, but dissolved into a time that didn't move forward; I was the only one who was swept away by the passage of the anxious seconds. Thinking that I was in a different time frame from theirs, I became as chilly and lonely, as if I were caught in a spring wind that blew only to spite the blooming flowers.

A comical-looking GI was leaning over at the portraits on display, crunching popcorn noisily.

"May I help you?" I asked, slipping back into my sales mode.

The arcade grew busier as the afternoon customers arrived. Misuk and I had to speak to them in English, adapting our tongues to its peculiar twists and rolls. After some time I noticed Ock Hui-do had started painting.

"I can't forget what you said this afternoon." Misuk ran to me after the shutters had come down.

"I'm sorry, I didn't realize that it was a curse word and that it is normally used for animals. I've heard it so often it didn't mean anything to me. When it comes to people, you say half-breeds, I guess." I apologized, stammering as we walked out onto the street together.

"It's all the same whether it's a mongrel or a half breed. The important thing is the prediction that I will give birth to children."

"Is that a prediction? It is only logical that married couples have children."

"That's what I mean. That's why I'm afraid."

"What do you mean?"

I was irritated because I knew she was going to get into something complicated. I wanted to be free from everything that had nothing to do with me. I needed to think of my own affairs, swaying my drooping limbs gently and gazing up at the stars and the lights in the stores. Then I would get on with business of my life, plunging myself into the darkness and cold.

"Where do you live? Don't you ride the bus? I walk home, you know."

I pulled her frozen hand toward the bus stop in a friendly manner. If she walked home, I could always take another road. The important thing was making clear that we were merely heading in our separate directions.

"Please, please talk with me for a while." She clung to me, her face puckered.

"You should go home now. Isn't your mother waiting for you?"

"Let her wait. Do you think I'm a child? Let's sit and talk in a tea room. It doesn't matter if I go home late."

I had no choice but to sit with her in a shabby second-floor tea room. Perhaps because of the whipping wind, her normally pink cheeks had grown pale. My face, reflected in the black windowpane, looked very tired. I was afraid that she would exhaust me. I closed my eyes, leaning the side of my head against the window. A sweet drowsiness spread over my body.

"Your coffee is getting cold." She hurried me without touching her own coffee. I covered the lukewarm cup with my hands, but I didn't know how to bring myself to drink that black liquid.

"I don't think I'll go to America."

"Why?" I was glad.

"Because of what you said . . . because of the mongrel business."

"Not mongrel again. Half-breed, I said. I don't expect prejudice against mixed blood is the same in America as it is here. Actually, America is made up of people of mixed blood."

"It's not that. I'm not afraid of that. What you said this afternoon made me realize something, something that I had forgotten."

"What?"

"There is something other than going to America. I began to think of marriage in more concrete terms. About the process of having babies. It gives me the creeps thinking of doing it with that PFC."

She frowned prettily, squeezing her eyebrows together.

I was exhausted, and I didn't understand what she was talking about.

"I want to go to America, but there's something more important."

"What's that?" I forced myself to ask.

"The dream that the first contact between a man and woman will be lovely. I can't let that PFC ruin that dream."

"You've been thinking those wild thoughts all day."

"No, that thought flashed through my mind the moment you said mongrel. Actually, I was thinking of that all along but I covered it up stupidly on account of my dream of going to America. You lifted the veil for me."

I smiled awkwardly, at a loss for words. Not knowing whether I had done a good deed or not, I just wanted to be free of her.

"All day I was thinking of ways to escape from the sewer without going to America. I decided to have a talk with you."

She gulped down the cold coffee as if drinking water, and her cheeks grew flushed.

"Can I stay with you at your house?" She asked it as if she had finally gathered up enough courage.

I turned toward the pane. The window didn't show any details of the dark back alley but my reflection. I pressed my forehead on the cold window pane and then my nose, distorting it. I shut my eyes and tried to devise a way to get out of an embarrassing answer, but I grew sick and tired of making silly excuses. I shook my head until the loose windowpane clattered. Drowsiness enveloped me like mist.

"I'll pay for my board." Having moved next to me, she was whispering, blowing a warm breath into my ear, her arm draped around my back. Her unique body smell reached me. It was a shame that she didn't know she was so fragrant in the midst of the sewage.

If the ground she was standing on was a sewer, what I was standing on was a terrible land parched by a long dry spell demon. How could I explain that to her? It would be easier to explain Korea's *sijo* poems in English.

I really hated to feel burdened and distressed by other people's problems. I decided to ignore it.

"Let's go now. Our mothers will be waiting for us." I stood up, pulling her hand.

"Our mothers?"

"Yes, your mother and my mother," I said nonchalantly.

"You'll think about what I've just asked, won't you?"

"Put on your scarf. It's cold outside."

I wrapped my hair in my scarf, as if giving her a demonstration, pulling down several wisps of bangs over my forehead.

"I'll pay for my board. I earn enough for that."

"I'm rather hungry. All I had for lunch was a few rolls. Aren't you hungry?"

Ahead of her, I climbed down the dark, steep stairs expertly. The street was cold, and I hated to be alone in the cold. I wanted to be more friendly just because it was cold, but decided I'd better not. She seemed to expect to hear a definite answer. I said firmly, "Goodbye."

Walking alone, I sucked in my stomach, pulling my head into my coat collar. It was only then that I turned to look inside myself. My field of vision was as dark and narrow as that of a snail hiding inside its shell. But it was only there, inside that confined range, that I could feel at ease with the world around me.

I stood absentmindedly at a trolley stop. The trolley hadn't come for a long time, but the number of people waiting didn't increase. I was so tired that I wanted to ride if only as far as Hwashin. I was completely exhausted, having drummed up sales amounting to almost 200 dollars that day.

I suddenly realized that the most exhausted part of me was not my legs, but my mouth. After a day of repeating the same phrases over and over in my seventh grader's English, by evening my tongue was ready to go into fits.

"How beautiful she is!"

"May I help you?"

Thinking back, I realized that I may not have spoken my mother tongue all day. I was extremely busy, Misuk and Tae-su didn't come to talk to me, and I didn't have time to talk to Ock Hui-do. All of a sudden I was seized with the compulsion to speak my own language. I moved next to a middle-aged man who was standing nearby, although it was not clear if he was waiting for the trolley.

"How beautiful your wife is!" I muttered under my breath in Korean.

"What's her eye color?"

"What's her hair color?"

Fortunately, he couldn't hear me because I kept my voice so low. Low as it was, it was the first Korean I had spoken that day. But even if it was Korean, it wasn't my own words. I felt I would go crazy if I didn't say something that conveyed my own feelings. If not in words, I wanted to express myself in a cry or even a gesture.

The middle-aged man ambled toward the other side of the trolley strip. The trolley didn't come, and the number of people waiting for it didn't increase or decrease. I paced a while, then started walking.

A boy working as a hawker at a gift shop for American soldiers had latched onto a black man. I stopped to listen to his sad English.

"Hallo, Preese come, come. Rook, Rook. We have meny, meny, berry nice present."

"I don't have money. You give yourself a present, okay?"

The boy slammed down the brass ashtray and pipe he was hawking on the counter, and cried, "Damn it, you son-of-bitch!"

It was in our own refreshing tongue. I felt much better and asked him, grinning, "Hey, little boy, have you sold a lot today?"

This seemed like the first meaningful Korean I had used all day. Not waiting for his answer, I went on wearily, looking at the stores.

Bamboo baskets, pipes, A-frame carriers, wooden baskets, jackets with flashy embroidery on both front and back, faded pajamas made of coarse fabric, a grandfather with a horsehair hat, a wooden farmer doll with a fertilizer carrier on his back. All the goods were supposed to be typical Korean products, but they looked strange and foreign to me. There was not much to sell, but you couldn't survive without selling what there was; that must be the mark of poverty. I passed the shops and stood in a dark corner.

And then I ran. It wasn't simply because I was afraid. Something more urgent than fear had overcome me. I wanted to see the chimpanzee at the toy stall. I wanted to be with that pleasant friend caught in that frenzy of whisky drinking until he slowed down and returned to total emptiness.

The toy stall was surrounded by spectators as usual, most of them adults. I felt better seeing other grown-ups who liked toys. Among the piles of cars, trains, dolls, airplanes, swords, and guns, the chimpanzee drew the most attention, but he didn't seem to generate any income for the vendor. Today he had a helper beside him. A wind-up black doll, with bulging eyes and white teeth, was waiting for his master's festival to begin, a pair of cymbals in his hands.

The vendor yawned languidly, eyed the crowd with a sidelong glance, and stretched his dry wooden hand toward the chimpanzee, as if he were being forced to please the spectators. I held my breath like someone in a theater audience waiting for the opening gong. The vendor wound the screw on the back of the chimpanzee first, then he wound up the black doll, before setting them up side by side. They moved their shoulders rhythmically, one pouring and drinking whisky and the other clanging the cymbals. They were a becoming pair, for one poured and drank whisky faster and faster, while the other pounded the cymbals faster and faster.

The onlookers swayed their bodies to the rhythm, laughing and laughing. I laughed so hard that tears flowed from the corners of my eyes. While the onlookers held their breath, the pair's movement slowed down. When they came to a complete halt, I felt the energy draining from my body, almost melting to the ground. I brushed away my tears, while the crowd moved away and newcomers arrived. I kept staring absentmindedly. Nothing crept into my empty brain. Suddenly I realized that I could stand without crumpling to the ground because I was being supported by somebody. The support was so expert, so comfortable. A sense of recognition flashed through me.

"Let's go now," said Ock Hui-do.

A pair of warm, good-natured eyes was looking down at me. Happiness surged through me, as if we were meeting after a long, long separation. Side by side we threaded our way through the crowd.

"Do you still look at toys just like a child?" he asked.

"What about you?"

"Suddenly I had to see him. That drunkard . . . ," he said softly.

"Me, too. I ran all the way."

"I did the same thing. Why? I wonder. I couldn't resist the urge."

"Maybe we expected to see each other," I said.

"What do you mean? We've just been together all day."

As if showing that he had been really with me, he held my small hand. It thawed inside his thick, warm one, and his heat, his breath, his eyes conveyed an ecstatic joy almost as in a dream.

"It's been a long time."

I was thankful to see him there. He seemed to be a new person, different from the one I had been with the whole day.

"We've always been together." He squeezed my hand.

"What's the use of being together? We were so busy that we couldn't find a moment to talk. I was so lonely."

"Pitiful girl," he said in a half-joking tone, grinning, but his words had a special power that stroked my heart.

"Please, please don't make me a pitiful girl again," I spoke like a child, walking with my head against his shoulder. He didn't answer.

After the glittering lights of the dressmaker, the haberdashery, the shoe shop, and the jewelry shop, came the dim Chinese bun shop and the dark hill that rose toward the cathedral. I looked up at him by the 30-watt light of the bun shop. Usually good-natured, bright, and calm, his eyes were now burning with a strange fever.

Shocked, I shifted my glance. When I looked up at him again the next time, we had passed the brightness, and with the street lights behind, his face was shadowed, but his eyes were still burning.

I held my breath. Throughout my body, I could feel that this rock-like man was trembling from deep inside. I was trembling also. My hand in his was feeling something completely new. For a minute, I felt a resistance to the new feeling. I tried to pull my hand from his, but he was much stronger than I expected. I couldn't help but sense his masculinity.

My heart began to pound uncontrollably. I pressed on the left side of my chest with my free hand. My heart, suddenly transformed into a separate being, was about to jump from the ribs that confined it. He was dragging me. I missed some steps and lost my balance. He stopped abruptly and pressed against me firmly with all his weight.

I could see and feel his fever close up.

"Pitiful girl. You're trembling," he whispered in a shaky voice, which tickled my ear.

I knew he was deeply frightened of something. And I was frightened of whatever he was frightened of. I waited for the frightening thing to happen. I felt his breath, hesitating a little. I tilted back my head and looked up at the cross on the roof of the cathedral before accepting his breath. Strangely, I remembered the phrase of the poem I had forgotten when I had stood at that spot. Before I knew it, I was reciting the poetry haltingly.

Maria, only you should be merciful to us. We were born of your blood.
Who knows better than you how heartbreaking longing can be.

I had no idea why I had to spoil that precious moment by doing such a silly thing. His breath didn't come closer. I felt regretful and relieved at the same time. We started walking again down the hill and around the corner.

"Cold?"

"Yes, very."

"Today is Small Cold by the lunar calendar, isn't it?"

"It's strange that Small Cold is always colder than Big Cold."

"That's one of the tricks our ancestors played. They sneaked in Fall Begins in the middle of the hot spell. They figured they could alleviate the cold or heat by the use of language."

We crossed the street again and passed an alley without speaking.

"How far below zero do you think it is today?"

"This morning they said it was minus 15."

We regained our composure by exchanging such meaningless pleasantries. Finally we said goodbye politely, not having found the words that could connect the moment beside the cathedral to the present.

There was a strange jeep parked in front of my house. A jeep in front of that haunted house was as inappropriate as a reality that suddenly jumped into a dream. I hesitated about going inside the house and was irritated by the fact that this unexpected visitor wouldn't leave me in peace, but it was minus 15 outside and I didn't want to suffer in the cold. The gate stood open, and on the entryway step was a pair of shiny military boots and another pair of shabby boots. My cousin Jin was visiting us. As I took off my shoes, I noticed the long rows of holes for lacing the boots. I felt sorry for Jin who had to put on and take off such boots.

It was a good thing that I could feel sorry for him, if only a little. It made me more comfortable in facing him, something I had been worrying a lot about.

Jin was sprawled on the warmest part of the floor, and a sergeant, apparently his driver, sat awkwardly on the colder side.

"Do you always come home this late?" Jin spat with a disapproving air as he pulled himself up.

"I'm rather late today."

I was in the habit of acting subdued in front of him and I couldn't help it today as usual. The rows of holes on his boots weren't any help. His handsome face was pale, unlike a soldier's, and it still had its dignity and elegance. It wasn't simply because of his rank as lieutenant colonel; his unique dignity and refinement would have shone, even if he were thrown into a public bath. The so-called UN jacket, a shapeless winter coat that resembled a Chinese outfit, looked very good on him and didn't alter his appearance a bit.

As I took off my coat and put my lunch box aside, I could feel Jin's twisted smile following me, so disdainful of others and yet so becoming to him. But how could I escape being imprisoned by his smile?

I put my frozen hands under the quilt on which Jin was sitting and spoke to the sergeant first.

"It's cold. Why don't you come sit here?"

I felt closer to him sitting awkwardly in a corner than I did to my cousin. The sergeant pushed himself further away to indicate that my invitation was out of the question.

"How do you like your work?" Jin asked me.

"I like it well enough."

Conversation died, and I was as ill at ease as the sergeant in the corner, although I was sitting in a comfortable position.

Jin pulled out a Pall Mall, lit it and exhaled gracefully. The cigarette sent out a thin, bluish smoke. For no apparent reason it seemed extravagant.

My mother must have given *kimchi* soup to this precious eldest son of my father's older brother, the one who ate only the most delicious foods, who slept on the softest mat, who thought only the most refined thoughts. Or had she given him soy bean stew, with shredded *kimchi* in it? I regretted missing his face when he sat down to such a meal, but it cheered me to no end to imagine him being served *kimchi* soup.

"Shall I bring your dinner in?" asked my mother, sliding the door halfway open.

"Yes, but did you feed Cousin Jin?"

"No, he said he'd eaten already," she said in a bored voice.

"Oh, I've eaten, too. I forgot for a moment."

I hated the idea of lapping up *kimchi* soup in front of him.

"How can you forget eating your dinner so quickly?" he asked, twisting his cigarette stub out.

It sounded derisive, but what could I do? The more I thought about not feeding him *kimchi* soup, the more wronged I felt. It seemed unfair to have to skip a meal because of him, but it was better than drinking *kimchi* soup in front of a man who had such a lustrous sheen on his skin, as if he always had his fill of the most delicious food.

After rejecting the meal, I felt even more awkward and crushed. I found myself slouching as clumsily as the sergeant on the other side of the room.

"How can you live like this? Actually, I have been ordered to bring you back with me, by force if necessary." He smiled briefly, moving only the corners of his mouth.

"You can't," I retorted, looking him straight in the eye.

"You don't have to be afraid."

"Who's afraid? You always think everyone trembles in fear at the sight of you."

"You haven't changed a bit." He smirked briefly. "My father thinks it's his duty to take care of your family since you've lost the head of your household. He's afraid that other relatives will criticize him later if he neglects his obligations. That's why he made Mal write a letter and asked me to come and see you. I know my father's hypocrisy only too well."

"Why are you telling me this?"

"Because you're so cold. You seem to think I'm as hypocritical as my father for coming here. I came willingly. I kind of wanted to see you and I was curious about this old house." His smile seemed more gentle than before.

"I wish you and your father would leave us alone. We'll manage."

"That won't do. My father doesn't care if Nan frequents dance halls or Min causes trouble with women. His only concern is your family in Seoul. I mean the only concern he expresses. It's getting embarrassing. In fact, everybody knows that we owe your family a lot, so you can understand my father's distress, can't you, Kyong-a?"

I was suddenly afraid of where he was heading, but fortunately he must have been thinking of other things. He didn't delve any deeper.

"But it's all a waste of energy," he muttered.

"Yes, you're right. I won't go."

"I don't mean that. I mean it wouldn't make any difference whether my father worries about what other people think or not. Even if you do become a

Yankee slut because of your poverty, the relatives wouldn't blame us. It won't affect us. After the war, everyone will be busier and more selfish."

Baffled, I watched his mouth, which was twisted in a cold snicker.

"The concept of the family will shrink, too. Nobody will blame someone for not taking care of his niece. Forget about his authority as the head of the clan; people will have enough trouble disciplining their own children."

He spoke carelessly, pulled out another Pall Mall, and lit it. The metallic gleam in his eyes took on a shade of sorrow. Was it because the smoke was in his eyes? He had said some cruel things, but he looked more distracted than I was. He eyed me indifferently for a long while.

"Maybe in the future young people will be bolder in disregarding their family ties and breaking away from the bondage of convention. They'll take more responsibility for what they do, bravely and seriously. It will become the world of youth."

He seemed to be engrossed in his own problems and telling his own story. He was still a bachelor because he couldn't overcome his parents' fierce objection to his first love's inferior family background. But I couldn't tell whether he was simply reminiscing or if he was truly in pain. When he finished his cigarette, the sorrow I thought I had seen was not there. His eyes were still cold and his perfectly handsome face was expressionless. I wondered what kind of woman could have wounded this cold and impenetrable man, but he looked so unshakable that nobody's curiosity could find its way inside him. His dignity and elegance weren't part of his character. Rather, he was hiding behind those qualities.

I managed to ask, "What are you trying to say? How can I understand you if you speak in such an obscure way?"

"It's simple. You're free. You don't have to pay attention to adults," he said matter-of-factly.

I was suddenly furious.

"Ha! What a waste of energy! It's more a waste of energy than what your father's trying to do. My dear cousin, so cultivated and cool, came all this way to make such a long speech. I've been free for a long time, long before you proclaimed it. Do you think there's anything I couldn't do because I had to think about family appearances? I'm only concerned with my problems. I live as I please and I'll keep living as I please, so don't worry. I won't accept your family's help with our living expenses any more. Do you think I don't know what your family is up to? You've mouthed all this nonsense because you hate to part with money. Good! I won't accept it. I make my own money."

"Why are you so narrow-minded?" His low, chilly voice suppressed my fury. "Accept it. Your uncle is rich. You can even ask for more. Actually, we owe your family. Can't you read between the lines?"

He stopped and seemed to concentrate on my mother's room. It was quiet. There wasn't a hint of human life there.

"You don't understand. You have to free yourself from your mother and then from this old house."

"What?" I was jolted by his remark.

"First, free yourself from your mother."

"What are you telling me to do?"

"Your mother is already part of this old house. If she's most comfortable here, what can we do? But you're too young and too spirited to be part of this house. So don't bind yourself to any obligation."

"Then what happens to my mother?"

"Your mother is physically healthy."

He reduced my mother's health to her body. I didn't like hearing him speak like that.

"Anyway, she can take care of herself, and my father will contribute to the grocery bills. As I said before, your uncle is rich, and although I criticized him from time to time, he is a good man. He takes pride in keeping up appearances with his relatives. In other words, he is a good fellow representing the older generation. Lean on him. You and your mother can lean on him. Understand? You must come down to Pusan. You can continue your schooling and enjoy a life suitable for your age. Life can be a little brighter for you."

He pronounced the word "brighter" with such a fascinating stress that my heart began to pound: My longing for light and joy wrenched its head up inside me. The sergeant, who was dozing awkwardly in the corner, suddenly sprawled out and began to snore. His limbs spread out comfortably, he fell into a sweet sleep, pleasing to look at. A genuine smile spread over Jin's lips for the first time.

"That fellow, he must have been really exhausted."

I tried to calm myself by flicking Jin's lighter on and off until my thumb hurt. He observed me at leisure, confident of the effect of his words, but I tried to put on the most bored expression I could muster. However, I was severely torn between the longing for a brighter life and the resignation that I might never escape from my situation. I knew that this feeling, this pain, was obviously meaningless. I would never become a new person through that pain.

No matter what anyone said, I might never be free. Looking up in fright, as the war raged on, at the dark roof with one side shattered, hating my mother, eating *kimchi* soup; I might never be free from any of it.

Once again I realized that layer after layer of chains bound me. Where had those chains come from? Sometimes I tried to trace them back to the beginning, but I always gave up. With Jin's help, perhaps I could get a glimpse of their origin. But I was afraid of looking at them. I hadn't forgotten about them. I was just avoiding them as deftly as possible.

"The day after tomorrow when I head south, I'm taking you with me," he said in a bored but confident tone. "It looks like we are going to take someone along with us to help my mother with her chores. I heard that the sergeant's sister is quiet and nice, and I asked him to bring her along, so it's almost certain," he said, indicating the sergeant with his chin.

As if his mission were through now, his thin lips pursed and his eyes shone with their characteristically selfish gleam, completely uninterested in anyone else's affairs.

I kept flicking the lighter. The flame had long since been reduced to a putter of sparks. I pushed the lighter toward him, and blew on my thumb, red and swollen.

"I'm not going." I said firmly.

He didn't seem surprised, and he didn't try to talk me into going any more. He looked at his watch and told me to wake up the sergeant. It seemed that the slot of time he had set aside to pay attention to others had passed.

The sergeant was snoring noisily. He had stretched out completely, his big feet rudely directed to his arrogant superior. He was so deep in sleep that he wouldn't even have noticed if somebody had carried him away, but I felt as if he were the only one alive in the whole house.

"Let him sleep a little more, if you don't have to hurry," I suggested.

"I guess so."

Jin yawned languidly and pulled out his third cigarette. I struck a match for him. It was nice to look at the cigarette release a wisp of smoke between his delicate and yet masculine fingers.

"Have you ever been in a battle where people actually killed each other?" I asked contemptuously.

"Of course, but I'm not on the front anymore."

"Killing people and firing guns?" I showed my contempt more openly.

"I hate war stories."

He brushed aside my taunt in a matter-of-fact tone, but I was insistent.

"Still, you must have retreated and fled once when Seoul fell into communist hands. Calling it a strategic retreat. Ha! I can't imagine you fleeing." I wanted to crush his arrogance with my derision.

"Then how about imagining me charging into an enemy camp all alone, beheading tens of them? I'm sorry, but I'm not a noble *hwarang* warrior from the Shilla Kingdom or a righteous soldier from the Yi Dynasty."

He avoided my disdain with cunning and skill. The conversation stopped. We held our breath, listening to the stillness that filled the old house.

85

It was not that we couldn't hear the wind blowing; rather we were listening for a human movement.

It seemed as if nobody lived there, nobody had ever lived there. Even if a goblin materialized to search the house with his sensitive nose, he wouldn't have been able to sniff a human scent in this house. The stillness lasted a long time before Jin broke it.

"Are you planning to go crazy as well?" He spat out the words as he stuffed the lighter and gloves in his pocket.

"Sergeant Kim!" he called sharply.

The sergeant bounced up like a wound spring. As the two soldiers laced their boots, my mother stood silently at the edge of the wooden floor. I whispered to her that she should ask them to stay overnight to indicate her hospitality. Clearly Jin thought my mother had gone mad. I wanted to show him that she could be normal. However, she pretended not to hear me, accepted their bows wordlessly, and followed them to the gate with me. She gazed at the jeep until it turned at the end of the alley, then locked the gate and went into her room without a word.

I was hungry. I was sad, thinking that I was still hungry for *kimchi* soup, and I couldn't pretend I was not.

Are you planning to go crazy as well? Ha! I'm this hungry, so how can I go mad? Who does he think he is? Everyone knows the truth, no matter how he denied it. He fled at the beginning of the war, of course. He left us under that cruel, depraved rule. And now he pities us for having to endure all that and suffer from the aftermath. Disgusting! Who does he think he is, idiot! He looks down on my family because it's made of women and ghosts.

I tossed and turned on my mat, flinging one insult after another at him. But I didn't feel any better.

Coward. Bastard. Deserter. Everyone knows it.

I liked the word deserter and felt much better for having said it. I could hear a cough from the other room. A shutter clattered a few times. Then a deep stillness without even a rustling encroached again.

I knew I wouldn't go crazy. I knew I was intent on finding the joy of life, hidden deep in my heart. It lay deep inside, never losing its force, although it sometimes acted as if it were a separate entity, ignoring the fact that I had to pretend to live a dull life because I was not supposed to have any other choice.

That was why I fell in love. What a blessing, what a salvation it was to have met Ock Hui-do. If I hadn't met him, I would have crumbled all to pieces, the perfect target for Jin's pity.

I remembered an incident from my childhood. My father had loved me best. But because he was afraid that other people would criticize him for spoiling me, he sometimes acted with sudden severity, and at other times I was punished harshly for trivial things. I remembered he often argued with my mother because of that.

One day, when I was in the first grade, I was punished for having bought sweets with the money left over after I bought my school supplies. I was locked in the attic in the outer quarters. The door was locked outside. I knew if I cried loudly enough, I would be forgiven, but I didn't cry. I put up with the fright, pressing down on my pounding heart. I began to notice that it was not really dark inside the attic. As my eyes got used to the darkness and began to discern the shapes around me, I was surprised to find that the things inside the closet were more interesting than things outside. If you brushed off the dust, the toys my brothers had played with were almost new and all of them were in working condition. I could become a driver, a pilot, or put on a military uniform. I did it all, but I grew tired soon. I was anxious because I felt I had to examine the piles of wondrous goods that had been forgotten by the other members of the family.

A couple of times I dipped my finger into a honey jar and sucked it. Then I moved on to the books piled high in one corner. They looked fascinating but there wasn't enough light to read. At that very moment a beam of light miraculously streamed in. It was the afternoon sunlight, pouring through the gap between the west wall and the post at the corner of the room. I shuffled through the musty books looking for one with pictures. That was how I first got to know Hans Christian Anderson.

In that crowded attic a glittering and wonderful land of fantasy opened before me. I was a mermaid, a swan, a princess, all rolled into one.

Then I heard my mother's shriek as she returned home. The attic door was flung open and I was embraced.

"Oh, my, my, Kyong-a. Poor baby, you must have been scared to death. Did you cry?" She hugged me to her breast. Her heart was racing.

"What a rigid man. He's so inflexible. How could he lock our precious Kyong-a in here? Something terrible could have happened. What if you fainted out of fright? It was a good thing that I came home early. For some reason I wanted to come home early. Now I see why."

She fussed over me, pressing her cheek to mine and wiping my tear-less eyes. I sniffled a little.

"Poor baby! Even your tears have all dried up. Where is that father of yours hiding?"

I missed the chance to tell her that I had not been miserable at all, so I had to burst into tears just to go along with her. My father rushed to me from his hiding place, and gave me a spoonful of liquid medicine mixed with red powder. He said it was good for the nerves.

I couldn't remember whether or not I swallowed the medicine, but I was proud to remember that I hadn't felt dejected during my confinement.

No, I couldn't let myself become the object of anyone's pity. I began to appreciate myself. I couldn't let myself suffer from hunger. I bolted up and went to the kitchen, where I laid out a tray for myself quietly, so my mother wouldn't know.

Ten

Although Ock Hui-do and I didn't have a standing appointment, we met every evening in front of the chimpanzee. When it snowed or was especially cold, we were the only onlookers at the toy stall. On those days we didn't have the heart to ask the vendor to wind the toy up. We just stared at the chimpanzee's dull expression.

In fact, I didn't care whether the chimpanzee drank the whisky, or whether the black doll pounded his cymbals next to him. I was preoccupied with seeing Ock. I grew weary of all other things.

The weather seemed to have let up a bit. It had been cold for quite a while in spite of our old belief in the winter cycle of Three Cold Days and Four Warm Days, but now it started to snow. All in all, that winter was especially cold and snowy. The painters began to grumble.

"Damn it, it's snowing again. We're already weak from hunger, and then it snows so we can slip and fall on our faces."

"Has a hunger demon attached itself to you? Why are you always harping about food?"

"Fool! What in the world is more important than food? Tell me if you can think of anything more important."

"Money, of course. If you have money, what food can't you eat? Who cares if you play the harmonica on spareribs from morning till night? The target is money. Money. Don't you agree, Mr. Ock?"

Kim and Cash drew Ock into their squabble. Recently they had been trying to include him in their conversations, for no reason other than they felt that good manners dictated it.

Ock Hui-do put down his brush, saying, "That's hard to say," but he didn't continue. He pounded his shoulders with an exhausted expression and gazed warmly at the Yankees coming in the door, covered with snow like snowmen.

"It must be snowing really hard." said Misuk as she walked toward me with a bright face.

"Do you like it when it snows?"

"Yes, I wish I could make snowballs and throw them anywhere I wanted. At the back of the GIs' heads, at the display windows of the stores."

She laced her fingers and jumped up and down, as if she were about to do that right then and there. She was more attractive when she was talking

89

about a snow fight than when the topic was international marriage. She was still so young. It didn't look like jumping up and down on the tiled floor would satisfy her. She rushed into our shop and pushed the grimy grey curtain to one side.

"Oh, isn't it lovely!"

The snow was no longer a novelty, but everyone turned to look out at the snowy landscape, attracted by Misuk's childlike enthusiasm.

The snow fell calmly and abundantly. The environment that I had seen too much of looked barren and sad, like the final scene of some sentimental movie set against a blurry background of snowflakes; the passersby, mostly clad in military uniforms, the makeshift gift shops on the other side of the street, the ugly, skeletal trees lining the thoroughfare. Misuk grew quiet, and everyone seemed to imagine a sad, low music to accompany the scene.

"If there's a lot of snow, the barley harvest is supposed to be good." Chin's remark sounded hollow and pathetic, maybe because we were indulging in the luxury of emotion, however fleetingly.

"I know a story that has to do with snow," Kim said in a low voice.

"You mean it was a snowy night when you met her and it was a snowy night when you parted?"

"Hey, fella! I didn't part with her."

"Then the girl you met on a snowy night is your wife?"

"That's right, sir."

"What a silly fellow! You broke the mood."

Misuk dropped the curtain regretfully when we noticed that we were being watched from outside. Some boys holding shoe shine boxes and boards that displayed packs of chewing gum and American cigarettes were clustered at the window, gazing in at us curiously. They must have heard that the PX was filled with expensive goods, like Ali Baba's cave. Their eyes were filled with incomprehension and disappointment at the sight of a few shabby men sitting around painting pictures.

The painters resumed their work. It was snowing, but nothing extraordinary occurred that day, except for the momentary disappointment of the boys in the street. Only Ock Hui-do seemed to be oblivious to the drawn curtain. He sat gazing at the curtain for longer than usual. I fixed my own eyes on the back of his head, curious about his gaze, but he remained preoccupied. I grew more curious. I was anxious, longing for him to turn his warm eyes on me.

The longing transformed itself into a feeling of emptiness and hunger, which in turn brought about an impulse to cry out. I wanted to shout that I longed to meet his kind, honest eyes. I suppressed the impulse by piercing a sheet of notebook paper into small pieces with the end of my pen, taking up the habit Misuk employed when she was deep in thought.

Then I decided, if he didn't turn to me by the time I counted ten, to go to him and shout hysterically. I felt like I could cry out in a hundred different tones, in a hundred different emotions.

I started counting slowly. He remained as still as a rock. I forced down a scream. Then I made another bet with myself. If he didn't look back by the time I counted to ten again, I wouldn't go to the chimpanzee that evening.

Why did I risk such a precious thing? Our gratifying encounters before the chimpanzee, Ock's passionate breath on that dark street, my indiscreet attraction to that passion, and all the uncertainty laden with fright. I wagered all this and counted more slowly than before. I went up to ten, each number counted more slowly than the previous one.

After counting, I felt gloomy and disoriented, as if I had gotten off the train at the wrong station. Because no one had peered into my heart when I was counting, I was free to meet him, but I decided to stick to my contract. I was irritated enough to be persistent about my disappointment in him. I was nothing more than a small container waiting to be filled by his glance, but this time he refused to give me even that. Was it because of the snow?

Misuk polished the display case, blowing her warm breath on the glass. The arcade was almost deserted. Misuk's rosy cheeks glowed so beautifully that I began to envy her. I went to visit the brass section, as if I were drawn by her cheeks. Hugging her from behind, I buried my face in her back. The fluffy texture of her red sweater and her warm temperature were pleasing and gradually lifted my spirits.

"Have you sold anything today?"

"Nothing. What about you?"

"Same here. Do you still want to have a snowball fight?"

"Yes, I'm itching for some exercise."

"That must be why you're polishing the glass so hard."

We laughed. I suddenly felt wonderful about having this girl, who was healthy both physically and mentally, as a friend. Only a few days ago she had wept about her turmoil, a burden too heavy for her age. Amazingly, she was completely recovered in such a short time.

When she had wanted to share her distress, I had ignored her plea, an act I now regretted. I tried to think of something that would help her, but nothing presented itself. It was not that I couldn't remember a few famous maxims. I simply wasn't sure that I could utter them with a serious expression on my face.

I could see Diana Kim's neat profile in front of us. She was filing her nails earnestly, while Linda Cho yawned loudly and then put on another coat of lipstick. It was a slack afternoon, with only a few GIs browsing around.

Sergeant Balcom, who was in charge of the first floor, and Susan Chong were giggling together.

"Isn't she beautiful!" exclaimed Misuk, gesturing toward Diana Kim with her chin.

"No, not a bit," I answered shrilly, shaking my head.

As a token that I thought Misuk was one hundred times better-looking than Diana, I squeezed her short, slender fingers.

"She looks so young, but they say she has two sons."

"Really? I didn't know that. They must be mixed-blood children."

"I heard they are not. I heard the cleaning women say they were surprised, too. They said the kids looked like full-blooded Koreans no matter how they looked at them. And very handsome Koreans at that."

"So?"

"They said the reason she'll do anything for money is because of her kids."

"What an evil woman! Does she think she can do all those terrible things in the name of motherhood? Thick-skinned bitch!"

"Oh, my, my. You're being too harsh. Everyone says she is being so heroic." Misuk shot me a sharp glance.

I couldn't control my anger at all the good, naive people who were swayed by the word "mother." The fact that she was a mother couldn't reduce my contempt by even one-tenth.

"You're too cold sometimes. You don't seem to try to understand other people."

"Is that what you think? I don't care, but I will say I'm sorry if I've behaved that way to you."

"You've always been kind to me."

"I should have been more helpful the other day, but actually, I . . ."

I was not sure what to say next.

"I was grateful for that."

"What did I do? Actually at that time . . ."

"You reacted most appropriately." She cupped my hand in her plump hands as if I needed comfort and assurance.

"I thought I couldn't bear it if I didn't do something outrageous. If you had accepted my babyish plea, what would have happened to me? You didn't try to preach. You let me think it over and calm down."

"So what did you decide?"

"I decided not to flee. I will endure my problems at home and in my own country. That's the right choice, don't you think?"

For want of the right words, I had to nod.

"You've never asked about my problems."

"I'm sorry."

"That's all right. You didn't meddle with my problems, but you've already taught me how to live."

I was puzzled. How could I have taught anyone how to live? She understood and solved them on her own. Perhaps because she was young, she might want to believe that she had followed another person's directions instead of trusting herself to take the freedom to make up her mind. Anyway, she herself clearly knew how to live. Perhaps Diana Kim and Susan Chong knew it, too. The painters Kim, Cash, and Ock Hui-do must know it, too. Everyone must know except me.

I removed my hand from Misuk's grip but didn't know what to do. I felt as if I were excluded from other people's comfortable confidence and their frames of reference.

I was living amidst the cries and shouts of my many selves, selves that I had no control over. I hadn't thought of sorting them out or repressing them. Instead, the cries and shouts divided me up, spinning me to the point of dizziness.

Ock Hui-do was drawing something now. With his eyes fixed on a foreign woman, the eyes I had longed so ardently to have directed at me, he worked carefully. I was always envious and worried about the fact that everyone, including Ock Hui-do, knew how to live, but the question itself, "How to live?" sounded as difficult as a complicated philosophical conundrum.

I wanted to stand on my hands. I wanted to walk around the arcade on my hands, asking the people who lived according to their own rules whether or not I should go to see the chimpanzee this evening. I wanted to tell them I didn't even have an answer to that simple question. But instead, I sat there debating about whether or not I should go.

"A customer. Go ahead." Misuk poked at my side.

Several Yankees were looking at the portrait display. One of them, an older sergeant, handed me a family photo. An affable couple and three lovely girls, close in age, sat in the streaming sunlight on a green lawn, all smiling brightly. Bright and beautiful, the sure thing to bring a smile to an observer's lips, it looked more like a picture drawn by some amateur painter who loved life passionately. I asked the sergeant about his relationship with the happy family. He said it was his family and he was the father of the three girls. Because I looked surprised, he pushed his affectionate and innocent face closer to mine, as if wanting to prove that he really was the man in the photo.

"I'm sorry," I mumbled, embarrassed.

"That's okay. The uniform makes people look different."

"I'm sorry."

"I said it's okay. Don't worry about it."

I wasn't sorry about not recognizing him in the picture. Instead, I shrank back, filled with remorse, thinking he had given up his happiness and family in order to face death on brutal foreign battlefields, like "goddamn Chorwon," or "goddamn Changdan," or on a nameless plateau where the temperature fell to 30 degrees below. If he were to die, what would his cause have been? This war was a crazy thing created by the worst lunatics.

He chose a silk scarf for his family portrait and asked how much it would cost. We called it silk, but it was nothing more than a cheap coarse summer material, stiffly starched and ironed. I wanted to give it to him free of charge. Asking him to wait a minute, I looked back at the painters. In a gloomy mood they were drawing with the most calculating eyes, as if they knew what I had in mind. How about Ock Hui-do? He would agree to my suggestion. I hurriedly suppressed that thought. I needed to be calculating for Ock's sake.

Finally I realized that I couldn't give anything to the sergeant and that he was the one who had things to bestow on us. I sighed out of sorrow, out of sadness that we had to be the party that takes, never having the latitude and satisfaction of giving. Perhaps giving was the reason the sergeant was risking his life in a foreign land.

He seemed to think I was slow at arithmetic. Helpfully and generously he suggested that since the price for an 8-by-12 silk was five dollars, it would be 25 dollars for the five members of his family.

I accepted the 25 dollars and his photo and studied the photo for a long time after he left. Besides being a picture that brought a smile to anyone's lips, it produced a nostalgia for family and home in general. The green lawn lit by sunbeams, the good wife, and the angelic daughters. He was separated from them, now standing somewhere on a foreign street in the cold snow.

"Shit." Kim stretched his back.

"Damn." Cash threw down his brush, put a cigarette to his lips, and flicked his lighter. The old lighter produced a scattering of stray specks instead of a flame.

"Hey, fella. Do you call that a lighter? How about using flintstones instead? Flintstones, eh?" Kim lit his cigarette first and then threw his squashed match box to Cash.

"I thought my eyes were growing blurry. No wonder. It's almost closing time." Paek, the oldest and slowest painter, who rarely spoke to the others, wiped his nickel-coated pocket clock with his dingy handkerchief.

His was the only clock in the portrait section, but no one credited it as such. Kim collected his tools one by one, but in order to certify that he wasn't doing so because of that clock, he muttered, "Ahh . . . my stomach's grumbling. My stomach clock never fails."

The cleaning women sprinkled water on the tiled floor, while the salesgirls made up their faces for the evening. A sudden darkness descended outside and the shutters began to creak slowly down.

I no longer enjoyed watching the salesgirls put on their red lipstick. Instead of watching them, I began to do the day's arithmetic. It was one of the slowest days in a long while, but the figures came out wrong over and over again. I bit down on my lower lip and clasped my head in my hands, alternating between the thought that I should go to the chimpanzee and the thought that I couldn't. I was unable to concentrate on anything else.

"What's the matter? Aren't you feeling well?" Tae-su slapped my shoulder. I pushed the sheets of paper and the abacus toward him and said, "I can't add them up correctly today. Will you do it for me?"

"What? You have a problem with only this much? Oh, I know. You're depressed because business was bad today."

Burying my head in my arms on the counter, I sensed he was looking down at me with pity. I lifted my head and gave him a dull smile.

"You look really tired. Are you sure you're not sick?"

He put his head next to mine, so close that his breath tickled me, and studied my face. It was then that I realized how tired I had grown of debating whether or not I should go to the chimpanzee. I wanted to rest a bit, to escape that monotonous, incessant worry. I leaned my head against the back of my chair because his face was too close to mine. His hand touched my forehead. It was cold.

"I think you have a fever, too. What shall I do? I was going to ask you to spend some time with me," he murmured in disappointment.

"Why? Was there something special on your mind?"

"No, I was just thinking of having dinner with you and chatting. But you look like you have a cold. With that fever, I'll bet it's the flu."

"No, I'm all right. I'd like to eat something delicious tonight. I'll go with you."

I felt cheerful, having made up my mind. Finally I could escape the tedious question of going or not going.

"Thank you. I also have something to tell you, but it can wait until later. Are you sure you'll be all right?"

"I'm all right. How about checking my forehead again?"

"Thank you for coming with me."

I looked up at the young face filled with longing and desire. I pitied his eagerness and reached up to hold the hand on my forehead. I caressed his large, manly hand. It didn't feel bad; in fact, it felt quite pleasant.

However, that hand didn't have to belong to Tae-su; it could have belonged to any man. The mysterious power of the opposite sex stirred me; I loved caressing his hand. Tae-su pulled his hand away, stuck it in his jacket pocket and turned his head, embarrassed. I could see part of his flushed cheek. I suddenly wished I had another Tae-su. I thought I needed one Tae-su whom I could neglect and another Tae-su whom I could love and touch when I wanted. It was cruel of me to alternate between attachment and neglect for one. Still, the pleasure of touching lingered in me.

"Let's go somewhere quiet and have dinner together," I whispered sweetly.

"Wha . . . what?" He was flustered, as if I had caught him off guard.

I finished the accounts with Tae-su's help and went out with him. It had stopped snowing but the snow on the ground reached our ankles. I made several snow balls with my bare hands and flung them toward the streets. The muscles in my arm felt refreshed.

"What are you going to buy me today?"

I wanted to eat a pungent vegetable, hot and spicy fish soup, and a thick and tender steak broiled just right, all at the same time. My mouth watered with an intense appetite.

"Would you mind if we ate Chinese?"

"I've never eaten Chinese food except for black bean noodles, you know. How about something else?"

"To tell you the truth, I have another appointment tonight. My brother and his wife are waiting in a Chinese restaurant."

He seemed so distressed that I decided to give up my hopes for a good meal today.

"That's all right. You can buy me dinner tomorrow. I'll just go home. Don't worry about me."

"No, it's not that." He grabbed my sleeve. "You should be there. To tell you the truth . . . Please don't get angry with me. I told them that I'd bring you with me to dinner. I'm sorry for not asking you first. But please don't say you can't. Please?"

He clung to my sleeve frantically like a child.

"It's all right with me, but why do I have to be there?"

"It just happened that way. It's not important, so please don't worry. Just come with me."

"If it's not important, they won't mind if I don't show up."

"Well, the truth of the matter is, it's not like that. My brother and especially his wife wanted to meet you. That's why it was arranged this way." He was utterly at a loss, still holding onto my arm.

I grew interested. "Why? Why do they want to meet me? Don't act so embarrassed. Just tell me." I walked along beside him, without trying to get away any longer.

"My brother's wife is a very good person, but she has a wide skirt, so to speak. She's always worrying about other people. She says she can't get a decent night's sleep because of me."

"You should be grateful to her, but what kind of terrible things have you done to make her so anxious?"

"It's not that. She worries about me living by myself, cooking myself, so she finds all sorts of girls to introduce to me, and I couldn't stand it, so . . ."

"So?"

"I'm sorry. So I lied to her. I told her I have a girlfriend, someone I've promised to share the future with. I thought it would satisfy her. But no, she insists on meeting my girlfriend. I told her she didn't need to, but she says to think of it as a chance to meet the future in-laws, not as a formal viewing by the future in-laws. I guess they mean the same thing, and I'm sorry. Nothing will happen. Just sit there next to me. You don't have to say anything. Please go with me!"

I had heard such dull stories many times before. I yawned and nodded my head.

"Thank you. It won't be too difficult for you. You can just sit next to me. My sister-in-law is very talkative and can be a bother, so just keep smiling and think of other things."

I nodded again.

"And don't treat me too coldly. Pretend we're in love. All right?"

He grew bolder just because I kept nodding. I snorted, looking at the display windows of shops and at the grey sky. After a while he pushed open the glass door of a Chinese restaurant called Poksun-nu in a back alley of Myong-dong. I couldn't help but laugh because it sounded like the name of a country girl and suggested what I'd have to endure that evening. Humorous and somewhat boring, friendly and clumsy, I thought. As we climbed the creaking steps to the second floor, Tae-su winked and offered his arm. I linked my arm in his and walked up carefully, entering the room, before which a pair of men's and a pair of women's shoes were laid.

His brother, who looked like an aged nervous petty clerk, remained seated, but Tae-su's sister-in-law jumped up and exclaimed, "Oh, my, my. Brother-in-law, you . . ."

She kept smiling in a strange way. When I was sure that they had seen us arm in arm long enough, I took my arm away and bowed deeply. I tried to smile as sweetly as possible, as I sat in a docile pose on a dirty cushion.

Tae-su's sister-in-law had a large mouth, and her front teeth stuck out. Her teeth gave the impression that she was good-natured, but at the same time she was very talkative, as Tae-su had said.

"Why, Brother-in-law! You really do have a girlfriend. I can believe it now that I see her with my own eyes, but what in the world . . ."

"Why, you don't like my girlfriend?"

"What are you talking about? I'm just amazed and pleased. I thought in the Hwang family, where all the men are so proper and decorous, they would die bachelors if their parents hadn't found brides for them. Oh, my word, Brother-in-law found a girlfriend on his own. Oh, my gosh. You can see her now, too, darling, can't you? What a bore you are!"

She pinched the leg of her husband, who kept blinking his small, cautious eyes.

"Yes, but how old are you? Let's see if your horoscopes match up first." She was flexing her fingers, ready to count out the Sixty Year cycle.

"I was born in 1932," I said rather maliciously.

I thought it would take her some time to figure out my age first, and then I could be at peace while she made predictions about my future. She didn't fall for my trick, though. She didn't try to figure out my age, let alone tell my fortune, but kept asking whether my parents were alive, which school I graduated from, and so on, without waiting for my answers.

"Why don't you order some food, eh?" muttered Tae-su's brother for the first time, and as Tae-su raised himself rather self-consciously, she exclaimed, "Oh, my, what am I doing?"

She clapped sharply to summon the waiter. It seemed that she would take charge of ordering the food, too. She ordered what she wished without consulting us. The oddly named dishes she asked for didn't include black-bean noodles. In a way, I was relieved. When the food arrived, she stopped speaking completely, which was fortunate.

It was a pleasure to watch her eat, for she ate so ravenously that it whet our appetites. I ate a lot of the sweet, greasy food. I began to like the woman with the buck teeth, if only because she had the good sense not to combine eating and talking. I even put twinkles in my eyes, thanking her after we finished eating. I didn't know what she had on her mind when she moved next to me. She held my hand and began to rub it with her palm.

Her gesture was not awkward, and it revealed a kind of trust and affection that couldn't be expressed by words alone. Her palm was rather rough and scratched my hand with a pleasing coarseness.

"I can't believe this pretty girl will become my sister-in-law."

She stopped rubbing, squeezed my hand until it hurt, and said to her husband, "Darling, let's hurry up the wedding. Let's welcome this fine girl into our family as soon as possible."

"They have to decide on their own."

"What a silly man! Do monks shave their own heads?"

Listening to them disinterestedly, I remembered that Tae-su's brother was an old friend of Ock's. I grew uncomfortable and began to lose confidence in my false role. I fretted because I couldn't play the part Tae-su had asked of me.

"Marriage is the most important event in the course of human life. Shouldn't the elders start the process? What if they make a mistake in some hot-blooded moment?"

She refused to leave her husband alone. She was even kicking him under the table.

"I should go now. My mother is waiting for me." I managed to speak politely, but I shook her hand away firmly.

"What's there to be embarrassed about? You're a modern girl. In fact, the process should be discussed with the elders. Isn't that right, darling? When can I visit your home? I will come soon, so tell your mother to expect me."

She gathered her long skirt and moved next to her husband. She discussed the process with a "don't you think?" at the end of every sentence, and he responded only passively, either with "Yes" or "Well."

I felt nauseated, as if the greasy Chinese food and her chitchat had mixed to cause indigestion.

"Let me go," I whispered.

"It'll be over soon. Please hold on for a minute. Just a little longer."

"I don't think I can take it any longer. I think I might make some terrible mistake. I'm sorry."

I stood up, tired of asking in whispers for Tae-su's permission to leave. He stood up along with me, awkwardly. I leaned against him because I had a headache. I left the room, holding Tae-su's arm just as when we had entered.

Without a word his sister-in-law followed us with her eyes, as if to say, "What an impertinent thing! Why does she have to show off, holding onto him like that in front of us? Who does she think she is!"

As we walked along the snow-covered street, I kept holding onto Tae-su because it was slippery. We had never shared any passion, and yet we were walking arm in arm. Nothing had changed, but we walked as if we were enjoying an amiable stroll.

I was unconsciously leading Tae-su to the toy stall. The vendor had already gone home and only the board that normally held the toys, including the chimpanzee, was leaning against the wall under the eaves. There was nobody, no Ock.

There weren't many people in Myong-dong late at night, nor were many lights on. It was hazy, as if a drowsiness had descended over the neighborhood. Tae-su and I parted in front of the toy stall. Leaving Myong-dong, I had no choice but to head for home.

The darkness was grey because of snow and the snow was grey because of the darkness, and as I lifted my head the sky was dark grey, blocking the lights of the stars from coming through. I walked on hurriedly, enveloped in different shades of grey. Hard as I tried, I couldn't free myself from the layers of greyness, but I experienced some splendid lights that were like fantasies or recollections. The lights were those encounters with Ock Hui-do at the toy stall. They were too splendid to be recollections, too alive to be fantasies. I soon forgot about Tae-su and what had happened with his family. They were only a part of the obscure greyness.

Eleven

Today I wanted to be there for him in order to make up for his futile wait the day before. I hurried out of work and stood at the toy stall. Before long, I felt him behind me. I was relieved, and everything around me took on an interesting, exciting look. When the performances of the chimpanzee and the black doll came to an end, I enjoyed the vivid colors and movements of the other toys. I squeezed the belly of a blond doll to hear her monotonous cries, pushed a red fire engine, and pulled the trigger of a pistol. If at that moment Ock Hui-do had handed me the miniature dish set for three, with its small stove, pot, bowls, and plates decorated with yellow flowers, my joy would have reached its peak. I could have asked him to give it to me as a present, but I refrained. I was cautious about attaining happiness so easily.

After enjoying the show, we started to walk away slowly. The passersby hurried along, their heads buried in their collars. Most of the men wore military uniforms or thick dyed military jackets and the women were dressed, at best, in coats made of dyed military blankets. The mannequin in a display window, however, was dressed in a gorgeous spring coat, the color of azaleas. I bought a handful of peanuts from a boy in front of that impatient mannequin. I mashed the nuts between my molars, swallowing the juice as slowly as possible. With lingering steps I approached the darkness of the cathedral.

I clung to him, shifting my weight.

"Let's walk slowly. I'm tired."

"Are you? Pitiful girl!"

He supported me calmly. The brightly lit stores came to an end, and the dark hill that led to the cathedral started. The steep slope made us pant, but we were both careful to hide our gasps from each other.

"Why didn't you come yesterday?"

His voice was hoarse and split like somebody else's. I chomped the nuts noisily, quickly sucking in the juice.

"Do you know how long I waited?"

He grabbed my arm. He seemed so manly I was afraid of his sudden change and I stepped back a little, but he grasped me again.

"Do you know how long I waited?"

I tilted my head back, trying to see the cross at the top of the cathedral, but all I could see were ugly square houses. Those square roofs couldn't bring back the lines of the poem I had forgotten, with which I could cool his passion.

Defenseless, I submitted to his rough, unbearably sad touch, but he didn't go any further. He hugged me violently, released me, hugged me again, with the bristle of his chin rubbing my forehead until it hurt. Gradually I began to think that the object of his sad touch was not me but himself.

"Why didn't you come? Do you know how long I waited for you?"

It was a soliloquy that didn't require an answer, but I had to say something, however useless, as I couldn't stand his pathetic actions.

"Yesterday . . . I met the people who might become my in-laws."

I regretted saying it even before I finished, but it was too late. His arms slackened, and I was released.

"I didn't mean to go, it just . . . happened. I really didn't intend to go. You know Tae-su's brother. I was viewed by him and his wife."

"Tae-su's brother?" He had finally spoken.

Encouraged, I began to make excuses in earnest. "Tae-su made up the whole thing, pretending I was his future bride, without my knowledge. Without even telling me what was going to happen, he took me to meet his family."

The slope down to the street was very icy. I slipped several times, and each time he supported me calmly and led me to a less icy spot.

"If I made a mistake, please forgive me. I really didn't mean to go. Please don't think of the relationship between Tae-su and me as something strange."

"What do you mean by strange? I always thought you two looked good together."

He had regained his composure and was being affectionate and brotherly.

"I don't like it when you joke. What's the point of looking good together? I love you. You know that."

I spoke clearly, but I was shocked by my own words. It was the first time I used the word "love" to him, but it sounded very hollow. It had been used by so many people that it was too worn-out to describe my passion for Ock Hui-do.

People were spilling out of the theater where the last showing ended, and they dispersed reluctantly. I felt heartsick as if I were one of them.

"I think it's a greater blessing to look good together than to be in love."

His words rang sad and hollow, as if he, too, were one of the movie-goers heading home reluctantly. I swallowed a sigh and looked up. I tried to imagine the hundreds and thousands of light years that separated those densely packed stars. The words I had said to Tae-su, just for the sake of saying something, rang hollow now, but I shook my head as if that would push them away.

"I love you. I could die for you. You love me, too. That's the important thing. All other words are meaningless and superfluous."

I had no choice but to emphasize the word love, but I felt we needed another word to describe our feelings. Sad, strong words that no one had used before.

"For me, now, looking good together seems better than anything. Harmony and balance."

I covered his mouth with my palm, pulled his hand toward me, and showered kisses on the back of it for a long time, as if I were a poor dog pleading for her master's trust and affection.

"Ah . . . What are we going to do? We . . . I'm not some immature boy." His deflated voice trembled with weariness.

"I'm not a child, either."

"I have a daughter who's almost your age."

"I know."

"We shouldn't. Really, we shouldn't."

He determinedly stopped in his tracks but he grew despondent, as if he were not confident.

"Why? Does Not-Looking-Good-Together mean we have to worry about appearances?"

"Not-Looking-Good-Together isn't restricted to mere appearances. The relationship between a man and woman is like the foundation of a tall building. You can build up a future as you please, but in our case we're building a sand castle that will crumble before our eyes. It is all right for me, but I can't lead you to ruin. What am I doing? I should have some discretion."

"But, if it's my fate to live a short life, that's all right, isn't it?"

"What do you mean? You're so young, Kyong-a. You're so young that I'm afraid and envious."

He put his arm around my shoulder and caressed my cheek with his palm. He was again trembling a little. I wanted to reassure him, so I pulled his trustworthy hand from my cheek and kissed it with reverence.

"Don't worry, just love me and take me. I won't have a long life, anyway."

"Why? Why are you thinking like that? Is it because of me?"

"It is not because of you. It's because of the war. This insane war will kill us off one by one. Nobody can be free from its crazy hand."

I spoke as confidently as a shaman possessed by a spirit.

"Don't say such a thing! The war will end soon, and you will live on, Kyong-a, and you will live a long, happy life."

I chuckled.

"I had no idea you were thinking such strange thoughts. It's because of me. Yes, of course. Of course, it's because of me."

I mumbled to myself. I didn't insist that it was not the case. The fortune I was telling revealed the life deep inside me, which belonged only to me and did not require anyone else's understanding or sympathy. Furthermore, clarification about whether it had to do with someone else was unnecessary.

We reached the fork of the road where we had to part. I leaned against the gaunt trunk of a naked tree. He stopped and looked down at me for a long time. I looked up at him. What joy and at the same time what heartache there was in gazing into his eyes! I was the first to avert the gaze. I sighed into the grey opaque space. I knew he was sharing himself generously, but he was not willing to give me his complete self. Besides he seemed to be keeping the most important part of himself from me.

Suddenly I wanted to gaze up at the stars through the thickly tangled branches of the trees. The stars seemed to be hanging from the tops of the branches, but they were so far away. I could see signs for *sollongtang* soup and *komtang* soup and *ttokmanduguk* soup under the lamp in the distance and followed the lights of the passing trolley with my eyes.

"Well, it's time we went."

"Go ahead. I'll rest a little here."

"You can rest at home. Your mother will be waiting for you."

Insulted, I hurried across the street. I wove around several corners in order to be out of his sight quickly and then began to think. How did people in love get to the ecstasy and satisfaction of becoming one from the terrible sadness and hollowness of being only a half? Couldn't I stop being my mother's daughter, just once in a while? Couldn't I make my mother wear her false teeth again? Yes, I'd make her wear them. As I couldn't avoid being her daughter, no matter how cumbersome it was, my mother couldn't be free of her false teeth even if they were a bother.

I'll make her wear those false teeth, by force if necessary. I'll plead. Then I thought I wanted to die. Then I changed my mind quickly, thinking I wanted to live. My conflicting desires, death vs. life, were equally strong so that I couldn't settle on either side.

My mother came to the gate like a shadow and opened it. I wondered what she had been thinking during the long day but didn't ask. I already knew her answer. Nothing. I was sure that would be her answer. A being without a thought. Complete hollowness. I couldn't even imagine what it was like. Perhaps it was because of my mother's complete emptiness that I hated her, at the same time fearing her might.

I didn't pull my eyes from my mother's face as she ate. Tangled strands of grey hair hung over her forehead and ears, but there wasn't a wrinkle on her

face except for a few spidery lines around her toothless mouth, making it look
like an old wound sloppily sewn up.

Suddenly I felt the courage to bring up the false teeth.

"Mother, what did you do with your false teeth?"

Since the two of us had begun to live alone, I had taken on the habit of
alternating between calling "Mother" and "Mom," depending on my mood.
Today it was "Mother."

"False teeth? What do you mean?"

"Your dentures."

"Well, I haven't worn them for so long."

"Find them and put them in."

"No."

"Why?"

"They're uncomfortable. Do you realize how they make my gums hurt?"

"But you always wore them before. Nobody even knew you had false
teeth."

"Did I? Well, but it's different now."

"What's different? I'm asking you what's different!"

"Child, you know perfectly well what's different! Tsk, tsk." She
clucked and put down her spoon.

"Different? What's different? Put them in. Find them and put them in.
I'll find them myself."

I pulled open the wardrobe, the blood rushing into my head. I searched
the large drawers of the three-tier chest, the drawers of the low desk, the large
drawers of the quilt and clothes wardrobe, and into the deep corners of a small
chest. She didn't show any interest. She simply gathered up the bowls and
plates and slowly raised herself with a crack of her knees. She left the room
carrying the tray.

As I dug through the darkness of the drawers, I began to notice
something extraordinary. They were neatly arranged. My mother had always
been a diligent housekeeper, but she had often elicited my father's complaints
for messing up the drawers trying to find something. The drawers had been
always messy, and nobody but my mother could find anything.

We had hardly lost anything since we were among the last to flee Seoul
and the first to return. It was amazing that she could find the time and energy
to straighten the overflowing drawers. Drawers which used to be filled with
mainly useless items now held neatly folded clothes arranged according to
seasons. Had she thrown out all the junk? The drawers were so neatly arranged
that she could be ready for an outing in no time. Everything was arranged
perfectly, and yet the drawers lacked a living smell. They seemed to be
enveloped in cold, like the relics left behind by my mother as well as my father

and brothers. These drawers looked as if they had been preserved in the same condition forever and would never perform their original function again. Deflated, I stopped searching. Those lifeless drawers, so like my mother's empty head, didn't seem to allow any thoughts. I gave up searching altogether. I felt the relics in the drawers didn't welcome my touch. I shut the wardrobe door as tightly as before. I realized how meaningless it was for me to try to force my mother to wear her false teeth. It was obvious that the false teeth were among the trash she had thrown out.

She was still washing the dishes, occasionally clattering the aluminum bowls. I thought I could imagine her lips in a derisive smile. I tore at my hair and went into my room to sprawl on the floor. I had a terrible feeling that I was living all alone in this old, haunted house. I tried to appease myself by remembering that people lived outside of this house. I decided to communicate with one of them. I pulled out some writing paper and a fountain pen.

I wrote, "To my beloved . . ." and considered whose name I should put in the blank. The longing to love someone was so strong that I had to start the letter that way. At first, I thought of Ock Hui-do. But "my beloved" was not glorious enough to crown his name. And "To my beloved Tae-su" sounded exaggerated.

How about writing a letter to Pusan? "To my beloved Mal." As she was always anxious about other people, I certainly would get an answer. But I wanted to write a letter that didn't solicit an answer. I wanted to write a letter that wouldn't make me worry about getting an answer.

"To my beloved Cousin Jin." I pictured his metallic eyes and thin pursed lips. He would never bother writing back. "To my beloved Cousin Jin." Come to think of it, he might be my favorite relative.

To my beloved Cousin Jin,

Before even saying hello, I want to tell you how normal my mother is. She has the most carefully arranged drawers. I just realized this today. I believe that a woman's drawers and purse reflect her frame of mind. My mother must be pure and peaceful, both inside and out. People are crazy when they have too many things on their mind, when their mind is messy and convoluted. I have been thinking of so many things today. I thought of the rather embarrassing things that girls my age often think about and some things nobody might have thought about before. I wanted to live and to die. Both those wishes were completely sincere. Do you know why I say this? Because I imagine you've had similar contradictory wishes in the past. If I am wrong, don't be offended. I wonder what you did in your case. You don't have to answer, though. My beloved Cousin Jin, I want to address you this way, though it's a little embarrassing. It might be because I'm living in a vast house where even the bark of the neighbor's dog can't be heard. I believe that in order to endure this perfect quiet, I need many people to love; a man to love, a friend to love, and relatives to love. Goodbye.

I heard my mother's dry cough and the cry of the paper doors and the rattle of the shutters in response.

"Lately I often think of strange things," said Ock Hui-do, holding my hand as we stood absentmindedly in front of the chimpanzee after his performance, which had long since grown boring, had finished. By Ock's voice, I knew that his eyes had a disheartened shine, a bleakness, instead of their usual warmth. My heart ached just imagining his eyes. We had no other choice but to meet in front of the chimpanzee, never missing a day. We really had no alternative. I stood next to him in silence.

"I want to buy something for you," he said.

I felt depressed, somehow thinking that it might be our last meeting there in front of the chimpanzee.

"Tell me. Anything you would like?"

"Well, I don't know."

"Silly! Don't you know what you want?"

I wanted to shout that I wasn't a child who wanted a toy. Today he seemed to want to make me a child who would like a toy, and I thought I couldn't go against his wishes.

"Will you buy me the dish set?" I pointed to the set with the stove, pot, and the plates with yellow flowers. When Ock asked for it, the vendor looked surprised, as if thinking, "I thought he was a permanent onlooker, but he's actually buying something. Of course, he should act his age once in a while. How could he watch so long without buying anything?" The vendor's thin smile seemed to say these thoughts, while his hands moved swiftly, wrapping the purchase.

Even after Ock had received the package, I found it hard to leave.

"Let's go."

"Just a minute."

"Do you want anything else?"

"Yes. I want to buy something for you."

"For me? A toy?"

For the first time, I found him detestable.

"No. For your youngest son."

I thought of the solid boy who had crunched an apple on my lap, of his vigorous appetite, his health, and his lovely smell. We were trying to restrain ourselves by doing silly things. I fingered the toys without thinking what kind of things the boy might like. I decided on a red truck at random and asked the keeper to wrap it up. The truck was big enough to hold the pretty stones the boy might pick up in the street and it could even cradle his shoes. We left the toy stall and walked away, slowly exchanging the gifts.

"Are we wise or stupid?"

Since I was thinking of one of the O. Henry's stories, Ock's comment didn't come as a complete surprise.

"We're neither. It might make sense if we said we are sly," I said to hurt him a little. Fingering the stove, pot, and plates through the wrapping paper, I deliberately walked a little apart from him.

A good-looking couple was stepping out of the Western dress shop with grins on their faces as the shop owner bowed deeply behind them. The woman was holding a gift tied with a beautiful red ribbon in the shape of a plum blossom. I followed them with my eyes until they were far away.

"Are you envious?"

"Yes."

"Of what?"

"At least she had something better than a child's dish set."

He sighed deeply.

"Forgive me for saying that."

"No, I'm envious, too."

"Of what?"

"Of them looking good together. Of them being a lovely couple."

This time it was me who sighed. He was about to start again on his dull old theory, and I was not sure if I could draw him into my crazy ideas. We started up the steep hill toward the cathedral.

"I always have strange thoughts when I see that chimpanzee." He returned to the same topic he had brought up at the toy stall.

"What kind of thoughts?"

"I feel as if both you and I have turned into chimpanzees."

"Isn't that reverse evolution?"

"Yes, that's right. At first it was wonderful to watch him drink when he was wound up, but then it grew boring and hateful. He seems to hate himself. That's why he has such a sad face. Still, he has to do his silly routine whenever someone winds him up. That endless, boring repetition. Isn't he the same as us? Every time we smell dollars, you speak halting English with a sad face and I draw the same damned mongrel faces over and over again."

He shuddered. His trembling was not because of me now. We reached the cathedral. He embraced me. I could feel the pulse on various parts of his body. Of course, I didn't recite a poem or talk about a meeting with my future in-laws. I couldn't do something regrettable three times in a row.

I entrusted my body to a sense of joy and fulfillment. As his lips approached me, the toy truck clanked down onto the street. Soon the dish set dropped from my hands, and I wrapped my arms around his neck. We desired each other painfully, shivering with a yearning that couldn't be satisfied. He pushed me away and picked up the toy truck. I gathered up my dish set, which was strewn a little further away.

After the ecstatic kiss, a painful, deep sorrow lingered. We walked down the hill, cooling our passion. The last show was ending at the movie theater. The audience surged out and scattered. The dark theater could be seen through the wide open doors. On the huge billboard at the theater, Moira Shearer was dancing a crazy fateful dance, her swollen bloody feet wrapped in pink toeshoes.

"Let's come a little early tomorrow. Let's stop watching the chimpanzee and see a movie instead," I suggested.

He fumbled around for a cigarette in silence, lit it, and took a long draw. His expression was not different from before the kiss, but he was immersed in an agony that I couldn't fathom. I was nervous and anxious.

"What are you thinking? I wish you wouldn't put on that kind of expression. If you can't be sure that I'm real from an embrace alone, do whatever you want with me. But please, don't look like that."

He threw his cigarette butt far away, ran to it, and crushed it with his heavy boot much longer than necessary.

"I need to have a break for a few days. A few days will do. That's all right, isn't it?"

"Why? No, you can't do that." I opposed quickly.

"I must," he said more firmly. "I want to find out whether I'm still an artist."

"What? What do you mean?"

"I haven't been able to paint for a long time. Too long! It's been so long that I wonder if I'm still an artist. I'm more afraid that I'm not an artist than that I'm not a person. I can't imagine what I would be if I weren't an artist. Let me be an artist for a few days."

"Do you want to be an artist that badly?"

"I just want to paint. I'm going crazy because I'm not painting. I want to be engrossed in hard work and concentrate for hours and hours."

He was sizzling, panting without the slightest embarrassment. It was not because of me any longer. He had his own work and he didn't need a companion. We parted at the same corner as always.

Once alone, I felt the breathless scene near the cathedral was no longer real. It didn't seem that the strong man had trembled because of me, that he had flushed because of me. It could have been a fantasy I imagined in the middle of a night. Like the poor match girl's dream, her hungry fantasy about a turkey and a warm stove, her lonely fantasy about a warm-hearted grandmother. I must have been imagining what I craved.

The gift of the toy dishes was the only thing I had for sure. I hurled it to the frozen ground. That was not enough for me, so I ran to each of the pieces that were rolling on the ground and crushed them with the heel of my shoe. It sounded like a freshly baked crispy Japanese cookie being crunched between molars, and a similar pleasure traveled all through my body.

Twelve

Holding the rail of the center staircase, Sergeant Balcom appeared to scold Tae-su. Tae-su, with several tools peeping out from his back pocket, was smiling sheepishly, scratching his head. Then Balcom replaced his serious expression with a generous one and rapped Tae-su on the shoulder. Then the sergeant circled the arcade, still wearing that benevolent face.

Tae-su looked somewhat subdued. He leaned against the rail the sergeant had been holding. He searched his pockets for a cigarette. The houseboy, the sergeant's helper, was ascending the stairs. He put his hand up to his neck pretending to chop at it and asked in broken English, "Fire?"

Tae-su answered in English, "Not yet," and, with that short exchange, seemed to recover. His face regained its usual comical look as he pulled some tools from his back pocket. He clattered them against each other, approaching me.

He slid onto my desk carelessly. I pulled the remaining tools from his back pocket with a clatter and asked about their purposes.

"What do you use this for?"

"To strip electrical cords."

"And this?"

"To cut electrical cords."

"This?"

"To cut iron pipe."

"Hmm, you could rob a bank safe with all these."

"What! Do you think robbery is easy? You don't know what I just went through."

"What was it?"

"I was spotted sneaking out with some bulbs in an empty box. Did I steal them? No, sir. I paid for them in dollars, but they treat me like a thief."

"Where did a mere Korean think he was, presumptuously buying something with dollars?"

"It's more difficult to make money than it looks."

His expression grew dark and confused. It did not become him.

"Did you get the axe?" I asked him, pretending to chop at my neck like the boy had done earlier.

"He said he'd let me off this once. Damn it."

"He's giving you another chance."

112

"Other people do that kind of thing all the time, by the truckload, but I get caught with a box of bulbs! Do you know how much I had to invest? I followed Susan Chong at the electric goods section for days and days to get this first bit of business, but all I got was disgrace."

"Shit!" Kim stretched and threw his brush down.

"Mongrels!" Cash seconded him, throwing down his brush.

The boredom and exhaustion of the afternoon was settling in.

"Shit, what mongrels!" Tae-su outdid them all with his loud curse, arched his back, and laced his hands behind his head as he tilted it back.

The one-hundred-watt bulb under its dirt-covered glass shade sent its light right on top of him. He seemed to be preoccupied for a while. His eyes were still clear. I wished the point on which his eyes rested was something other than the bulb. Even a piece of sky would be better.

"Aren't you sick and tired of it all? Don't you want to escape like Mr. Ock?" I asked.

"What? Mr. Ock has fled?" he asked, straightening himself up.

"Not really," I muttered vaguely. I wanted to be the only one who knew about Ock's business.

"He's not in today. Did you say he's fled?"

"I said no. He said he'd take a few days off. Anyway, haven't you ever wanted to be something besides an electrician?"

"How can I dream of becoming something else when I'm not even a good electrician? Why? Is there a good opening or something?"

"I don't mean changing jobs. I'm not talking about making a living. What I mean is . . . don't you want to be engrossed in something?"

"Well, that's a vague question."

"Even if it's vague, and if only sometimes, wouldn't you like to be something else other than the person you are at this moment?"

"What are you leading to? I have one thing that I want to be. If I could be your boyfriend or your fiance, I wouldn't mind being an electrician for the rest of my life."

His eyes were pleading, like those of a child. I put the wonderful tools back in his pocket one by one.

"Now go. You've been scolded by the sergeant, so it won't do you any good if you idle away your time like this."

He obediently went back to being an electrician, and the painters started drawing again. I waited earnestly for a naive GI to materialize in front of me. Readying my mouth for a "May I help you?" I swallowed a yawn.

Everyone seemed to be tired of working, but nobody was able to break out of the routine. Yawning, Misuk approached me.

I squeezed her plump hand and asked, "How's it going? Anything special happening? You haven't done anything outrageous, have you?"

"Don't worry."

I released her hand slowly. At this point I was not interested in people who never caused trouble. Gradually I came to wish I could stir up some trouble. But the trouble I could make wouldn't amount to much. I wished I could sweep around the arcade on my hands or scream from the top of the central staircase. However, these were only ideas, and I knew I would never act on them.

A sturdy Yankee dumped an armful of goods he had bought onto my desk and began to write addresses on a pile of envelopes. It looked like a good chance to improve our business, and I gulped and waited for him to finish writing.

He wrote addresses rapidly in typical reckless Yankee handwriting. I couldn't stand watching, and I blurted out, "Be careful."

"With what?"

"I'm afraid that the letters and the addresses might be mixed up."

He stopped writing for a moment, twisted his mouth in a frown, and shrugged, spreading out his arms in the typical Yankee gesture, which meant he didn't care.

I still hoped to make him my customer, so I smiled sweetly and commented, "Is it really all right if you write so fast?"

"No problem. The contents are similar."

"But the people who get them are all different."

"They're all girls. I know what kind of things they want to hear."

Amazed, I couldn't continue. He had deep green eyes. They were beautiful. His nose was arrogantly high with the end bent a little like a hook, and his thin lips were closed, tucked inward. He looked as selfish as Cousin Jin.

I gave up the idea of selling him a portrait. From my experience, I could tell potential customers after exchanging a few words with them. Either they had to be on the stupid side or they had to be so curious that they wanted to do everything in sight. Or they had to be the excessively sympathetic type, disgusting enough to assume every transaction with a Korean as an act of charity. This fellow didn't belong to any of these categories.

His eyes didn't look like they belonged to someone who could be easily bought, and they were shrouded with a boredom that wouldn't be easily stirred by curiosity.

"If you send so many letters out, you'll get as many answers."

"Maybe."

"What kind of answers do you usually get?"

"Something similar to mine."

"I wonder what they are."

"I love you. I'm thinking only of you."

"Oh, my."

He smirked and shrugged again.

"You have good luck with women. Must be a happy man."

"No, not at all."

"Why?"

"I don't believe them."

"Why?"

"I lie to them. If I don't believe what I tell them, how can I believe their answers?"

"Then why do you bother at all?"

"Bother? It's not. Sometimes I have an urge to say 'I love you' even to the thin air."

I suddenly glimpsed a hunger hidden behind his boredom. I was jolted. Confused, I said something I should not have.

"You should have bought a woman."

"Who said I haven't bought women? Who in this country could avoid that? The cheap women. Five dollars, okay, one dollar, okay. The cheapest sex in the world. But afterwards, I feel like it's all a waste of money. Korean whores are the world's worst! They're like vending machines. They don't know the first rule of business: That products should offer the buyer the pleasure of shopping in addition to being practical. These women just go crazy when they see dollars."

He challenged me as if I too were a sham, his penetrating beautiful eyes burning with anger.

"I'm sorry." I apologized in confusion, as if I had cheated him already.

"Why are you sorry? You look like a *tong bang yeui jiguk* yourself."

His Korean pronunciation was awkward and I assumed he was saying some difficult English words I was not familiar with. I kept asking, "I beg your pardon?" Finally I realized he meant "The Country of Courteous People in the East," Korea's nickname, but I was still in the dark.

"What do you mean?"

"The women who aren't whores. When they see GIs, they put on such demure faces you'd think they'd had their sex organs removed long ago, and if a GI as much as winks at them, they act as if he's trying to rape them." No longer in a fury, he explained this haltingly and with such a bored expression that it could have induced sleep.

"Bye, bye, *tong bang yeui jiguk*," he said dully and was gone. I watched him as he raced up the stairs two at a time. He was one GI I would not easily forget.

Perhaps he went to the post office upstairs and mailed all those love letters, knowing that he would have to buy from a vending machine that very night. I began to regret that I didn't tell him I was neither a whore nor a *tong bang yeui jiguk*.

It had been three days since I had seen that GI, so it was the third day Ock had not been in.

"He must be sick again. He looks strong and sturdy but he's not even as healthy as we are. Tsk, tsk."

"Miss Lee, let's all go and see him. Talk one of the Yankees into buying a few cans of fruit for us."

"What nonsense! I'm already nervous because all the GIs have their eyes on Miss Lee. Why should we make it easy for them to buy her for the price of a few cans of fruit?"

"What are you talking about? Do you think she'd fall into their hands for a couple of cans of fruit? She's pure gold. Right, pure gold."

I gave each painter a larger work load and told them not to worry about the fruit because Ock was not sick, that he had some business to take care of at home.

How many more days would he need to prove that he was an artist? I sat in his chair, staring at the grey curtain. Originally it had been pale blue, but now it was a faded grimy grey. He had escaped this greyness, enjoying the opportunity for concentration and hard work, experimenting with vivid colors to his heart's content.

I felt anxious as if I were stranded all alone in the midst of confusion. I was so anxious I wanted to shout to him for help, but he was as far away as my dead father where my shouts could not be heard.

The grey curtain didn't flutter even a little, and I was stirred by the desire to do something. If I couldn't escape this greyness, I at least wanted to crack or chip away at its thickness.

"Miss Lee, a customer." Chin poked me with the end of his brush.

A young, disagreeable-looking PFC handed me a receipt. He didn't ask me to wrap the portrait up but gazed at it with a frown, his head cocked as if he were about to cause trouble. I pretended not to notice his expression because I decided I'd rather have his portrait drawn again than try to placate him in my broken English.

"Ah, this looks great. A work of art."

I looked up and found Joe, the green-eyed man I had met a few days earlier.

"Hey, Miss, which painter drew this?" he added, pointing to the portrait the PFC was holding.

He winked at my surprised face. I went along with him, pointing at Chin, who had the most dignified appearance of the painters, and said, "He drew it. He's a very respected artist. Anyone who can have one of his paintings is lucky."

"That's great. Ask him to do mine."

Joe fumbled noisily in his inner pockets, presumably looking for a picture. The PFC slowly lost his frown until his face went blank and asked me to wrap his portrait up. I mischievously said if he was not happy with it, I would ask one of the other painters to do it again, but he said he liked it all right.

After the customer left, Joe slowly returned his photo to his pocket.

"You don't want a portrait?"

"I know the worth of a dollar better than most people."

"Thank you for helping me, anyway."

"Any time. Don't hesitate to ask for help."

"I'm glad to see you again."

"Really? Have you thought of me?"

"No, but I think I will from now on."

"Thanks," he grinned for the first time. Unexpectedly, his smile revealed a dimple on his right cheek. That dimple didn't diminish his masculinity a bit, but softened his brashness and made him look so sweet that I could have plunged into his arms.

I felt a fondness for him. We didn't speak to each other but looked at each other. The curtain of boredom in his eyes began to open, and I felt myself being sucked into them as they showed unrestrained hunger.

"I want to whisper in your ear that I love you." His voice sounded very sexy all of a sudden.

"Didn't you write any love letters today?"

"I might be able to skip them today, thanks to you."

I disguised the shortness of breath I felt with a sigh. In his hunger I saw myself, and I interpreted it in my own way. He was an insatiable person. He had an extravagant spirit which couldn't be consoled by sex from a vending machine, and at the same time he possessed a sex drive which couldn't be satisfied no matter how many love letters he wrote. He was an insatiable man who insisted on pursuing both at the same time.

He shifted his eyes, which had been locked with mine, pulled out an Old Gold, and inhaled it with pleasure without the slightest movement. I felt a strong physical attraction.

I found myself waiting for Joe all the next day. Finally he came and squeezed my hand hard with his strong, hairy one. His thirsty, hungry eyes, like those of a starving animal, seemed to lick. As if by magic, I felt I was being transformed into a female animal.

I retrieved my hand from his, remembering the watchful eyes of the painters. I couldn't extricate myself, however, from the embarrassing consciousness that had been awakened within me.

"What do you want from me?" My voice sounded strange and split.

"I want to love you. We can have lots of fun. I want to love this country through you," he whispered enthrallingly in my ear.

Dreams began to form in his hungry eyes, making them shine with a dazzling light. My thoughts wandered wildly as I shuffled through the paperback he had brought.

His arrogant high nose and selfish-looking thin lips didn't suggest that he wanted a lasting love with a foreign woman. Perhaps he simply wanted to enjoy the feeling of love, to have a woman in his arms.

A love affair in a foreign country, something more than simple sex. Did I need to be the victim in his love affair? I could be a co-conspirator. I could conspire in a fantastic love affair with him. I could enjoy conversation with him, and better yet, I could listen to music, looking into his eyes. Sitting by a warm stove, listening to stories about his childhood. My own childhood would make him laugh. I could enjoy his dimple to my heart's content.

I closed the book. Slowly the flashy color illustration on the cover began to register in my mind. A woman with one strap of her slip hanging from her shoulder was leaning back on a bed, and a man was kneeling at her feet, tearing his hair. By the way their faces were distorted with lust, it was clear they were in a prostitute's room. I read the title of the book. Unexpectedly, it was *Crime and Punishment* by Dostoyevsky.

I hadn't read Dostoyevsky's works carefully, but influenced by my brother Hyok, who had been a literature fanatic, I had a deep respect for him tinged with awe. As I thought of *Crime and Punishment*'s Sonja as a saint, I was offended by the illustration. I turned the title page facedown.

"Why the sour expression? You don't like the illustration?"

"It's too much for *Crime and Punishment* even if it is only a cheap paperback."

"What's wrong with this picture? This is the true nature of a man and woman," he challenged, furious.

"Still . . ."

"You're a *tong bang yeui jiguk.* I almost forgot."

His anger cooled as quickly as it had erupted, but for some reason his face took on a strange look. His eyes, full of expression only a moment ago, were suddenly hidden behind a blanket of boredom.

"I almost forgot that you're a *tong bang yeui jiguk,*" he said again.

"Why do you have to bring up that *tong bang yeui jiguk* all the time? What right do you, a foreigner, have to slander this country by ridiculing its time-honored values by turning them into some trashy slang?"

"At least I came to fight for this country. I could die here although I don't want to. I want to know more about this country, especially the women. But the women are hidden behind a thick taboo that a foreigner can't ever penetrate. I use the term *tong bang yeui jiguk* to refer to women who can't be bought. If I was wrong, forgive me," he said gravely.

"You're exaggerating about the awkwardness between strangers."

"Exaggerating? Hardly. I was curious about the life behind the windows and high walls. I wanted to peep behind the curtain of mystery through you. But you can't do it. If you are not a whore and if you're from a good family, you can't invite me to your home, can you?"

"Well, that's . . ."

I was embarrassed. I couldn't imagine knocking on the gate of my house and introducing this man to my grey mother.

"I fantasized about walking with you in the beautiful palaces when the grass turns green. I wanted to caress you, roll on that grass. Are you brave enough? If you are, you're a whore."

I remembered Misuk worrying about being called a Yankee slut even if she legally married an American soldier. She was more afraid of other people's criticism than of the marriage itself. Come to think of it, we were all so sensitive to what others thought. Yankee slut. Would I have the courage to ignore the derisive eyes?

"Would you walk with me on a busy street, go shopping with me, and listen to music at a coffee shop? Would you permit that? If you did, you sure aren't from a good family."

He kept jeering at me. He insulted me squinting his eyes, on which the boredom had already descended.

"And finally I wanted to strip off your clothes. Like this."

He turned the paperback faceup.

"You'd never do anything so terrible. One look at the picture and you flush. A woman of *tong bang yeui jiguk* would never take her clothes off in front of a man. Right?"

His taunting stopped there. It seemed our meeting had come to a disastrous end.

Still, the next day I waited for him. I went about my work listlessly trying to spot him among the military uniforms milling in the PX. I knew he would come back. He had left his paperback behind. We had an excuse to see each other again.

I wanted to see him. But at the same time I felt uncomfortable as if his hungry eyes had remained on my body like a sticky liquid.

My recollections of him weren't clear, so I couldn't decide how I felt about him. In my confusion, I was directing my nervousness to the act of waiting for him. The sense of waiting was vicious, quite different from waiting I had experienced before. Perhaps I had been contaminated by him.

"Shit!" Kim wadded a scarf in a ball, shoved it aside and stretched. It was the second scarf he had ruined that day.

"Hey, what's wrong? Did you eat something you shouldn't have before coming to work this morning?"

"Shit! My wife nagged me this morning, so now I can't do a decent job."

"Same here. The day after tomorrow is lunar New Year's. We've got to work harder if we're going to provide rice cake soup for our families and buy our wives velvet skirts or something." Cash sounded weary.

I was suddenly conscious of Ock's empty seat. Was he willing to starve his children in order to prove that he was an artist? Even if it meant no rice cake soup for New Year's? And had he ever imagined how much better his long-necked wife would look if she took off those shabby army fatigues and wore something more feminine, if not a velvet skirt? What was he looking for? My disappointment in him surged inside me, like an uncontrollable cry.

I realized that I was waiting for that sticky Yankee because of Ock Hui-do. I wanted to do something out of the ordinary because of him. I could have remained a good girl if he had kept his gaze on me, but he had rejected my wish and sought his own work. Just to spite him, I had to do something.

I was determined, even if nobody cared about what I did. Joe hadn't appeared by the end of the day, and I kept his paperback deep in a drawer.

"Please help me," Misuk called out from behind.

"What?"

"Please go to a tavern with me."

"What are you talking about?"

"Do you think I'm asking you out for rice wine? I want to buy some mung bean pancakes. Pure mung bean pancakes."

"Do you crave them so?"

"No, my mother loves them. She's had a terrible cold, and now she simply doesn't have an appetite for anything. I want to buy some for her. My boss says there's this tavern where they fry pure mung bean cakes with lots of pork in them, but I don't have the nerve to go there by myself."

"No problem."

My heart warmed, and I thought I might buy some as well. My mother used to like them, too. I remembered that around the end of the year, when she made mung bean pancakes, my mother, who rarely sampled anything in the kitchen, would squish up her eyes and eat the first fried cake, dipped in the soy-vinegar sauce, without bothering to offer it to anybody, saying it tasted best straight from the frying pan.

Misuk led me down a dark, secluded alley which seemed quite out of place in Myong-dong. Although narrow, it was filled with the delicious scent of cooking odors and a noisy din.

"There it is."

Misuk pointed to a tavern with a shapeless wooden board instead of glass. The door opened smoothly. It was warm inside, and the dim light was hazy, either from the smoke or the heat.

It was not that we weren't curious about the men drinking, but we headed straight to the proprietor inside without giving the men a second glance. In a vast frying pan, several pancakes and a yellow lump of fat sizzled together. The pan was as big as the lid of the cast-iron cauldron in every kitchen.

I felt flushed with the noise mixed with singing and the thick odors of food, wine, and people.

"Give us hot ones. The freshest ones."

Misuk bought five pancakes and I ended up buying five myself. We left the tavern as if someone were chasing us, breathed a sigh of relief and smiled at each other. We were proud, as if we had just accomplished something very difficult.

As I walked, the pancakes became a burden. I was irritated and blamed Misuk for making me buy them. Oblivious to what I was thinking, Misuk opened her coat and clasped the cakes to her chest.

"What are you doing? Your clothes will smell."

"That's all right. Mung bean pancakes are no good if they're cold."

After saying goodbye, I didn't know what to do with my five pancakes. They were gradually losing warmth in my hands. At a corner I finally opened my coat, and going one step further, I pulled my sweater to put the cakes against my undershirt. I adjusted my sweater and closed my coat, hugging the pancakes in my arms.

"What a pain! All because of her."

I still blamed Misuk for the purchase, but as I neared my house, I found myself expecting something extraordinary to happen. Perhaps I could bring some kind of emotion to my mother's dull eyes.

I shook the gate, calling out for her loudly. My chest felt warm. It was because the pancakes were still warm. I drew close to my mother, one hand holding hers and the other hugging my chest.

"Mom, Mom, do you smell anything? A good smell. Can you guess what it is? Hum, hum?"

"Smell?" my mother answered flatly. The dry wood of her hand didn't respond to my squeeze. I stood on the front step, and my mother went into the dimly lit kitchen.

"Mom, mung bean pancakes!" I handed them to her quickly. "Have some before they get cold. I put them under my clothes to keep them warm."

I stared in her eyes, hoping to find some meaning. She simply put the bundle down, and went about her regular routine, warming up the soup, setting out the spoons, chopsticks, and bowls on the tray. Her eyes revealed nothing but a stubborn determination that said she was living only because she couldn't kill herself. I regretted buying the mung bean pancakes. And embracing them under my clothes.

And I especially regretted telling her, "I put them under my clothes to keep them warm." If words were tangible, I would have snatched them back.

I stepped into the house. The spot on my chest where the pancakes had been was burning with fury. I shoved open the northern window, which hadn't been open all winter.

The fierce, cold wind whipped in. I should have brought that Yankee home. Maybe Joe will come tomorrow. If I knocked on our gate with my arm hooked in his, my mother's eyes couldn't remain expressionless. They would have to show some emotion. I had to invite him here behind these high walls, behind these intricately latticed window.

She couldn't help but be shocked. I'd ignore her reaction and walk with him around the house. She would be horrified, of course. I would let him sit down on my father's overstuffed chair, let him touch my brothers' things, and I would broil marinated beef for him in the kitchen.

The trees in the backyard sent out a blast of wind toward me, shaking all over. Still, the spot where I had held the pancakes had not cooled.

I would tell him what a splendid yellow the trees once were, although they're miserable now. How they spilled their yellowness to the earth continuously. I would whisper to him in front of my mother. Then she wouldn't be able to gaze at her daughter with those lifeless eyes.

The event that was to shock my mother didn't happen the next day, either. Joe didn't show up although I thought he surely would. Since it was payday for the painters, I had Ock Hui-do's earnings with me. The painters were discussing the best way to utilize their meager earnings over the holiday season.

In my head I tried to squeeze rice cake soup and new clothes for the children out of Ock's earnings, less than 50,000 won, but there were so many children that I gave up in dismay. Fortunately, the allocation of his earning was not my job. The only use that money had for me was that it provided me an excuse to see Ock.

I left work with the money in my inside pocket, but it wasn't easy for me to go to Yonji-dong. I wished I didn't need an excuse to see him. I wished I didn't have to see him in the presence of the five children and wife.

Perhaps tomorrow he would surprise us by coming to sit in his chair. Maybe he was standing in front of the chimpanzee at this very moment. Yes, he must be there. Savoring that hope, I went to the toy stall. It was deserted. There were no spectators. The vendor looked up at me, half-dozing, and seemed to recognize me. The chimpanzee and the black doll were gone. They must have brought the vendor some money, finally.

I felt helpless as if I were a lost child. I pressed the belly of a doll my hand happened to touch and said, "You must have sold the chimpanzee."

"They're expensive but they go as soon as I get them. I haven't been able to get hold of any lately," he explained kindly with a yawn.

Then it had not been one chimpanzee but a series of chimpanzees, coming and going.

"But have you seen the man who used to come with me?"

"No, I don't think I have."

"Think harder, please?"

I wanted to believe that he had rushed from his concentration and hard work to wait for me here, but the old man shook his head three times running.

Then hadn't he stepped away from his concentration and hard work even once? I was swept up by a desire to do something. I headed for Yonji-dong.

"Oh, my. What brought you here at this hour?" Mrs. Ock asked.

"It's payday."

"Well, how thoughtful of you!"

She squeezed my hand. I couldn't shake her hand away. Dejected, I was angry at myself for not being able to dislike her.

"To tell you the truth, I couldn't say anything to the children's father, but I was dying for the money, knowing today's payday."

I whispered in her ear, "Why didn't you tell him to go and get it?"

"How could I? He's painting for the first time in a long while, and I couldn't worry him with a trivial thing like money. It's been so long since he painted."

Her face was happy as if she wanted to be congratulated because her husband had started painting again.

"Yes, that's right. And as he was off this week, he won't be paid next week. What will you do?"

"Thank you for your concern. We'll get by somehow."

She put aside the worry about money as trivial and said, "Please come in. I'd like to serve you tea."

She was excited. Was it because she had money or was it because her husband had started painting again? She looked much younger and more vivacious than the last time. She was wearing something more feminine, a purple Korean blouse with a neat white collar. Over it she wore a shabby, yet feminine sweater. She was certainly aware of her appearance. That was why she always accentuated it with clean collars.

"Darling, it's Miss Lee. Today is payday, she says. She came here because of that. We had forgotten all about it, hadn't we?"

"Tell her to come in and warm up before heading for home."

The whole family was together. Ock Hui-do, who was reading the newspaper with the youngest son on his lap, looked rather gaunt. As I entered, the other children slid back toward the colder part of the room and only the youngest remained on his father's lap.

"Didn't you bring apples this time?" he asked.

"What an impudent boy!" Ock said, bouncing up the boy with his thigh. The boy's bottom landed on his father's lap with a slap, and everyone in the family laughed. They were the picture of the happy family enjoying an evening together.

I smiled with them and looked around the room. There wasn't a trace of his painting to be seen. She served me ginger tea in a thick heavy cup. The yellow liquid was hot, spicy, and sweet, perfect for the cold weather.

"Have you finished painting?" I cautiously brought up the subject. That was what I was most curious about. "Where is it? Can I see?"

The youngest bolted from his father's lap and slid open the paper door leading to the next room. Then I realized why his wife hadn't sent the children to the other room. It was not clear whether there was no electric light or whether it was not turned on, but the room was dark. A large canvas was leaning against the wall and things were strewn about in the tiny space, with hardly an inch to spare. I could smell turpentine.

On the canvas was a tree. It gave me a terrifying sensation. The old tree, with neither flowers nor fruit, stood bleakly against an almost grey space. That was all. The whole space had a sandy texture, with different shades of black and white, like a mosaic. Neither the sky nor the earth were visible, and the old tree floated like a monster in the grey confusion.

The tree might have died from the dry-spell demon; if so, where was the cruel sunlight? A dry spell without sunlight. If such a thing were possible, it was a dry spell in thick mist. The sandy grey texture was like a thick mist. Why had I seen a dead tree killed by a cruel dry spell on his canvas? The child couldn't stand still a minute and shut the sliding door quickly. The fragrant ginger tea had cooled, but I had lost my appetite for it. I didn't have any specialized knowledge of art, but I had always loved it. I loved paintings, from the ones on the wall of my elementary school classroom, to professional painters, famous and nameless, to the beautiful prints in albums of famous artists' works.

I didn't understand the language of those works, but I enjoyed their light and colors. I loved paintings that expressed the joy of life in various colors and shapes. My taste for art was as simple and down-to-earth as a child who longed for colorful balloons or a woman admiring bright colors in front of a fabric shop window. My simple taste was perplexed by his painting.

The boy sat on my lap.

"Will you bring apples next time?"

"Yes."

I gave him two 1,000 won bills and stood up, leaving the cold ginger tea untouched. I wanted to sort out my bewilderment alone. Ock Hui-do and his wife didn't try to hold me back. They had been silent since the child opened the sliding door.

The wife followed me to the alley.

"Why did he paint that kind of thing?'

"Why? Don't you like it?"

"Do you?"

"Of course. It's his."

"Don't you think you should do something more for him?"

"Of course I do. I'm embarrassed that I can't fix it so he can paint without having to worry about the family finances. We have so many children that . . ."

"You're talking about his difficulty making a living."

"I'm ashamed, but, yes."

"You should be ashamed of something else."

"What are you trying to say? I don't understand."

"In my opinion you're not qualified to be an artist's wife."

She halted in her tracks. I stopped and we faced each other.

"What? I've been taking care of him for almost twenty years."

"Ha, do you think you can be proud of that?"

"What does a young lady like you know? You mean I shouldn't be proud of taking care of a man who knows nothing but painting for twenty years?"

"You're really confident."

"Listen, young lady. You're making me nervous. Why do you want to argue with me all of a sudden?"

"I'm not trying to argue. I simply pity Mr. Ock."

"Don't say everything that pops into your head. Why do you pity him? There's no reason why a young lady like you should pity him. I know because I've been the wife of an artist for twenty years."

We faced each other, eyes burning in the dark night. There was not even a waning moon in the sky. Twice she called me "a young lady like you." I tried hard to get back at her for her insult.

"You couldn't even read the desperate poverty in his painting."

"Is our poverty my sole responsibility? It's difficult enough for me to act as a buffer, protecting him from feeling the poverty on his skin."

"I'm not talking about material poverty, but about the poverty of light and colors that indicates starvation for the joy of life."

"You are too young, and you don't know much about works of art. Colorful paintings aren't always the best."

She was trying to teach me in a dignified manner. I wanted to crush her.

"Painting is a visual language. In his painting, I see poverty and desperation. You could have given him more of life's joy."

"Nobody can take care of him better than I do."

"I can."

"How? What do you want?"

"I'd rather take off my clothes and let him paint me, instead of watching him paint dead wood and things like that."

I hadn't thought before I spoke, but once the words were out, I thought that was what I really wanted and in order to save both myself and Ock Hui-do I really had to do that.

"What? I'd take off my clothes before I'd let you do that."

"Have you forgotten you've given birth to five children? Who do you think he would prefer?"

"Who on earth are you?" She clearly was terrified. Her voice quavered.

In the dark I could see the white collar and her slender, elegant neck. I knew that neck could carry a burden several times her own weight if it were for him.

And I liked this woman. Still, I had to make her angry with me. I was rebelling against her for no reason. I had not expected or planned to do it, but I couldn't stop once I had started.

"Don't you realize who I am?"

"No, no. Who are you? Who?"

"I'll tell you by and by."

I ran down the alley, leaving her standing there. Immediately I forgot about her distress and thought only of that tree standing dead in the mist.

Of course she wasn't to blame for that painting. It must have been that grey curtain, that glum curtain blocking his view. That curtain must have repressed his inspiration, his imagination. No, maybe it was those painters. How he must have suffered because of those impoverished talkative philistines!

Maybe it was the war. Perhaps it was the bleak streets, the grey buildings, and the skeletal trees.

It could have been all of these. They could have combined to drive him to starvation. He must be suffering from a hunger, different from that of the green-eyed GI. I sadly realized that I couldn't relieve Ock's hunger, although I could alleviate the GI's.

Thirteen

"Hi, baby."

It was Joe, back after a long absence. I had been waiting for him earnestly, but once I saw him I was neither happy nor sad.

I pulled his book from my drawer and handed it to him calmly. It was to convince myself that he had just come for the book.

"I missed you."

His deep eyes licked my whole body. I hurriedly lowered my eyes. My attraction to him was shallow and sensual, so I could forget him when out of his presence, but when I was with him, it pained me.

"Me, too," I whispered, betraying myself with a complicated expression.

I was ashamed that my voice sounded hoarse, ringing strange to my ear. If he wanted me to, I had a feeling, well, rather a belief, that I might do something with him.

Under his sensual gaze, I felt all the joints of my body loosen, making it easy for him to break me apart. I was not the least bit frightened or sorry about imagining myself broken apart.

It wouldn't be my responsibility if I were broken apart. It was not important that I was the one who might be broken apart. To me, the fact that I was not responsible was important. I wanted to shout it, so everyone could hear.

What really mattered to me was having an excuse, to be able to say it was all because of Ock Hui-do, that nothing like this would have happened if only he had been with me.

"Can we meet somewhere today, somewhere besides here?"

"Shall I invite you to my home?"

"Are you serious?"

"Of course. This evening is fine."

He seemed to think for a while and said, "Let's forget it. I mean let's forget your invitation."

"Why? I thought you wanted me to invite you to my house."

"You shouldn't be so easy. You should remain a girl from a good family. I don't want to think of you as a whore."

"How about walking together in a busy street? How about going shopping together? You could buy me some beautiful shoes and drape a beautiful silk scarf."

"That won't do, either. You should be wrapped in layers of mystery. That way you won't seem like a whore to me."

"You are being very difficult."

I studied him carefully. What was he trying to say? Beautiful, but hungry eyes. I felt an inexplicable chill and thought of the naked tree Ock was painting.

"Can I have a pen and paper?"

He drew a map and put in the street names before explaining it to me. He apparently wanted to show me the way to a hotel in a back alley of Hoehyon-dong.

"It's called the Kyongso Hotel. If you are thinking of a large building, you won't be able to find it. It's a Japanese-style building with a rather large garden. Room seven. I have a reservation. You can come right in. You don't need a key. The room has a Japanese sliding door. I'm telling you, don't picture a real hotel just because it calls itself a hotel. There's a sign. It's an old Japanese building hidden behind the trees in the garden. I'll be there. You'll come to see me, right?"

"What do you want?"

"Well, I want to take off your clothes."

"Do you really think you can? I'm a girl from a good family, no whore. Besides, who knows? I might be a *tong bang yeui jiguk*." I mimicked everything he had said.

"I don't care."

"You sure are confident."

"You bet I'm as confident as you have a belly button."

I opened my mouth wide and let out a high-pitched giggle. He laughed along with me. His cold, thin lips opened and a dimple appeared on his cheek. I suddenly felt conscious of my belly button.

"What about it? You do have a belly button, right?"

"Well, I'll have to check. If I do, I'll go to room seven, and if not, I won't. I don't want you to waste your time."

"You have one."

"Maybe not."

"You do."

We laughed again. Gradually I felt as if my belly button were growing larger. I laughed once more, thinking of the old saying, "The belly button is larger than the belly." Giggling like an idiot, all I could feel was my belly button.

"Why are you laughing?" he asked, puzzled by my prolonged laughter.

However, I didn't try to explain why the old saying made me feel light-headed. It seemed that was something that would be funny only to me, and that we couldn't laugh about it together. He left, confidently reminding me that I had a belly button. I folded up the map he had drawn crookedly, putting it in my purse.

After closing, I carefully brushed my teeth in the rest area on the second floor and chewed a piece of gum which a cleaning woman had given me, rolling it into every corner of my mouth.

Once in the street, however, I turned my back on Hoehyon-dong, and headed for Myong-dong. I rushed to the toy vendor as if I had some urgent business there. It was almost deserted. I felt dejected because there was no chimpanzee.

"Excuse me. Don't you have the chimpanzees any more?"

"They aren't available any more. They are not made in Korea. They are imported directly from Japan. Did you want to buy one? If I happen to spot one, shall I hold it for you?"

"N . . . no."

The toy stall didn't provide me with relief any more. I climbed up the hill to the cathedral and then continued down on the other side. I didn't go home directly and I felt myself consciously resisting the call of my belly button. I walked the avenues and roamed the alleys lined with taverns exuding the smell of mung bean pancakes. I was cold and a bit tired. I opened the door of a pretentious-looking Western cake shop, with a decorated cake in the shape of a building still in the display window, although it had been made for Christmas. I slumped down near the stove. The green tea was fragrant and hot.

I was finally at ease. With the tension gone of my body, I grew drowsy. I leaned back in the chair and closed my eyes.

"Are you alone?"

Diana was sitting on the other side of the stove. I smiled, embarrassed to be caught dozing, and opened my eyes wider than was necessary. Opposite Diana sat two cute little boys side by side. They must be the sons of the Korean father, as Misuk had said. The children were healthy and even had an air of elegance about them. Diana, wearing subdued makeup for once, was gazing at her sons with warm, calm eyes.

"If you are by yourself, come join us."

I was looking at the boys distractedly.

"Are you waiting for somebody?"

"No."

"Then come on. Let me treat you to some pastries."

She laughed a warm, natural laugh. Today her wrinkles didn't look ugly, possibly because her sons were sitting with her. In fact, she and her sons looked quite happy together. I moved next to the boys, not next to her.

"Say hello to Mommy's friend. This auntie works at the same company as Mommy does."

"How do you do?"

"What nice manners you have! Who's older?"

"I am," said the bigger boy, puffing his chest out.

"They look like twins."

"Yes, they are only a year apart."

She ordered some cakes and pastries and warned the boys, whose cheeks were already bulging, to slow down and chew carefully, and to drink some water between bites. Her warnings didn't sound like nagging.

Goodness, is it because she's a mother? Shit, how could she be a mother?

My anger boiled up and a curse lodged in my throat.

"How old are you?"

"I'm six."

"I'm five."

"They're so smart and so handsome. They don't take after you."

"They look exactly like their father."

She was unruffled. I was not particularly curious about their father. The conversation stopped. I was uncomfortable because I was not familiar with this woman who was affectionate and almost elegant.

They left before me. She made her sons say polite goodbyes, walked them in front of her proudly, and paid my bill along with hers.

Ripping open an eclair to lick the cream, I pondered who the real Diana Kim was. She had several selves, changing them frequently, as if she were changing outfits. Which was the false Diana and which was the real Diana? The name Diana must be false as well. Her real name could be something as provincial as Poksun or Sunduk.

She clung desperately to money, slept with niggers, and had given birth to two sons only a year apart. On top of that, she was wife to their father, and she had insulted Ock Hui-do. Some of these roles must be faked, and she must prefer that of mother, wanting it to be the real her, but I made up my mind not to be deceived by her lies.

Maybe she was a fake through and through, and if you peeled off the mother, the whore, and the miser, she would be a hollow cave, completely empty like my mother. I felt good imagining her like that.

Having finished the eclair, I kept eating more pastries. There wasn't anyone to tell me to drink water between bites so I stupidly kept eating until my throat was stuffy and dry. I sat there for a long time after I had finished everything. Suddenly my coat was unbearably heavy.

The stove was hot and all the windows were covered with thick wool curtains. I took off my coat, rolled it up, and put it on my lap. I wanted to take off all my clothes.

I wanted to peel them off one by one and kick them away. It was not solely because of the pleasant room temperature. I would have felt the same way if I were roaming about in the street.

Yes, I wanted to go to the Kyongso Hotel. I wanted to be stripped by Joe. He would certainly take off my clothes. At the same time he would help me get rid of all the layers of taboo. My heart pounded with another expectation, perhaps the most important of all. Through him I wanted to step out of all those superfluous layers of myself. I wanted to throw off those selves, the ones that sometimes tore me to pieces, that hid behind myself and transformed with such dizzying speed without ever consulting me.

With Joe's help, I believed I could. He certainly would show up the real me. I wanted to see my body and soul in all its nakedness.

I wished I could gaze boldly at the distorted roof without fear.

I wished I could look smack at the hole on the ridge and at the splintered tiles. And most of all, I would have liked to have been able to face my mother without hating her.

Joe would take off my clothes, and through him I hoped I could rid myself of the tatters of my soul.

I put on my coat and pulled out the map from my purse. Having memorized the way from the map, I stepped out to the street.

The red neon sign on the iron gate made it easy to find the Kyongso Hotel, hidden behind the evergreen trees and otherwise indistinguishable from the other Japanese-style homes in the neighborhood.

The gate was wide open. There were stepping stones to the entrance. The garden, without lights, was dark and the evergreen trees were snow-capped. The spacious glass-doored room at the entrance was empty, and I could see some clothes hanging from the wall.

I found room seven without being seen by anyone. I hesitated for a moment. I was only thinking of lucky seven. It was a Japanese-style house, but contrary to what Joe had said, the sliding door had been replaced by a Western-style door. I twisted the handle open smoothly.

Joe was sitting on the window sill reading a thick book. I sat next to him. The *tatami* room was large. On the platform was a flower arrangement, yellow chrysanthemums interspersed with pine branches. A double bed, with a pink spread, occupied one end of the room. I felt a bit apprehensive at the idea of a western bed in a *tatami* room. Furthermore, the pink bedspread was a shade too tacky for my taste.

"Is it cold outside?" Joe asked, helping me off my coat and expertly hanging it on the rack. I shook my head and leafed through the thick brown book he was reading.

"Is it a novel?"

"No."

He pushed the book away and stared at me with his hungry eyes. The handsome eyes of a male animal were changing me into a female animal very fast, but when he leaned toward me, I pushed him away abruptly and asked him another question.

"What is that book about? I'd like to know what you were thinking about before I came here."

"It's a kind of history book."

"Which country's? Yours, of course?"

"No. A history of the human race. It's a story about how people evolved from animals to create culture and the arts."

"Sounds interesting. Will you tell me about it?"

"I want to teach you something more interesting."

Joe opened the top buttons of my warm sweater and ran his lips along my neck. I twisted my body to extricate myself from his embrace and pulled my collar together.

"You must have studied something like that in your country. What's it called? History? Sociology?"

"I was just reading it because I was bored waiting for you. Please don't put such stupid things between us."

He pushed the thick book further away with his foot. His green eyes were bloodshot with anxiety and thirst. I was nervous, too. I didn't have to know about that brown book, but I wanted to know more about him before I took off all my clothes. I thought I should know something more about him than that he was an attractive male.

"I love you," he whispered in a sexy voice.

The bristles on his chin pricked my neck. The front buttons of my sweater had opened. I couldn't pull it closed again. I suppressed my panting with all my strength, however. It seemed like I had to do something before taking off my clothes.

More conversation or something to deepen the thoroughly superficial attraction between us. I had no idea why I began to feel I needed that kind of step before taking my clothes off. If I had known, I would have put off the visit to the room with the pink bed for a few days.

The room was designed for taking off clothes, nothing else. The pink bed eloquently said that, and the crimson shade on the lamp next to the bed said that, and the nude photos of people that were attached to the low walls at the eye level of someone lying on the bed said that.

The brown book was too far away to be of any help to me. I began to respond to his caresses more fully. My violet sweater came off and was thrown on top of the book. It would take ages to remove all the undershirts I was wearing, though, for I was more sensitive to the cold than most people. He caressed me leisurely, peeling my clothes off one by one. I abandoned myself to the pleasure of having my clothes taken off.

My varied colored clothes were strewn all over the *tatami*. I had selected them so carefully, but now they looked like mere rags on the floor, ugly and useless rags. I had the vague feeling that something was being cast off within me. No, I hoped that it was so.

I thought it seemed as though I had wings that could carry me out of that thick cocoon. Wings that could free me from the stifling cocoon. Wings.

Finally I floated up to the air, as if I really had wings. There was no resistance that could deter my flight. I was weightless.

I was in his arms with only a thin slip, hanging by one strap over my shoulder. He was carrying me to the pink bed.

It was fine with me. I would have wings. I would spring out from the narrow confinement of my chrysalis. The soft bed engulfed almost half of my body. I could feel his weight as he lay beside me. His lips and hands explored every part of my body. Like a magician, he found the hidden points of sensuality and offered me a fascinating feast of the senses. His breath came in gasps.

Still, I was the guest at the feast. For a guest invited to a gourmet meal, I was a shade too conscious. I knew too much about the flavors of the food. I tasted the flavors so clearly, distinguishing between the savory taste and all the other different flavors.

Perhaps one could get sick and tired of a gourmet meal too easily. A gourmet meal was a gourmet meal, and it could not change the fact that the host was the host and the guest was the guest.

Something was missing in our feast. A flavorful, exquisite wine that could enhance the feast and intoxicate the host and the guest, and that could transform the tastes of other dishes to a perfect harmony.

Joe seemed to sense that. He kept whispering "I love you," but his caress grew more nervous and intense. I accepted his expert caresses with delicate appreciation, but they didn't intoxicate me.

"How about turning off the light?" I suggested, growing more nervous.

The switch was on the wall next to the door. He sauntered to the door and flicked the black switch.

Darkness wrapped around us. His breathing grew shorter and louder. His strong body smell, like that of an animal, assaulted my nose. I was afraid of him changing into something fierce in the dark.

"Turn the light on. The light!"

He didn't answer, but snatched down the strap that was hanging precariously from my shoulder.

"Turn on the light, I said!" I screamed, grabbing hold of my slip.

He mumbled something that sounded like a curse, and raising his upper body, he fumbled about at the head of the bed. He must be looking for the lamp with the crimson shade. The switch clicked on. The crimson bulb came to life under the crimson shade. Before looking into Joe's face, I saw the bedspread dyed in a deep blood-red. The blood-red sheet . . . the blood-red sheet. Ah, the blood-red sheet!

My memory dashed into the past like water flooding down from a broken dam. The yellow ginkgo leaves. The yellow ginkgo leaves dropping endlessly to the ground. The splendid yellow, beautiful to the point of sorrow, couldn't manage to stop my memory going back.

Like a smack on the face, I encountered the memory that I thought I had forgotten, that I thought I had been avoiding so skillfully. I then accepted this memory, giving in like a person cornered in the dead end of an alley.

The ghastly blood stains on the bright white sheet that my mother had so carefully beaten to a stiff smoothness with her ironing bats, the young bodies so mercilessly ripped. Those gruesome bodies that showed in full horror how tender young bodies could be mangled before their souls departed, the crimson blood, still warm, which had flowed from those horrible bodies. I had seen them.

"Ahh!" I screamed with all the might my lungs could muster, and fell to the *tatami* floor, clutching my slip.

"What's the matter with you?"

Shocked by my sudden outburst, Joe raised his body from the bed and approached me.

"Ahh!" I shrieked again, shaking the whole building.

I couldn't express the horror I felt. I felt as if my body would be mangled by Joe at that very moment. Like my brothers Hyok and Wook, I thought I would be hacked to pieces, drenching the bed with my blood.

I had to flee. I had to.

"What's the matter?"

He came closer again.

"Oh, no. Please, please don't break me."

I pleaded, rubbing my palms together. Joe, with his hairy arms and chest, looked like a huge gorilla. I could hear talking outside, and there was a knock on the door. It grew noisy as if the whole building had been awakened by my screams. Joe opened the door a crack and said something. I quickly put on one of my undershirts. The door closed, and I was left alone with Joe.

"What's the matter? Are you crazy?"

I nodded, gathering up the clothes. I didn't mind being crazy. I wanted to get away from the squirting blood, the butchering, the ugliness, and the pain.

"Don't be scared. I'll help you put on your clothes."

"Oh, no. Please don't break me."

I pleaded, rubbing my palms together and slipping on my layers of clothes numbly. When I was finished, he tried to put my coat on, but I jumped and shrieked, "Don't come any closer. Just throw it to me."

He cursed, using a word I couldn't understand, and threw the coat to me. I picked it up and pushed the door open. Several people were gathered outside. I flew down the corridor without giving them a chance to ask any questions, put on my shoes in the foyer, and ran through the long garden.

Having passed the gate, I hurried up the steep road. Looking back, I could see the vivid neon sign "Kyongso Hotel"

I dashed on again. When I got to the main street, I looked back again. Nobody was following me, and the red neon sign was no longer in view. Exhaustion engulfed me, and for the first time I felt the chill of the night. Not bothering to put my arms into the sleeves, I hung my coat over my shoulders, hugging a tree trunk in the street. I rubbed my cheeks on the rough bark and shed tears of relief.

My head cleared and those forgotten days rushed back to me vividly.

Fourteen

Strangely, I don't recall being particularly saddened by my father's death. Although I nearly monopolized my father's love and his death was so sudden, my failure on the college entrance examination was a much greater shock than my father's death. Of course, the death of the head of a household can hardly be compared with a girl's failure to get into college, but perhaps my recollection of my father's death was lessened because I had shared it with my brothers, while I had to deal with my failure to get into college on my own.

Anyway, his funeral didn't seem to be a particularly gloomy affair. My brothers Wook and Hyok sobbed uncontrollably but soon recovered from their sorrow. I remembered vividly that the pain of loss I felt during the rite held on the forty-ninth day after his death was sharper than what I had felt at his funeral.

The memorial chant sung by the rosy-skinned nun, her face so young and absolutely beautiful, resounded clearly through the hall.

Oh, the efforts and cares our parents devoted to us as we were growing up! Our mothers lay on the wet spots, placing us on the dry side, they tasted the food first, eating the bitter and giving us, their babies, the sweet . . .

The courtyard outside the temple was filled with marigolds and moss roses. Unexpectedly a cannon rumbled in the distance. My mother placed crisp new money in front of the Buddha and bowed over and over again. Her face was calm and extremely solemn. Thin wisps of incense continued to curl upward and the chanting continued to resound clearly.

A cannon boomed in the distance once more, but the temple was as silent as creation. The plump marigold blossoms grew hazy and my nose stung, but I didn't think it was because I was saddened by my father's death. Rather, I was moved by the sorrowful chanting and also by the young resonant voice of this world.

My mother wiped away her tears with a handkerchief. My brothers, who had been standing by quietly, their faces gloomy, took their handkerchiefs from their sleeves and dabbed their eyes. The chant was doleful and melancholy.

Seventy years of human life is a joy, eighty years longevity, and ninety years a spring light, but even if we live one hundred years, our lives are as fleeting as dew. If we subtract the days of sickness, sleep, and the time filled with anxiety and worries, we live no more than forty years. When you die, sprouts or shoots won't spring from your body. Life is but an endless sorrow. Wild roses in Myongsasipni, don't cry when your flowers fall . . .

On our way back home from the Forty-Ninth Day Rite we felt lighthearted. Of course my brothers, having changed from the mourning robes into Western suits, were careful with their usual jokes, but their faces were bright as they supported my bereaved mother by either arm. She looked contented and comfortable with their support.

"He could have lived a little longer. He didn't have any ambition at all, dying early like that! We can expect only happy things from now on, welcoming daughters-in-law and a son-in-law, but he will miss all the fun." My mother sighed, sitting on the wooden floor, taking the food from the memorial out of the basket and putting it onto plates.

"Mother, don't think of Father any more. You have to live a long time. You have to live father's unused share, too," Wook said in the nasal voice of a child, shaking her knees.

"Yes, that's right, Mother. You won't see just the daughters-in-law. You'll welcome your grandchildren, too. And your granddaughters-in-law! You're young, and you'll live a long, long life," said Hyok, rubbing his cheek against Mother's.

"Oh, go away, what a crass thing for a grown man to do!" said my mother, but she was grinning for the first time.

She was beautiful. She hadn't applied any oil to her hair since my father's death, so some dry wisps stuck out, but her lustrous hair was neatly combed and the contours of her face were beautiful, as were her teeth.

I liked my mother very much. But my brothers had already said what I wanted to say and had played the baby, too. I didn't think I could say the same thing to her without embarrassing myself. I kept quiet. I was lonely. I had always been my father's girl, while my brothers were closer to my mother. I wanted to share my mother now, but my brothers didn't seem to notice.

A cannon went off in the distance again, then more loudly, as the booming came closer. At times the reverberations were long, with a series of explosions that rumbled like frying beans. However, nobody seemed nervous.

The elegant old house, sitting on its 7,000-square-foot lot, was even more quiet and peaceful than the temple from which we had just returned. In the backyard the roses, blooming for the second time that year, were shedding a petal or two.

The next day was somewhat different. Cannon balls exploded nearer, and we were told that the avenues were packed with people taking flight. Because our house was situated in a back alley, however, we didn't actually see any refugees.

My uncle stopped by several times, as did my brothers' friends. By twilight my uncle's face had grown pale, and he had a long talk with my mother. They seemed to have agreed to send their sons away. There were only four sons in the two households and since Jin, my uncle's eldest, was already an officer in the South Korean army, his family was nervous and frightened.

My mother was busy, grinding glutinous rice powder, making rolls of seaweed rice, cooking side dishes. I helped her pack my brothers' underwear and sew their rucksacks. It was dark by the time the three bulky bags were ready.

My brothers didn't seem to consider the war a reality. They left the house in a boisterous mood, as if they were going hiking. They cracked jokes as they said their goodbyes to the neighbors who, worried about the situation, had spilled out into the alley. Before they left, my brothers stopped to buy some snacks at the corner store like small children. Their noisy departure in full view of the neighbors was to be significant in the coming days, for they came back at dawn. They had stopped at too many friends' homes to say goodbye and to look for friends to join their party that they failed to cross the Han River before the bridge was blown up. Fortunately, when they came back, nobody saw them. The neighbors thought my brothers had taken refuge in the south.

Cousin Min, who had left with my brothers, went back to his home, and my brothers began their stifling life in hiding. We had enough grain and staples to get by. We were considered good neighbors and we were buried away from the busy street. During the war, when the rest of the world turned upside down, we lived an unbelievably comfortable existence, however stifling and boring. Of course we prepared a careful hiding place to protect my brothers from the sudden visits by communist sympathizers working for the newly formed neighborhood and women's organizations. There was a crawl space between the sturdy wooden ceiling of the pantry and the attic, and my mother and I pulled down a panel and made a secret hiding place inside.

Even though their secret space had a guitar, an electric lamp, and books, my brothers couldn't stay put for long periods of time. They climbed in and out several times a day. They wouldn't be forced to abandon their habits, just because there was a war. They would come down to report exciting news they had heard on the radio, to search for snacks, to smoke, or to cool their feet in cold water. Considering their youth, we could hardly deny them the exercise.

My mother hated to see my brothers roam around in the yard. No matter how large it was, no house in Seoul was totally isolated from the outside. An elementary school was clearly visible from the front yard, and sometimes men in military garb could be seen strolling on top of the building. My mother believed that they went up there just to spy on our front yard. The backyard was cool and dark during the hottest hours of the day thanks to the untrimmed pines and Chinese junipers. My brothers would often nap in the shade of the trees, but they were in full view of our neighbor's second-story window.

"Hey, get back up there. What if the head of the district comes again?"

My mother feared the head of the People's District Office, who visited almost every day. She removed all the men's shoes and dried my brothers' laundry in a corner, constantly worrying, all because of the head of the People's District Office.

But everything went smoothly. Things seemed to be going well in the outside world as well. My brothers were excited, anticipating their freedom.

"This is not the way for men to live. As soon as our army comes back, I'm going to join up to get my revenge."

"I'll join the army, and you take care of Mother, Big Brother. The eldest son should always take care of his precious body."

They were visibly excited, flexing the muscles that they had strengthened with iron dumbbells.

"I wonder if Jin's still alive. I heard our side has had lots of casualties," said my mother, reminded of him by the mention of the eldest son.

"Mother, Cousin Jin isn't a foot soldier. Do you think a major could be shot so easily?"

They seemed to believe that a major's insignia was some kind of shield.

"Well, I just hope your uncle's family is hiding somewhere safe. I shouldn't have let Min leave us."

My good-hearted mother often sighed over my uncle's family. On the day the boys had returned from the Han River, Min had gone to his home immediately, worrying about his family, and we hadn't heard anything from them since. Concerned, I once went to my uncle's house. I couldn't get near it, however, for the sign of a communist organization was attached to it. Asking around the neighborhood, I found out that our relatives had fled at the beginning of the war, frightened of their status as a military family. Fortunately, no one seemed to have been caught.

The bombing grew more frequent and cannon shells roared overhead day and night. My brothers relayed the news that Inchon was being hit by concentrated artillery attacks. The large city groaned in a desperate attempt to turn the world upside down once more.

As the relatives of refugees, we gradually began to attract the attention of the head of the People's District Office and the members of the District People's Committee. We were conscripted to dig trenches along the Mapo River and were visited by people in nondescript military garb who left dirty footprints as they searched every nook and cranny. We were not sure whether they were looking for grain or people, but they found neither.

We compared our suffering to labor pains. It was a frantic but hopeful pain, and so we comforted each other, encouraging each other to hold out a little longer. We believed that with the growing intensity of their persecution, our liberation from the pain came closer.

On one of those days we were visited by my uncle and Cousin Min, from whom we had heard nothing for a long time. They were unrecognizable, emaciated in their beggar-like rags. They had been hiding in the countryside, moving from one of my aunt's relatives to another, but it had become more and more risky as conditions worsened. They had left the women behind to seek us out. Being a military family was a crime that prevented them from finding shelter with relatives.

My mother hastily cooked them some rice mixed with barley, and they emptied their bowls in the blink of an eye. Through them we finally learned the cruel tidings: How many innocent people had been arrested, how many had been killed, how many were starving. We realized that it was a miracle that the demon of disaster had ignored us thus far.

From my uncle we learned that almost all our male acquaintances had either been arrested or become communist sympathizers. My mother and I came to believe that Hyok and Wook were the only young men left behind in the whole world.

My mother clasped her hands together and announced solemnly, "It's all because your father is watching over us."

We took it for granted that we should hide my uncle and Min in our house. We took pity on them because of their ragged appearance, and my mother was even offended that they hadn't come to us sooner.

Up to this point, my memories are of "us" as a family, and our joy and sorrow were my joy and sorrow. But then, during the night, as they were sleeping under our roof, I was terribly anxious. I didn't know why, but I couldn't reveal my anxiety to anybody.

The sound of the cannons was so loud, so close. The war was approaching, and soon it would fly over our heads.

Please let it pass, without hurting anybody in my family, I prayed. I was reassured, remembering my mother's saying that it was all because of my father's care. I was his only daughter, and he never refused my requests when he was alive. Now he was a being more than human. A god? A superbeing? A ghost? It didn't matter. He must be up there. He could protect us with his mysterious power.

All that night I couldn't sleep a wink because of the constant explosions of the cannon shells. I carried on a conversation with my father and prayed desperately for my family's well-being.

I was still anxious when the sun rose. I felt guilty that my family alone had been fortunate and at peace until then. The eye of the demon of disaster had accidentally passed us by, but somehow I had a feeling that an even more terrible evil was awaiting us, as in the old saying that it was better to be the first one to be spanked than the last. Cannons boomed closer still, and my brothers went back and forth from their hiding place in the ceiling. I thought they were acting more childish than I. It seemed like the demon of disaster would spot them. I wanted to hide them somewhere more impenetrable.

"Child, where shall we put your uncle and Min?"

"I don't know. The ceiling over the pantry is too small for all of them."

"Besides, we could hardly put them all together."

"Why not? Uncle would understand. After all, it's wartime."

"I don't mean it would be uncomfortable."

"What then?"

"We divide up the grain when we hide it, don't we? If something happens, we don't want to lose everything."

I considered possible hiding places, and slyly decided to find a safer place for my brothers.

"How about the closet in the servants' quarters?"

"But it's so isolated."

"But nobody has even bothered to open the servants' quarters yet. Nobody's even glanced in that direction."

"It hasn't been used for so long, and it's so old."

"That's why it's so perfect. Let's put them there."

"Perhaps you're right."

My mother seemed to be tempted. The servants' quarters had never been opened or cleaned since I was a child. The outer shutters were closed tightly, the paper faded and torn. Although the building was not locked, there had been no reason to open them.

Since we had done away with servants, the servants' quarters naturally had become little more than a forgotten corner. Because we didn't need to rent the space out and we had enough room for our own family, there was no reason we should bother fixing up a space with the lowly name of the servants' quarters.

"Let's put my brothers over there."

"Are you sure?"

"I think it's safer there."

"How could you . . ."

My mother was shocked and embarrassed, but she seemed to agree with me. It was only natural to value one's closest relatives most. I began to clean out the closet in the servants' quarters. I swept out the spider webs, dusted, mopped, and spread a woven mat on the floor. My mother, who was particular about cleanliness, seemed concerned about the dirty walls, but I convinced her by reminding her that it was wartime. My mother spread the snow-white sheets that she had beaten with her ironing bats on top of the thin reed mat and placed mattresses over them. My brothers moved in without a murmur. I helped with their belongings.

"We should have moved. I'm sorry for causing you this trouble," said my uncle apologetically.

"No, Brother-in-Law, how could we put you in those dirty quarters?" said my mother, seemingly shocked.

Wook, who had jumped in first, blurted out, "It's cozy, but it looks like the inside of a coffin."

"What? How can you be so ominous?"

My heart began to beat crazily, as if two ironing bats were pounding at it from inside.

"You can't help being a girl, I guess. Imagine being worried about ominous things already."

The closet didn't have an inch to spare when the two of them lay down.

"Oh, it's tight, isn't it? We should have found a larger place," I said.

"It's all right. Let's make this our last move."

Cannon balls began flying overhead now. The explosions and the hissing sounds grated on my nerves, making me cringe. They began with a dragging sssshhhhh and ended with an eardrum-splitting echo.

The bombing went on throughout the day and night. Fire reddened the sky. Still, the city was in the hands of the Reds. Unlike the beginning of the war, the battle didn't move quickly. It hung overhead, its madness in full swing.

It was a frightfully bright moonlit night. I couldn't fall asleep far into the night, taking in the incredible quietness of the moon and the crazy din of the war. I struggled to calm my anxiety and fright with careful, persistent prayers. I kept calling my father.

"If the war ends, the first thing I'll do . . ."

My mother said in a clear voice next to me, as she couldn't sleep, either.

"The first thing you'll do?"

That common expression "If the war ends" sounded like something impossible we say in the subjunctive mood, as in "If I were a bird . . ."

"Is to marry off your brother."

"Mother, why is his marriage so urgent?"

"His marriage may not be so urgent, but my grandsons are. When the world is like this, we need to catch your brother's seed as soon as possible."

This instinct to preserve the species was rather stupid and cruel. I turned my back to her.

"Do you think he will listen to me?"

"Well, I can imagine him being married, but I don't want to imagine him being a father. He's too young."

"Who's too young? I married into this family when your father was only sixteen and I was so shy that I couldn't look him directly in the face for over a month."

"Then you must have seen only his profile."

"What?"

I turned toward my mother again. I wanted to see my mother's profile. Her profile as she recollected her happy days and her dreams about the happy future, her profile in the bluish moonlight.

However, I never got to see it. Instead, my mother and I shrieked and hugged each other. The floor shook violently and my ears rang. The blast was only the reverberation as the first explosion had been too loud for our ears. We could only hear the lingering sound of the explosion, shaking the pillars and shattering the mirrors and windows.

Realizing that some part of our house had been hit by a cannon ball, I moved my limbs with my eyes shut and touched my mother's face.

My mother yanked my hand away and raised herself, screaming. "Where is it? Where is it?"

She dashed out like a crazy woman. My ringing ears heard her bare feet crunching the shards of glass strewn about on the wooden floor. Goose bumps sprouted all over my body.

I bolted upright, staring at my mother running through the dust and blue moonlight and out the middle gate. Soon a terrible scream pierced the air like the tearing of silk and then everything went quiet.

Actually the din of the attack couldn't have stopped just for us, but in my recollection there could never be a silence so long and miserable as the lapse between my mother's scream and the moment my uncle clambered down from the crawl space, his face pale with fright.

"Kyong-a! Kyong-a! Are you in there?" My uncle hovered before our room.

"Yes," I managed to make a sound, barely moving my tongue.

"So you're alive. Then is it the servants' quarters?"

The servants' quarters! The servants' quarters! My brain grew transparently clear, and I too sprinted over the shards of glass scattered on the wooden floor and the entryway steps, through the yard, to the servants' quarters.

My mother was lying flat on her face on top of a pile of dirt and pulverized tiles where she had fainted, and I saw the terrible scene in the moonlight that poured through the hole in the roof.

The white sheets were stained with the dark pools of fresh blood. Lumps of torn flesh wriggled, perhaps in a desperate attempt to cling to life.

I staggered as if my feet were caught by a red sheet, and then a red sheet covered my eyes. Caught in the red sheet, wrapped by the red sheet, I rolled over and over on the floor and gradually lost consciousness.

I was lying in a clean, soft bed like a princess in a fairy tale.

Perhaps I am a little sick. Or maybe I'm pretending to be sick. I mean I don't hurt anywhere in particular.

Still, I was being treated like an intensive care patient by my uncle, aunt, and cousins. They took turns coaxing me to eat tasty foods, reading me poems, and arranging bouquets of fragrant flowers in my room.

That was how I knew I was sick. I was comfortable. Lying on the bed in Mal's room on the second floor of my uncle's house for days and days, I didn't have the energy to refuse the apple juice, milk, and soft-boiled eggs. Every morning I washed my face and brushed my teeth in bed and looked at myself in the mirror. The thin face I saw didn't have any color. And so, I swallowed the bitter Chinese medicine without a murmur.

I knew my mother was lying ill somewhere in that house. I knew things had changed in the world. And I knew why my mother and I couldn't recover quickly.

It was because of the salvia. My uncle's cozy garden lay in ruin over the summer, but in the corner of the garden clumps of crimson salvia were blooming relentlessly.

I liked salvia. I liked its healthy look, neither weak nor sad. The crimson strength of its life struck me as almost solemn. I would fall asleep, gazing out at the salvia through the window. Then I dreamed of the crimson sheets. The nightmare of being wrapped in the bloody sheets visited me in the daytime, and at night I couldn't sleep. I wanted to go home.

I began to believe that I was having nightmares because of the crimson salvia, nightmares that were eating away at me. Was my mother lying in some room, forced to look at that sea of crimson? Poor Mother. She had to gaze out upon that color. Nobody else would understand. Nobody would understand why she shouldn't look at that color. Poor Mother. I sobbed secretly out of pity and love for her.

"Let us go home," I asked Mal, who came and stayed with me most frequently.

I wanted to go home as soon as possible, especially for my mother's sake.

"How can you go in this condition?"

"When you're not feeling well, it's best to be in your own home."

She was friendly and kind, so I pleaded with her repeatedly.

The temperature was comfortable, the sky deep and distant, and the salvia bloody red day in and day out.

Then one day Mother and I were loaded into Jin's jeep. My aunt supported my mother and Mal helped me. I finally saw my mother without her false teeth for the first time. She looked twenty years older than the mother I used to know, and her eyes were strange and dull. I shifted my eyes away since I didn't know where to look, blinking to hold back the tears.

The street was busy. It was fascinating, like a street in a foreign land. Even more fascinating were all the healthy, strong young men. I couldn't bear to think that my mother had to see them, too, just as she had had no choice but to gaze out at the salvia.

Passing the familiar corner store, the jeep turned up our alley. I saw my house. The house, with one corner of the roof blown off. I wanted to scream but couldn't. My lips trembling, I buried my face in Mal's skirt. I shut my eyes, but the crimson spread before my eyes. At first, it was the salvia at my uncle's house. Only the blooming salvia, without the green leaves or blue sky.

Repulsed by the color, I shook my head. The more I shook, the darker the color grew. Finally it diffused into a sticky liquid.

"No, no," I mumbled, shaking my head.

"Poor Older Sister." Mal rubbed my back, sniffling.

The jeep pulled up to the house, and we walked through the old gate, the middle gate, the inner yard and up the three entryway steps. The inner quarters had been completely cleaned up. The glass in the front door had been replaced with a new pane of thick glass etched in a wave pattern.

My mother lay in her room and I lay in mine. A helper from my uncle's house came along with us and my aunt stopped by every day.

"You have to recover soon. Think of your mother."

My aunt took better care of me than my mother who didn't seem to distinguish one day from the next.

"Pull yourself together. If something happens to you, what will your mother do?"

Hearing those words, I gulped down even the bitterest Chinese medicine without complaint.

"We're so lucky Kyong-a wasn't hurt. What if something had happened to her!"

Yes, what would my mother have done? Poor Mother! I took care of myself, thinking I was indispensable. I recovered quickly. Soon I could eat a real apple with the skin on, instead of drinking apple juice, and I preferred rice to smelly milk.

The high windows of the Korean house allowed only an armful of blue sky in, and the sliding door commanded a view of the condiment jars on the platform in the inner yard and of the stone walls decorated with mosaics of deer, pine trees, and the legendary herb of eternal life.

Gradually I could help take care of my mother, who didn't improve. She lived in a state of stupefaction. It was impossible to tell if she was conscious of what was going on around her; her eyes didn't betray even the slightest emotion.

"Poor Mother!"

I grew healthier and took a greater role taking care of my mother. I made nutritious gruels, combed her hair neatly, and changed her clothes frequently. She accepted it all like a well-behaved child. My aunt felt sorry for me.

"Tsk, tsk. I thought you were a mere child, but you've grown up instantly because of that terrible experience. You're doing all right. You're all your mother has. Take extra good care of her. You shouldn't ever hurt her feelings. Never. Never."

My mother sometimes had a fever and lost consciousness for days on end. At those times, her tightly shut lips refused even boiled rice water. I would call my uncle's house, a doctor would be sent, and he would silently give her a shot. I would spend the night at my mother's side. I was worried but contented in those nights. I could still caress my mother's delicate hands, and whisper what I was thinking. In fact, I was afraid of my mother when she was awake. I shrank under her apathetic eyes. My affection and my dreams withered before them.

"Poor Mother!"

I caressed my mother's dry hands until they turned soft, enjoying my love for her and my future dreams.

"Poor Mother! Why did you have to see it? I never dreamed you'd have to see something like that. But Mom, you have to live for a long, long time, even if it is only for me. You have me, your daughter. I'll make you happy. I'll make up my brothers' shares. Poor Mother. Get well soon."

Lifting my mother's hand between my hands, I wished for her recovery as if in prayer. She opened her eyes suddenly. At first she squinted as if the light hurt, but then she opened her eyes wide, meeting mine.

"Mom. It's me, Kyong-a," I blurted out happily.

For the first time the dull mist in her eyes disappeared and feelings were clear. Afraid that her spirit would leave her if I dared to glance away, I met her gaze.

She squinted her bright eyes as if she were irritated, and wrenched her hand from mine. She turned away from me and sighed so deeply the ground might have shaken.

"The gods are so cruel. Why did they take all my sons, leaving only the girl behind?"

I scrambled to my feet. I managed to slide the door open and went out. My eyes grew fuzzy and dim. I blinked, trying to remove the hazy blinders in front of my eyes, and opened the window to the north. A chilly draft of wind swept my skirt. The wind rushed through the backyard. The trees moaned refreshingly but coldly. For the first time I saw the ginkgo trees, the dazzling yellow. They were splendid.

How many layers of clothes were they wearing? They were still beautiful, even after discarding so much yellow. The leaves were more brilliant than flowers.

I stumbled into the backyard. Under the trees the ground was soft and comfortable. I threw myself down onto the luxurious carpet. Leaving only the girl behind! The words rang in my ears like a horrible curse.

"Stop it! Stop it!"

I shook my head over and over again. When that was not enough, I rolled over and over. The gold leaves sometimes dropped by ones or twos and at times by fits and starts.

Suddenly I stopped rolling and sobbed violently. Once I had started, I couldn't stop. I cried on and on like the yellow leaves dropping endlessly. As long as there was even one leaf left on the trees, the leaves would keep falling, and I would weep until I was drained of all the tears imprisoned in me. My weeping was pure, not tinged with sadness, and I fell into a deep sleep on the soft carpet.

From that day forward, I spent more time under the ginkgo trees than by my mother's sick bed. The gold that had seemed so endless grew scarce. Lying on the thick yellow carpet, I could stare up at the blue sky through the sparse yellow leaves. I liked those moments. I liked them because I didn't have to feel sorry that I was the one who was alive.

I avoided my mother as much as possible. Whenever I saw her, I felt so guilty about being alive that I shrank away. The only place I could escape her was under the trees. There, I was cultivating a hatred for my mother without knowing it.

I wanted to make her miserable, to make her feel at least a fraction of the misery I was feeling. What will your mother do if something happens to you? That's what my aunt had said. I'll make them pity my mother. I'll make her a poor woman without any children, not even a daughter.

I wanted to die. I wanted to die. But the ginkgo trees were so splendid, the sky so blue, the air in the backyard so refreshing and clear that I wanted to live. I wanted to die. I wanted to live. I wanted to die.

Suddenly I wanted the war to sweep down over us. I could accept the fact that I had survived my brothers' deaths, but I couldn't stand it if others lived on after I died. If only the war would come back. The only way I could be saved was by the war.

My yearning for the war started this way and grew stronger and stronger every day. I wanted it to keep raging on forever. However, along with the word "war," an image of the bloody sheets and the mutilated chunks of young flesh darted before me. I shook my head and rolled on the soft leaves to forget. I writhed on the bed of leaves each day, and the leaves piled higher and higher, embracing me cozily.

My mother seemed to regain her strength without my nursing. To be more exact, her body began to return to its old habits. She suddenly started mopping the floors and washing the dishes. She answered simple questions, her eyes still dull. People meeting her for the first time would have thought her a quiet, lifeless, but normal old woman. They couldn't know how active and how positive my mother had been.

The girl who had been helping us returned to my uncle's house and the visits by my uncle's family grew less frequent. My mother took on the responsibility for housekeeping once more, and I had no choice but to face her again. Her eyes always inspired fear and hatred in me.

I began to mumble excuses. The war would return soon, and this time nobody would survive it. I had to make excuses, feeling embarrassed about my survival.

Sometimes my brothers' friends visited us. They offered their awkward condolences as if they couldn't accept the reality of my brothers' deaths. In fact, it would have been strange if anyone that age had known how to express their condolences gracefully.

I wanted to put my hand over my mother's eyes to prevent her from seeing their youth and energy. When they left, I would say, "The war is not over yet. They say it won't come to an end so easily. I supposed they won't survive it, either."

My hesitant and somewhat frightened incantations grew in shrillness each time they were repeated. Somewhere along the way the wish that I had created for my mother had become my own.

Emotion didn't return to my mother's lifeless eyes. They seemed to say that she was living because she couldn't kill herself, rejecting life more completely than people who committed suicide.

The Chinese army intervened in the war, which had seemed to be leading to the victorious unification of Korea, and the UN army began their retreat once more. Seoul was abuzz with rumors, and the people, with apprehension, packed up to flee south. The war was coming back overhead. As I had predicted.

I thought my mother's blank eyes were constantly following me. They seemed to be ordering me to sit back and suffer the war.

I packed without her knowledge, unpacked, and packed again. It was part of my struggle, more complex and desperate than mere hesitation. I had already lost the soft piles of fallen leaves, onto which I could have thrown myself. Fall had already become winter and the ginkgo leaves that had witnessed my bloody remembrances had faded to a dark, ugly color, mere trash piled beside the wall.

I packed and unpacked, torn between my desire that the war would come to kill off everyone and my fear that the war could rush upon me at any moment. This contradiction was not solely due to my mother's curse or the recollection of the bloody sheets; it was simply my own. I had already forgotten about the crimson sheets along with my mother's lament about leaving only the girl behind. They belonged to the rotting leaves and were no longer mine.

Having inherited the contradiction without its roots, I let myself be torn apart. One cold day my mother and I were loaded onto a large truck, as if we were bundles, along with several families and their belongings. My uncle's family considered that taking us to a refugee shelter was their responsibility, and I accepted their offer reluctantly. We were carried down to Pusan like baggage.

In Pusan life with my uncle's family was busy. I avoided my mother as much as possible. Even if I had tried, it would have been hard for the two of us to have had a quiet moment together. But I was more afraid of my mother than ever, having lost the excuses I used to mumble whenever I encountered her.

With the words, "The war's coming again," I had asserted that I would die when the war came back to us; I didn't have the courage to look at my mother now because I had fled the war.

For a few days my mother seemed puzzled and docile, but unexpectedly she began to make noises, demanding that she should go home because she couldn't leave her house unattended. Nobody could convince her that Seoul was not a place to go back to. Nothing, not the war, nor the Chinese army, was an obstacle to my mother. To her the old house, even with part of its roof blown off, was everything. She grew haggard, pining for her old house in Seoul.

As soon as Seoul was retaken, we returned to the empty city through the good offices of Cousin Jin.

Fifteen

When I fled the Kyongso Hotel, I had dressed hastily, so now my clothes felt uncomfortable and twisted. I reached inside my sleeves and pulled down the bunched undershirts at the elbow, buttoned the buttons, and pulled up the zippers. Then I put on my coat. I straightened my hair and put on my scarf. I was heading home, but all of a sudden I hated the idea.

I doubted whether my relationship to my mother could change, just because I could remember a few moments from the past. I wouldn't know until I saw her whether it would change a little or a lot, or for that matter, whether it could change at all. However, I wanted to make up my mind before I faced her. I hated surprises.

I wanted to make up my mind first whether I was going to keep hating her or whether I was going to pity her. It was like a difficult math problem that I might never be able to solve.

I was doctor and patient at the same time, but it was hard to combine the two. Still, I couldn't delegate either of those roles to anyone else. Exhausted, I couldn't think any further. I wanted to rest, somewhere other than at my home. I hugged a tree on the street. Its rough bark scratched my cheek. I thought of the woman with the long neck. If only I could bury my face in that elegant, warm place where her neck flowed down to meet her shoulders!

Forgetting how rudely I had behaved to her only a few days before, I simply hoped she would hug me. I decided not to go home. My face buried in my coat collar, I felt relieved just thinking of her.

A trolley stopped. I hesitated about whether or not to take it. The conductor pulled the cord and shouted, "Last car! Last car!"

It felt good to be on the last car. The trolley was so empty that you could even lie down on the seats, but we soon reached Chongno 5-ga. I thanked the conductor, got off the trolley, and went down the alley in Yonji-dong. It was too late to visit anyone, but I thought it would be all right since I was not really visiting. Visiting meant leaving after a while, but I was going to sleep there.

The light was on in his room. Instead of shaking the gate, I tapped on the window.

"Auntie, auntie," I called softly.

I could hear someone moving in the room, and soon the gate opened. She was in her daytime clothes, not in her night gown. Without studying her expression, I rushed to her and buried my face in her beautiful neck. It was fragrant and warm.

A sticky sadness rushed up in my throat, but it didn't provoke tears. It was lodged in my throat, too thick and sticky to flow as tears.

"What is it? Kyong-a, has something happened?"

She called my name for the first time, instead of "young lady." I was grateful for that.

"I want to sleep here. Please let me."

"Your mother must be waiting for you. You said she's alone."

"I just came from home. I told her." I lied.

"Really? Come in," she urged me, but I just stood there in her arms.

"Well, let's go," she prompted me.

"Please let me stay this way for a little longer. I'm so cold."

"Oh? It's warmer in the house."

Still, she kept hugging me tightly. Those large, comfortable breasts, her warm body, her generosity in not questioning anything. It was comfortable.

"Who is it?" Ock Hui-do called out from inside.

We let go of each other and went into the room. The children were sleeping side by side, and Ock was lying down, too. She must have been knitting while her husband and children slept. Her knitting things were at the head of her sleeping space.

"Kyong-a wants to sleep here."

Ock Hui-do, without a word, picked up a cigarette packet, and lit one. She pushed the children toward their father's side, making a place for me at the end of the room.

"Take off your clothes and lie down. You must be freezing."

She picked up the knitting and smiled at me with her eyes.

"Where are you going to sleep, Auntie?"

The room was the perfect size for her family to sleep all together, and I felt guilty squeezing in.

"Don't worry. I can wriggle in somehow."

"Still . . . I should sleep in the other room."

"I said not to worry. Haven't you ever ridden a crowded trolley? We can still take in several more people." She laughed clearly and innocently.

How could she accept poverty so elegantly? I took off some of my clothes and lay down. I tossed and turned, pulling the quilt over my head, but I couldn't sleep.

"Darling, turn off the light. Kyong-a seems to be having trouble falling asleep."

"Oh, you're right. I didn't think."

She put her knitting aside and turned off the light. A thick darkness blanketed us. I could hear her taking off her clothes. I held my breath and waited. I wished she would lie next to me. I wanted to fall asleep with my head against her large breasts or warm neck.

The rustling of clothes and adjusting of quilts stopped. It grew quiet. However long I waited, the silence continued, and I didn't feel squeezed. Obviously Ock had made room for her. Taking care that the children weren't squashed, he must have turned sideways and pulled her close in his arms. She must have curled up in order not to wake up the children, melting her body into his. The couple must be trying to make their bodies as small as possible for the sake of the children and me.

I pushed back the covers carefully and opened my pupils as widely as possible, holding my breath. It was strange, yet thrilling. Since my childhood, I had not slept with a husband and wife in the same room. Willing my pounding heart to be quiet, I waited for something I vaguely expected to happen. But no matter how I tried, all I could see was the outline of the quilts, and all I could hear was the breath of the sleeping faces. Nothing happened.

It grew warmer inside my quilt. My space was neither too tight nor too wide. It was perfectly snug. But I still felt I shouldn't fall asleep. The woman clinging to Ock Hui-do was not just the generous motherly person who had comforted me when I suffered from my sticky sorrow. She was also the woman who had shuddered and screamed, "Who are you?" a few days before.

The two women in her were totally different, but that was hardly strange to me. If what I was waiting for happened, I would scream loudly. I harbored the nasty thought that I would wake up the children to witness their parents' ugly act. But for a long while nothing happened, and they breathed quietly; I told myself not to fall for such a trick and tried not to fall asleep.

Every member of the family was breathing evenly, my body was thawing, and I was exhausted. When I realized my own breathing had grown even, I opened my eyes in surprise and rubbed them, but soon I was drawn back into that breathing.

I was lying sideways on a soft bed. It was Ock's studio. On one side was a huge window, covered with a heavy pleated velvet curtain that could be drawn against the light. The studio was submerged in pale light.

My bed was soft and fragrant. I was almost buried in a pile of multi-colored flower petals. I was naked, parts of my body buried in the petals. It was glowing and rosy. I was satisfied. I knew my body was far more beautiful than the flowers.

The flowers lost their vividness before my naked body; they were reduced to nothing more than a fantastic screen. I was the only living organism against a beautiful fantastic background that was to enhance my beauty.

I was posing for Ock Hui-do. I was glad that I could be a perfect model for him. But where was he? Why hadn't he exclaimed at my beauty and picked up his brush? I began to grow nervous. I was hoping that he could capture me on his canvas before my glowing rosy body faded like those brilliant flowers that had withered so fast.

I spotted Ock, crouching in one corner of the dark room. Kneeling in a pious posture, he was caressing something. It was a white porcelain wine bottle with a long neck. It was an unusually beautiful and elegant white piece from the Yi Dynasty. Totally absorbed in the act of stroking, he didn't toss even a glance at me. His attachment to the bottle was so extreme that I felt a little jealous. I tried to get his attention by saying something, but the words were caught in my throat.

He held up the bottle in awe and slowly began to kiss it from the mouth to the neck and downward. It was a sensuous gesture, much more than an expression of simple respect.

I burned fiercely in jealousy. I wanted to cry out, but my throat wouldn't allow it. I wanted to pick something up and throw it at the bottle, but I was surrounded by the soft petals, and because I was the only thing tangible, I floated, unable to grasp anything.

Unable to cause even a rustle, I had to endure my sizzling jealousy. It was the cruelest sort of punishment. His lips passed over the long, white bottle and headed toward the body. The clear, cold bottle began to glow. His lips grew more passionate and his eyes burned like those of a possessed man.

Then slowly the white bottle turned into an elegant woman. She was certainly Ock's wife, the woman with the long neck. Cursing and raving, I tried to dash toward him, but my body wouldn't move.

I couldn't move an inch. Was I alive? Afraid, I looked at my body. Why, my body had lost its radiance, its splendid rosy color. It was meager and ordinary.

How could I take off my clothes to reveal this emaciated body? I wanted to find something to cover it, but the petals and fantastic colors were gone. There was only a grey confusion. In the midst of that greyness, my ugly nakedness was conspicuously exposed.

I wanted to writhe, to lament in a loud voice, but couldn't. Finally I managed to squeeze out an animal-like moan. I was awakened by that hateful sound.

The room was wrapped in the feeble light of the studio in my dream, and fortunately nobody had been disturbed by my groan; it was as silent as the studio in the dream.

Lying next to Ock, her neat face emphasized by the spotless white sheet, she looked more beautiful in the dim light. The husband and wife, the five children, and me, who was superfluous by any standard. For the first time, I began to regret having come. Although I didn't regret not going home, I was lonely, like an orphan.

I buried myself deep under the quilt. I heard her getting up and the youngest child rising noisily and peeing into the chamber pot, but I held my breath, pretending to sleep.

"What shall we do? It's already eight o'clock."

"Let her sleep. She seems very tired. Nobody will say anything if she's late."

They must be talking about me. I pretended to yawn and got up. Thanks to her considerate help, washing up and getting ready for work in a strange house was neither uncomfortable nor embarrassing.

She served me a breakfast tray of warm bean sprout soup and toasted seaweed. I was surprised by the food, as if I were an orphan invited to someone else's house for a meal.

"When are you going to come back?"

"Well, I was thinking of going today because I wanted to see you, but since I've seen you, I might as well take a couple of more days off."

If he had said it in secret, I would have been happier, but he said it quite brightly, sitting at the breakfast tray with his family.

"Have you finished with the painting?"

"Yes. I need to work on the details, but I'll get around to it by and by."

Glancing at the sliding door, so tightly shut, I recalled the old tree set against its chilly background. In contrast, Ock's expression was bright and calm.

Had he put in some flowers or leaves? Had he let some birds land there? I suddenly wanted to open the door but couldn't.

I left their house, the children's loud goodbyes ringing in my ears. His wife followed me out to the alley.

"I packed your lunch, but I don't know whether you'll like it or not."

"Thank you."

"Even if you're late for work, stop by at your home first. Your mother must have waited for you last night."

"So you knew. Why didn't you make me go home?"

"It was so cold and late." She was apologizing cautiously for what she had done in order not to offend me.

It was a cold, clear morning. The whole neighborhood seemed empty. Her neckline was always loose. Was it because she had a slender neck, or was it because the loose neckline made her neck look thinner? Her fresh white neck appeared weak and frail, so unlike that of a woman going on forty, and this morning she looked rather cold.

Still, she was elegant and neat in whatever she wore. But to me she was the woman who had been passionately kissed by Ock. I felt a fierce hostility toward her. My heart writhed with a hatred that extended to every corner of my body. I was satisfied with the animosity I felt toward her. Finally my feelings about her had become clear. I realized for the first time that hating someone could be satisfactory and pleasant.

"I owe you so much. I'll repay it, so be prepared."

"What do you mean, Kyong-a?"

She muttered something more, but I pretended not to hear her and escaped down the alley, hitting the frozen earth noisily with the determined click of my heels. I never realized there was such satisfaction in hating somebody, a satisfaction that one couldn't possibly attain through love.

Not taking a trolley, I headed straight home. Of course it was not because she had asked me to do so. The air was fiercely cold, but it was a bright, splendid morning. If the sunlight grew stronger, it would be a rather warm winter day. Big Cold had long since passed, so Spring Begins was around the corner; it might have passed already. I tried to think what day it was today but couldn't remember.

I walked slowly up the alley. I stood at our gate, gazing unflinchingly up at the roof, without changing my posture or breathing. The old house with its gate to the east was calm and quiet, frost clinging to the roof tiles in the bright morning light. The frosty old house was beautiful beyond description.

I stared at the roof tiles, the missing corner, the ugly hole surrounded by dangling lumps of clay, the ragged eaves.

"Was it because of me?" I asked hesitantly.

"Was it because of me?" I faced the problem more boldly. What I had been terrified of was not the wrecked roof but the feeling of guilt. The idea that I had been responsible for my brothers' deaths. I was the one who had come up with the idea of hiding them in the closet in the servants' quarters.

I was so afraid of the thought that I was responsible for my brothers' deaths. That was why I looked at the damaged house in awe as if it were an idol. If I had not hurried my brothers into the casket-like closet, I might not be shuddering at the sight of the wrecked roof, even if the terrible thing had happened anyway. It had lost one wing, but the house's remaining eaves arched into the sky, and its patterned stone walls looked dignified and elegant despite their age and scars from the war.

The beautiful old house. I could understand why my father, a second son, had given up other property to inherit this house when his father divided up his estate. I asked once again, "Was it because of me?"

I escaped the arrow of my own question with room to spare. Of course it was because of me, but also because of the war, and perhaps it was their destiny. I wanted to believe that I had suffered long enough. I could share the blame with other reasons. I had suffered for what I had done. Once so stupid and small in the face of my idol, I was more relaxed and calculating in the face of the truth now. I decided to emphasize the other reasons for my brothers' deaths. And I resolved to be more generous with myself. What a virtue it was to be generous!

For the first time, I gazed with pity and affection at the old house and its wounds from the war. It had been a long time since I looked at it as just an old house.

Liberated, I thought I could already feel spring in the bright morning sunlight. I didn't knock at the gate. Instead I flung around, turning away from the house. Although I felt generous with my own faults, I couldn't be generous toward my mother. I would never forgive her.

"Leaving only the girl behind!"

I would never forget that hateful comment. Certainly my mother had not worried about me that night and I was not worried about her well-being, so there was no need for me to knock on the door and check on her.

I came out of the long, winding Kyae-dong alley, my heels clicking noisily as when I left Mrs. Ock. The click of my heels sounded refreshing and my whole body was charged with energy.

During the lunch break I opened my lunch box and was puzzled. The side dishes, other than the *kimchi*, looked odd. Toasted seaweed in an envelope, stewed black beans, and egg rolls. They were Mrs. Ock's careful elaborate creations. Feeling proud, I enjoyed my meal slowly. There was no reason to hide my lunch when the salesgirls passed by.

Diana entered with a large red bag slung over her shoulder.

"You're eating your lunch late today."

She must have been on her way back from lunch. She wiped off her faded lipstick with cold cream, then painted crimson lipstick to make her lips larger than their real size. She patted her face, rubbed the wrinkles around her eyes in a circular motion with her middle finger, and shut her bag noisily.

"Thank you for the pastries yesterday," I said sweetly, thinking I had grown very sociable recently.

"Don't mention it."

"Do you often go out with your children?"

"They want to, but I rarely have time. I had meant to take them out for days but it was only yesterday that I managed to do it. Even when I do go out with them, there aren't many places to go to. I mean, places to go with children."

"Are there many places for grownups to go to?"

"Sure. Dance halls, hotels, theaters. It's wartime in name only. There are lots of places where we can enjoy ourselves."

I smiled stupidly, wondering whether I was a child or an adult. I had only climbed up and down the hill from the toy stall to the cathedral. I was not familiar with the places adults went to; on the other hand, how many mature moments of torment and ecstasy I had experienced!

"Your children are so handsome."

I thought I had said the same thing yesterday, but I said it again all the same.

"They are exactly like their father."

I thought I had heard the same answer the day before.

"Their father . . . Where is he?"

"Huh?"

"Is he dead?"

"Dead? He's as alive as you and me."

"Then do you live together?"

"What an obscene thought! What do you think I am? Do you really think I'm a whore? If I had a husband, would I sleep around, with Yankees and niggers?"

She shuddered as if she were disgusted.

"Then is he in the army?"

"How can you be so cruel? Do you think I'd send my husband to the battlefield and when I couldn't stand waiting anymore I'd take . . ."

"I . . . I understand," I broke in, as she was about to say the same thing all over again.

"What do you know? What do you understand? How can you even imagine what I've been through?"

I really didn't want to know what she'd been through, so I wrapped up my lunch box, put it in my bag, and ignored her by brushing my teeth.

"We're in the middle of a conversation. Why are you trying to avoid it? You should listen to the end."

"That's all right."

"What's all right? It may be all right with you, but it's not with me."

"I said it's all right."

"Do you think I like the idea of you thinking I'm a whore?"

"Then what do you want me to think of you?" I answered seriously.

"See? You really do think I'm a whore. There's nobody more pathetic than me."

"Okay, make it short. My shop is unattended."

"Yeah, yeah. I have only ten minutes left myself. The kids' father lied to me. He told me he wasn't married. He has a wife and children."

"So?"

"What could I do? I had to give him up."

"Why?"

"What do you mean why? Could I be his concubine? Or could I take away another woman's husband? Giving up was the cleanest and most rational thing to do."

It was disgusting. She felt moral satisfaction about her decision.

"You're worse than a whore."

Without waiting for her response, I slipped out of the rest area. I didn't really think that, but I needed to fling some kind of insult at her to demonstrate my contempt.

Sitting in my chair, I felt my delicious lunch churn in my stomach because of her. I was nauseated not only by her, but by morality in general.

Before, I had not felt at all strange about my love for Ock Hui-do despite his wife. I hadn't been able to hate Mrs. Ock. It was because of the war. My mad belief that the war would end everything had made it all seem trivial.

But it was different now. I didn't need to wait for war; I didn't need to expect anything from it. I could be a little afraid of the war but could become braver as I kept my happiness safe from it. I wanted to build a long future with Ock Hui-do, to snatch him from the long-necked woman and make him concentrate on me. I couldn't be bothered with things like ethics or morals. I had to summon all my strength to repel everything moral.

"Shit, why can't she just admit she's a slut?" I was unnecessarily angry with her. Come to think of it, I liked her because she was a whore, a miser, an unscrupulous person. I didn't like her maternal role, but then, even animals were mothers, so I could look down on her for taking pride in being a mother. Yet I couldn't stand her when she pretended to be moral.

"Look after my shop, will you?"

Misuk picked up her lunch box and skipped up the stairs like a child. Cash came back from lunch, split a match and began to pick his teeth.

"Hey, you! You're disgusting. Stop trying to act like you had spareribs for lunch," Kim said.

"It's not that. A piece of ginger is caught in one of my rotten teeth. It smells horrible."

"To fill up your stomach with water, you must have gobbled down the *kimchi*. If something's free, you don't care whether it's sweet or bitter. Tsk, tsk."

"To tell you the truth, if they made a rest area for men, we could bring rice from home and eat our fill. With a bowl of noodles, my stomach doesn't even get the message that I ate."

"Stop it. I didn't even get noodles for lunch. If you keep talking about food, my tapeworms start squirming."

"Eat! Eat! Do you think you can make a fortune by skipping meals? Eat! In this kind of world you never know when you are going to die."

"It's really tough these days because my wife is sick."

"That's too bad. Poor people need their health. Did you take her to the doctor?" Cash had a serious, worried look now.

Kim was about to light a cigarette butt in silence when Chin threw a whole pack of cigarettes to him. It was rather funny to get such instant sympathy because of a wife's illness. Kim pulled out a single cigarette and threw the rest back to Chin, who also lit one.

"What happened to Ock? Perhaps his wife is sick, too."

"You should work faster. We have lots of orders to take care of." I interrupted their conversation. "Mr. Ock is painting now, so don't worry about him."

"What? Is he painting at home? What kind of painting?"

"He's an artist. He's a real artist recognized by people in the know."

"We figured as much. We knew he shouldn't be idling away his time in a place like this. But did he get a good commission?"

"He must have. I don't know for sure, but I heard some paintings bring in more than a million won."

"Who in Seoul is rich enough to order that kind of picture?"

"As I said, we need to hurry with these paintings. Please get to work," I said irritably, sorting out the orders to be finished. I drew the curtain at the window.

The ugly, cold sidewalk, the hurried pedestrians, the bare trunks of the ugly trees; they forced me to remember the old tree he had painted. I relived the shock I had felt when I saw it for the first time. I felt he was far away. Loneliness assaulted me like a sudden chill.

"I asked you to watch my shop." Misuk playfully shot me a sidelong glance.

"I'm sorry, really sorry."

She didn't go to her shop but kept standing next to me. This tidy girl blew a puff of breath on the window and wiped it clean.

The crisp, clear sky and grey, old buildings. The bus stop for the Eighth Army post. Some tall GIs were standing there right in front of us, either waiting for a bus or for people, their hands buried deep in their pockets. The glistening yellow bus pulled up to spit out a group of the GIs dressed in similar color and carried off the same number.

The scene repeated itself over and over again. At times, boys clung to the soldiers' arms, hoping to sell something or just to beg, and even when they were pushed down to the ground with a curse, I didn't feel embarrassed or sorry for them. The things that happened in front of the PX were all boring to me. It was a scene that could not be expected to change. I sighed unconsciously, releasing a suppressed breath. A cluster of boys gathered and hung around our window. One made an obscene hand gesture to taunt us.

We were monkeys held in a cage. More and more onlookers gathered, giggling and snickering. We were just incompetent monkeys with no tricks to perform. Our desperation couldn't touch them, and their sorrow and happiness were alien to us. We drew the curtain.

Sixteen

I didn't grab my mother's hand when she opened the gate. I passed through the middle gate and the yard by myself. She didn't seem to wonder where her daughter had been the night before, and I decided not to show any interest in how she had been. She had already taught me that indifference could be crueler than hatred, and I decided to treat her with the same aloofness that I would show a mere boarder.

She brought in a tray holding simply one bowl of *kimchi*, not even the usual *kimchi* soup. She lay down on the mat she had already spread out.

"Have you already eaten?"

"No, I'm not feeling well," she answered dully, weakly shoving toward me a bowl of rice she had kept under the mat. From her coarse hand, placed feebly on the faded pale green quilt, blood vessels protruded prominently as if they were separate living entities. I touched her hand. It was hot. I touched her forehead. I could see she had a high fever. The pulse at her temple was beating rapidly.

"You have a fever. Where does it hurt? How do you feel?"

"Must be a cold," she muttered as if it were someone else's problem.

The black horn hairpin holding the loose knot of hair at the back of her neck lay at the corner of the pillow.

After eating, I sat next to her for a long time, unable to believe she had a high fever. I touched her forehead again. She frowned irritably and turned over so her back was to me.

"Just leave the tray and go to bed." She labored with that short sentence like a train chugging up a steep hill. Her chest heaved visibly, causing the thick quilt to ripple up and down like waves. Her nose dominated her thin face, the nostrils ballooning in and out rapidly with each painful breath.

I took the tray to the kitchen and washed the bowls out quickly. My mother's painful cough and wheezing could be heard in the kitchen. I went directly to my room and lay down. Her coughing continued. These were not as hollow as her usual coughs that rang like a stick hitting a wooden container. They were thick and agonizing. Listening to her cough, I couldn't fall asleep. And between the bouts of coughing, I could hear her wheezing across the wooden hall that separated our rooms, as if she were lying right next to me. Yet I couldn't hear her groan or mumble in her feverish state.

I held my breath and waited for her to call me. At least she could have called me for water or complained about the pain. But I heard neither groans nor moans, much less her voice.

I couldn't wait any longer. I went to the kitchen to make some barley tea. I put the water with a sprinkle of toasted barley on the stove before rushing out of the house. The drug store was far away, and it was about time to draw down the shutters. I was relieved to find the druggist to be an old man.

"I need some medicine. For a cold."

"There are many kinds of cold. What are the symptoms?"

"A high fever . . . very high, about 40 degrees Centigrade. No, it could be higher."

"And?" he asked.

"She coughs and is short of breath, and a strange wheezing sound comes from her throat."

"Oh? And?"

"And, her chest heaves up and down like this, and her nostrils move a lot."

"Oh? And?" The druggist's face took on a serious air, and he seemed to begin to listen to my story carefully.

"That's all. All the symptoms are very serious. Her cough has such a splitting ring to it that you can't help but imagine how painful it must be to her." Frowning slightly, I described the symptoms, as if pleading with him.

"How old is the baby?"

"Baby? She's an old woman. My mother."

"Is that so? How old is she?"

"Fifty-five."

"That's fortunate."

"Why?"

"I bet it's pneumonia, but it can be difficult for a small child or someone elderly. Fifty-five is the prime of life."

"Well, that's not her case. In fact, she's like sixty . . . no, seventy. She hasn't much strength."

He began to prepare a prescription. He wrapped the capsules and yellowish powder separately, kindly telling me to give her the powder after a meal and two capsules every four hours and to observe her condition.

With the drugs in my hand, I rushed home without stopping. The barley tea was boiling vigorously on the stove, the kettle lid bouncing up and down. My mother lay on her back, a high-pitched noise still coming from her throat. Her lips were parched because of the high fever. Blowing on the barley tea to cool it off, I shook my mother.

"Here, take this medicine. Please? Take the medicine."

"I don't need any."

Unexpectedly my mother was fully conscious. I was taken aback because I had assumed that she had lost consciousness. I was afraid that she would say, eyes filled with resentment, "leaving only the girl behind!" But her dull eyes were bloodshot on account of the high fever and didn't show any feeling.

I lifted my mother's upper body and urged her to take the capsules. She opened her mouth wide, gulped them down, and shook me off before slumping back.

"Now go to sleep. I won't be lucky enough to die from illness."

A faint smile spread over her lips. I dozed but woke again anxiously and remained at my mother's side. I wished that time would pass quickly, so that the medicine would dissolve and spread to her various organs. I also wished that the time for the next dose of medicine would come soon. My mother's chest heaved continuously, and I wondered where she found the strength to breathe with such intensity.

"My chest hurts," my mother complained for the first time, tearing at her chest with her gnarled hands.

"Where?" I asked, baring her chest. I was expecting to find a boil or wound on her chest, but there was nothing. Two dark nipples clung to her breasts, flat as a wall, and her ribs showed through her miserable skinny flesh. Her feeble body, which didn't seem to have any life left in it, was burning with the fever. How could that body, so like a stick of dry wood, produce such a fury?

Having pulled down her undershirt, I gave her two more capsules although only three hours had elapsed. My mother twisted irritably, frowned, and opened her mouth a little, still lying on her mat. I shoved the medicine onto her white-coated tongue and poured in some water. It gurgled down her throat but the capsules remained on her tongue, and she was seized with a fit of coughing. I raised her upper body, rapping on her back to get her to spit out the medicine and to alleviate the pain of the cough. She contorted her face, red from the cough, and reached around for something. I hurriedly placed a bowl under her mouth, and she spat out reddish brown phlegm along with the yellow medicine.

I quickly pulled out the third capsule, raised my mother, supporting her from behind, and poured in a spoon of barley tea into her mouth. She swallowed appreciatively and motioned for more. I poured the tea in a cup and dropped the capsule into her mouth. She firmly shook her head, spitting out the medicine, and said, "Water . . . water . . ." as if talking in her sleep.

I had no choice but to give her a cup of barley tea. She sipped at it and slipped from my arm onto the mat. When I couldn't force her to take the medicine, I began to think of the oblong capsules, in the shape of Korean pillows, as wonder drugs. If only I could push them down into her, she would make a miraculous recovery.

Oh, I should have gotten her a shot! I kicked myself for not going to a clinic, instead of to that drug store. I couldn't bear to hear the slow ticking of the clock, so I stood up and paced the room until I felt dizzy. There was nothing I could do for my mother, and light did not yet fill the window.

I understood vaguely that my mother's condition was serious. I had witnessed my father's and brothers' deaths, but they had taken me by surprise, not allowing me to prepare for sorrow or shock. This was the first time I had seen a person's life being extinguished slowly, like the oil in a lamp burning away little by little. I had to watch it all alone.

I fled to my room to escape my mother's wheezing and panting, as well as the thought that I was all alone. I pulled the quilt over my head. And like a child I fell into a deep sleep.

When I opened my eyes, it was an unbelievably bright morning. My mother's condition had not changed at all. A new hope swelled within me, however, perhaps because I had slept well, or because it was such a bright morning. My mother was suffering from a severe flu. If she had a shot, she would be fine. I went out to the main street. I didn't see any signs indicating that there was a clinic in the neighborhood. I walked almost as far as Anguk-dong.

Doctors were either in the military or were wealthy. They wouldn't be caught in a dangerous place like Seoul. I was irritated but not disappointed. There must be a doctor somewhere in Seoul. The problem was getting him to make a house call, so I wanted to find a doctor nearby.

I happened to glance down a tiny alley and spotted a shabby clinic, even shabbier than the drug store I had gone to the day before.

The doctor was a pediatrician, but he was old and looked trustworthy. I explained my mother's condition in detail as I had done at the drug store the night before, and he prepared for a house call alone, without a nurse. I carried his bag and led the way. His bag was rather heavy. It helped me believe he was a good doctor.

My mother was burning with fever. I couldn't tell if she was conscious of the doctor's presence. He placed his stethoscope on her chest and her back, rapped them, and looked into her eyes. I swallowed nervously, watching him.

He remained silent after the examination and gave my mother an injection in her emaciated buttock. While feigning to brush off dust from the shoes he had placed on the entryway step, I managed to ask. "Doctor, how is my mother? Will she be better soon?"

"I can't say anything definite yet, but she's in very serious condition."

"Please make my mother live."

"Are you her only family?"

"Yes. My brothers are in the army," I lied, trying to get his sympathy.

"That's too bad. I'll do my best. She needs one shot every four hours."

"What shall I do?"

"I'll come by every four hours. That way I can check her condition too."

"Doctor, thank you very much."

"Keep the room warm, and place some wet towels around so that the air won't get too dry. If she wants barley tea, give her as much as she can take."

The doctor came every four hours without fail and gave her a shot, but her condition didn't change. Fortunately, it didn't worsen either.

"Will you come during the night, too?" I asked as the doctor arrived for his fourth visit at 10:00 that night.

He examined her carefully and walked silently to the end of the wooden hall before he muttered, "I did my best."

"What? Isn't she getting better?"

"Tonight is critical." He looked at me with a sympathetic expression.

"Help us," I grabbed hold of his heavy bag, as if it were a magic bundle of miracles.

"Medically speaking, I've done the best I can. Now it depends on her will to live."

Her will to live, I thought, slowly releasing his bag.

"Don't be discouraged. As I said, we did our best, so let's trust her now. Don't worry. It might not be so bad tonight."

As the doctor said, she seemed to be all right that night. Toward dawn, her wheezing and panting subsided. A faint smile rippled over her face, as if she were having a pleasant dream. I could hear her mutter "Wook" and "Hyok." The expression on her face began to resemble the look she wore in her happy days. Was she with the dead in her dream now?

It looked like my mother was improving. Suddenly I was afraid that she might be getting better. She was happy now, but if she woke up, her spirit and her body had to be separated again.

Had the doctor been wrong? She was improving without the will to live, and I was more frightened of a life without the will to live than of death itself.

I went to my room to avoid her muttering. Knowing that she was recovering, I was assaulted by exhaustion. The windows grew light, and I was sucked into a deep swamp of sweet sleep. When I woke up, I didn't know what time it was but vaguely sensed it was broad daylight. I was stepping down to the kitchen to make some watery gruel for my mother when I collapsed on the wooden floor. My body ached everywhere.

"Now am I going to get sick?" I laughed bitterly, for I couldn't imagine being nursed by my mother. It was extremely quiet in her room.

I touched her forehead and felt a jolt of electricity. It was so cold. I opened her blouse to search for her heartbeat. Her heart seemed to beat faintly and then it seemed to have stopped altogether.

I flung open the gate and tried to run to the doctor's. My legs shook and they couldn't carry me as fast as I wanted. I was just barely scrambling out of Kyae-dong when I heard a voice.

"Oh, what do you know! I never dreamed I'd run into you here."

It was Tae-su's sister-in-law. I tried to pass her by.

"Kyong-a, look at me. Hee, hee, hee! I'm on my way to your house."

"Why?"

"What do you mean why? To help you tie the marriage knot. My brother-in-law wouldn't tell me where you live, but I pleaded with him and finally found out you live near here. But I wasn't sure if I could find the house. I never thought I'd run into you."

She giggled, showing her protruding teeth. She might have thought I was being shy. She looked coarse, her orange silk skirt drooping out from her heavy black overcoat, but she had an air of simplicity that drew people to her.

Suddenly I felt I needed her more than the doctor. It was intuition without any reason.

"Help me, please." I grabbed her large, coarse hand.

"With what?" she asked, stroking my hand with her leathery palm, as if she found me so wonderful. Her hand was rough, but its warmth comforted me in the cold weather.

"Please come with me. Someone is dying. My mother."

"What? What did you say?"

We galloped along, her hand in mine. My feet regained their strength as she pulled me along. She seemed to be asking one question after another, but I didn't listen. I just kept nodding or shaking my head.

Was it because we ran in from the outside? My mother's room was dark like a cave. I stood in a corner, blinking my eyes.

Without hesitation, she rushed to my mother and screamed in her ear, "Madam-In-Law! Madam-In-Law! Pull yourself up. Madam-In-Law!"

Her use of the term "Madam-In-Law" almost made me smile, and the tension that I had felt for the last few days disappeared. When my mother didn't answer, Tae-su's sister-in-law checked her pulse more expertly than a doctor and opened my mother's blouse to reveal her chest. She put her ear to the chest, lifted an eyelid, and announced solemnly, "She has passed away."

She pulled the white sheet over my mother's head.

"I was just a little too late."

Did she mean that she should have been there for my mother's last moment or did she mean she could have kept my mother alive? But her words were no less solemn than her previous announcement, "She has passed away." I was not sad. I was almost embarrassed about it. My mother had left her daughter's house, where she had been nervous and uncomfortable, to go to her sons' house where she would be more at home. That was all. All I felt was exhaustion. That was all.

Tae-su's sister-in-law, expertly and enthusiastically, took care of Madam-In-Law's funeral arrangements, as if she were born to the task.

She took off her gaudy orange skirt, and changing into my mother's grey one, she bustled about the business of arranging the funeral. I merely sat back and watched her, concerning myself with money matters alone at first, but soon I handed everything over to her.

She sent a telegram to my uncle in Pusan and notices to the painters and Tae-su. My relatives in Seoul, mostly elderly people, were notified. My grand-aunt on my father's side, who was over seventy years old, arrived first and by nightfall the painters came.

A place was prepared for the coffin, soup was bubbling in all the pots in the kitchen, and the wine jars were filled to the brim with milky white rice wine. A few people from the district office came for the wake, and some men I didn't know gathered and played flower cards in the outer quarters, which had been unused for so long.

The house was alive with the smell of cooking and high-pitched conversation. As I couldn't get used to the liveliness so close on the heels of my mother's death, I gazed through the northern window at the trees that seemed exempt from the sudden bustle.

So she has finally gone to my brothers' side, I thought. Was it because my mother had not clung to life? After her death there was not much trace of her left. In that house, where no precious objects of the deceased remained, Madam-In-Law, whom the deceased had never laid an eye on, whirled around in a frenzy of activities.

My mother was referred to as Madam-In-Law by a woman she had not known; the mother who was discussed that way couldn't be real.

My grand-aunt didn't ask her what kind of an in-law she was to us but began to call her Madam-In-Law out of convenience, and the men drinking in the outer quarters gradually caught on, calling out "Madam-In-Law! We need some more rice wine here. Madam-In-law, more stew here, please."

Without thinking, even I called her Madam-In-Law. I called her that the way my mother had called her housekeeper Sangju Woman. She was shocked and told me to call her Elder Sister-In-Law.

"What a disgrace! What if someone hears? You should call me Elder Sister-In-Law. Understand? Tsk, tsk, if I'd been a little bit earlier, I could have helped Madam-In-Law go happily. How must she have felt, dying before she could marry her daughter off?"

She sniffled, wiping what could have been tears or mucus from her nose with the hem of my mother's skirt. Sometimes she wept loudly, saying people would frown if loud wailing didn't drift out of a bereaved home. Her mournful weeping was so plaintive that it brought tears to people's eyes. I shed some tears myself, listening to her, but they were all because of her mourning, not because of my mother's death.

The funeral arrangements were made one by one. My mother had not used much of the living expenses my uncle had sent and had put away the money I had earned for buying rice, so we could arrange things without having to wait for my uncle to send money.

The only thing that was undecided was whether it would be a third-day funeral or a fifth-day funeral, and the next day was already the third day. This was because nobody had come up from Pusan yet. As the preparations had been made with a third-day funeral in mind, everyone had their eye on the gate.

Ock Hui-do came, his wife entering in front of him. The painters had come the day before and were the loudest mourners in the outer quarters, but Ock must have heard the news after them. I was awkward mourning for my mother, but they were equally clumsy with their condolences. Mrs. Ock particularly couldn't say anything but simply moved her lips, and soon her clear eyes were brimming with tears. Wearing a black skirt under a black serge traditional overcoat, she was paler than I. However, she didn't wail like Tae-su's sister-in-law. She just lifted her eyes toward the ceiling, removing her shawl which was made of the same material as her overcoat.

The narrow white collar of her overcoat and the elegant neck appeared. I flung myself at her. And I wailed for the first time, in a heartbroken way.

"How could this . . ." She sobbed.

I repressed my wailing and stammered, "It's all because of me. Because of me. That time. When I slept at your home, my mother waited for me in the alley all night long, trembling and shaking. She caught pneumonia in the cold and then . . ."

I resumed weeping.

"Oh, my goodness! So that's how it happened." She stroked my back. She didn't say anything, but I was comforted by her soft touch.

"So that's how it happened, tsk, tsk," Madam-In-law said, fighting back her tears and she dabbed her eyes with the tie around her waist.

With my confession, a whole different meaning was attached to my mother's death, and the women mourners sitting in my mother's room bowed their heads and didn't know what to say.

My wailing turned into a sniffling and finally stopped. Then I awoke from the fantasy that I had been responsible for my mother's death, as if I had been awakened from a dream. I didn't know whether I cried because of that outrageous thought or whether I made it up because I wanted to wail. Anyway, I had completely escaped that fantasy, but I was trapped. Why did I want to be blamed for another death?

No, that wouldn't do. That wouldn't do. It was that I had wanted to dream as I lay my head on the elegant shoulder of the long-necked woman. It was only a sad and beautiful, yet stupid fantasy.

Suddenly I hated my illusion and my habit of spinning fantasies. It was like the hatred that I had felt toward my mother when she was alive. As I had avoided and hated my mother, so would I avoid and hate my fantasies.

I pushed Mrs. Ock away firmly. Then I laughed cynically, surprising the people around me.

"Ha, ha! Did you really believe what I said? It's a lie. It's a complete lie. I just made it up. I didn't have anything to do with her death."

"Yes, yes, of course, you didn't," she said in a low voice filled with pity. Her face had a pinched look once more.

"In fact, my mother didn't pay any attention to me. Ha, ha!"

"We understand, so stop now. Of course, you didn't have anything to do with it. Madam-in-law's life was destined to be a short one, that's all," Tae-su's sister-in-law said in a voice bordering on a sob.

"Of course, of course. Poor thing!" My grand-aunt hugged my shoulders. I looked at her and knew that she did not believe me. She believed my first announcement.

This was true of everybody. Madam-In-Law, Mrs. Ock, my grand-aunt, great aunt, and other distant relatives all believed my first story and thought my last speech was a sad fabrication prompted by guilt.

All of them preferred a sad story and they seemed to want to make the only surviving family member a tragic character to be pitied. I screamed, saying it was not true. I screamed that I had nothing to do with my mother's death, but in their eyes I was becoming more and more responsible for it. I was imprisoned by the story I had made up, powerless to escape.

I rolled around on the floor, screaming that it was not true, but people looked at me even more sympathetically and cried more profusely, as if I had made them shed tears. I was helpless.

Weakened from insomnia and a lack of nourishment over the past few days, I was exhausted by my crying and struggling, so much like wrestling with the air. Madam-In-Law rushed to make red bean porridge and spoon-fed me despite my resistance.

"The bereaved is grieving too much. Tsk, tsk, what a pity!"

"Why shouldn't she? With her mother gone, she is all alone under the vast blue sky."

"Why is she alone? Her elder uncle is alive and well," retorted my grand-aunt in a proper voice. I lay exhausted, resigning myself to the fact that I was the bereaved who had grieved too much and ended up the cause of another death. I was made into another me at the will of others.

Unexpectedly, Mrs. Ock and Madam-In-Law knew each other well. But then it was unexpected only to me. To them, it was quite natural, considering that they were from the same hometown and that Ock and Tae-su's brother were bosom buddies. I couldn't get over how strange it was to watch them being so friendly together and having so much to say to each other.

Naturally, Mrs. Ock had to ask her friend why she was called Madam-In-Law and why she was taking care of everything for the bereaved family.

"You didn't know? Well, I suppose it's to be expected. Both your husband and my husband are so busy bringing home just enough to live on that they don't have time to get together. You know my brother-in-law, right? Yes, you're right. That small boy you remember is now old enough to be married. Hee, hee, hee! And he's promised his future to Kyong-a."

My grand-aunt, great aunt, and the others in the room whispered among themselves. My uncle and aunt who had come up to Seoul late that night heard the news, and everyone seemed to think it was all for the best. Nobody had to take responsibility for me any more.

From then on, Madam-In-Law was treated with the respect befitting a real madam-in-law. "In-Law-Elder" and "In-Law-Person" were titles used because of me. Fortunately, when they actually did bring up the subject of marriage, they stopped themselves, remembering that we were still in mourning. It looked as if a concrete plan would materialize soon enough. I watched and listened to it all, but I didn't have the energy to protest or explain. I had used up all my energy. I could explain later. I thought it could wait.

My mother was buried in the frozen ground next to my father and brothers. I had become the head of the old house. With the third rite after the funeral, my uncle would be able to feel he had done enough for my family if he could only settle on the matter of my situation. He couldn't leave a girl all alone in the old house, so he had two choices; he could either take me down to Pusan or ask Madam-In-Law to look after me. Madam-In-Law strongly favored the latter, and if I stayed with them, it would practically mean an engagement, a choice my uncle preferred. If he took me down to Pusan, it would be only a temporary solution.

In defiance of all their plans for me, I chose to live alone in the old house, continuing to make a living as a salesgirl. I even acquired a girl to help around the house. I was a little lonely and a little happy.

Ock Hui-do started painting portraits again and he was incredibly kind to me. If I asked him, he would accompany me down the lonely alley in Kyae-dong, and I would look up at the crumbled roof quietly, holding onto him as I walked, feeling neither lonely nor cold.

I could sometimes talk about the reason for the collapsed roof, as if telling an old story. I would ask him in to the wooden hall and let him sit in my father's chair while I made fragrant coffee in the kitchen.

Nothing could make me happier than that smile I glimpsed when I brought out his coffee. He would sit and look out at the trees through the north window, exhaling smoke from his cigarette.

"Do you like coffee or ginger tea?"

"Both."

"Both won't do."

"Your coffee is lovely. Your coffee is improving all the time."

He deftly shifted the topic of conversation, and I could see a pain, deeper than a broken heart, pass in his eyes. He tried to avoid even this small aspect of reality that would have to be resolved sooner or later. I didn't press for an answer.

This unresolved state, that vague and irresponsible state that provided me repose, was what I needed at that point. I was still tired. I had only been in mourning for a month.

Nonetheless, Madam-In-Law didn't want to give me that kind of respite. She frequented my house as if it were hers, taking care of the housekeeping and making a fuss over everything, never failing to bring up the subject of marriage.

"Now, think about it. I, a woman with five children, am having a hard time overseeing two households. What was I thinking? It's not two households. Three households it is because I need to take care of my brother-in-law, too. So consider my difficulties and hurry up with the wedding. I need to stay home and mind my own housekeeping."

I couldn't imagine her staying home, minding her own affairs. It was not that I couldn't think up some cruel remarks, such as pointing out that it was not I who made her manage three households but she herself who needed it. Yet I hesitated to say anything rude because I owed her so much for looking after my mother's funeral. Recently she had started calling me "Bride" instead of "Kyong-a." I wanted to be free from her now. The time of needing her had passed.

"Tae-su, do you have any free time today?"

"Of course." His face lit up because we hadn't had time together since the funeral.

"How about Utopia?" I offered.

"Okay." He grinned, whistling. For some time he had been trying to put on a somber face when he was with me, which embarrassed me.

"Will you buy me a cup of tea today?" I asked Ock Hui-do, walking home from work next to him as always.

"I want to drink the coffee Kyong-a makes."

"I want to drink the tea you buy me today," I said like a child and led him to Utopia.

Tae-su was already there. He was about to raise his hand when he spotted me, but he looked puzzled at the sight of Ock following me in.

Their conversation was sparse and dull. All they had in common was Tae-su's brother, but because he was such a boring man the conversation didn't lead in any lively direction.

Each of them, especially Tae-su, seemed to be wishing that the other would leave. Their awkward conversation came to an end.

"Mr. Hwang, I owe your sister-in-law so much for the things she has done for me," I said.

"Well, she only did what was expected, of course."

"Even when we don't mean anything special to each other?"

"What do you mean?"

"I'm grateful to your sister-in-law, but she seems to presume too much."

"I'm sorry. I understand. I know you're not in a state to think about those matters. I told her many times not to push so, but she's kind of inconsiderate."

He stopped, glanced at Mr. Ock, and said, "I apologize for my sister-in-law."

"I want to make something clear about us at this point."

"I said I'm sorry. Let's talk it over when we're alone," he said pointedly.

Ock stubbed out his cigarette in the ashtray and stood up clumsily.

"Sit down, please," I said firmly, pulling at his sleeve.

"It looks like I don't belong here."

"I arranged this meeting because I need both of you here."

Tae-su's face paled.

"Mr. Hwang! I want to make it clear that we are only friends."

"I know. For now."

"For now?"

"Yes, for now. I think we can leave some latitude for the future."

"We will always remain friends."

"Do you need a witness to make such an announcement?" He was still annoyed by Ock's presence.

"I invited him because it's necessary. Mr. Ock and I love each other."
I was embarrassed to see both of them startle at the same time and
avoided looking at either one. There wasn't any further reaction since I had
blurted it out as if I were talking about someone else.

"You're joking, right, Kyong-a?" Tae-su said rather calmly.

"It's true. Isn't it? Please tell him it's true," I urged Ock, in order to
prevent him from evading the question.

My reason for arranging a meeting was not only to be free of Madam-
In-Law, but also to force Ock to confront our problem head-on.

"Is it really true?" Tae-su asked Ock, seeing that he had remained silent.

"Yes, it's true."

I was relieved and triumphant, as if I had managed to climb up a tough
hill.

"How can you, how can you . . ."

Tae-su seemed to be more confused than indignant. When he recovered
from his surprise, in a relatively casual manner he lit a cigarette, something he
would normally refrain from doing in front of an elder.

"Kyong-a, what are you up to? It's so childish. Mr. Ock, you're old
enough to have more discretion. What are you going to do?" He was still in
shock and, as a result, he was neglecting the impact my announcement had on
himself. "Mr. Ock, it's a pity. How can you do this to Kyong-a? She's almost
like an orphan. You're supposed to help her find her way. You should think of
your wife, and what are you planning to do with the children?"

He stopped and sighed. He looked as if he couldn't go on with such
nonsense, but not because he didn't know what to say.

"I'm ashamed," Ock said.

"What's the use of being ashamed about a matter like this? I will have
to discuss this with your wife and try to come up with a solution to this
problem. I want to make it clear that I am not doing it for myself. I don't want
to solve my problem with your wife's help like some coward. First of all, I
want to prevent a tragedy from befalling all the people involved in this matter.
And I can't sit back and watch Kyong-a like this. She doesn't have anyone to
lean on. My problems come afterwards."

Ock Hui-do was driven into a corner, and even in my eyes Tae-su
looked more dignified.

"Please don't drag my wife into this. My wife thinks you and Kyong-a
are getting married soon."

"How can you be so shameless? What on earth do you intend to do?"
Tae-su swallowed as if he were holding down something even crueler, and the
flesh around his lips quivered.

I watched their battle with interest, intermittently looking up at the landscape on the wall next to me.

"I love my wife and my children," croaked Ock, squealing like a helpless animal driven into a corner. I stared at him with a gasp.

"What are you talking about? Please don't make me despise you completely. What if Kyong-a despises you? Consider your age. You have to say something believable that will make people understand."

"I don't expect others to understand me."

"Ha! You mean you're some high and mighty artist. You don't care about what the common people think."

"Please stop insulting me. I don't know how to talk in a fancy way. I just told you the truth."

"You've gone too far. If that's the truth, it's nauseating. If you're going to make excuses, try to come up with something logical."

"Logical? Is there logic when a man, delirious with thirst, sees an oasis?"

"What's your point? We're discussing the practical, urgent, and somewhat ugly matter concerning you, Kyong-a, and your wife, so why are you bringing up a bunch of abstractions to obscure everything?"

"Ah, how can I make you understand? The last few years have been so dark that they drove me to the verge of madness. The grey frustration and humiliations. I'm not talking about my family life, but my life as an artist. I thought I would suffocate. Was I a shameless dog because I lost my mind in the middle of a dull, frustrated life? Kyong-a was a colorful mirage to me. Was it really immoral to have a boyish longing for that mirage?"

"You sound like an enlightened monk. Have you forgotten about your body?"

"Why do you have to stab me where it hurts most? I am a human being, too. I was tormented because of that, but my only comfort now is that I didn't harm Kyong-a."

"You're pretty good at making excuses."

"I should have stopped seeing Kyong-a before being attacked like this. That was what I had planned to do, but I was too weak and Kyong-a's recent tragedy . . . well, maybe it was an excuse to delay, but anyway, my resolve was undermined because of Kyong-a's recent unhappiness. I felt justified and happy about sharing her loneliness. I'll leave now. It looks like I've spoken too much and I want to be alone."

"What am I supposed to do if you go?" I grabbed him, trying to pull him down to his chair.

"Kyong-a, you've got to let go of me. You don't love me. You were fantasizing about your father and brothers through me. You've got to be free from that fantasy now. You've got to be brave and learn to be alone. Be a brave orphan. You can do it. Accept the fact that you're alone, but don't be frightened. Start over as an orphan who is courageous and confident. You can start loving and dreaming all over again."

He left and the two of us were alone. Were we both orphans? Orphans have a hard time making friends with others. I stood first and we left the tea room together, but we deliberately chose separate paths.

I didn't know what to do after work. Misuk was walking ahead of me. I ran to her, breathless.

"Misuk, aren't you going to buy some mung bean pancakes today?"

"Well, mung bean pancakes, why on earth . . ."

She didn't finish her sentence, perhaps guessing that I was thinking of my mother. Why did everyone near me these days try to link me with my mother? I didn't even have the freedom to wear whatever expression I pleased.

"How about eating some mung bean pancakes together? My treat."

"Why mung bean pancakes of all things? Let's go to a bakery. My treat."

"No, let's make it mung bean pancakes. On me."

I forced her to go to the tavern where we had gone before. I pulled open the door and sat at a table made of a tin barrel turned upside down. I asked for an order of mung bean pancakes and stripped the paper wrapper off the wooden chopsticks.

"You're not going to eat here! I can't believe it!"

Misuk was flustered. It was early evening, so the bar was not very crowded. But all the drinkers' eyes were on us.

"Hey, I didn't know you came to places like this."

Tae-su, who had been drinking alone in a corner, approached me. I was surprised.

"Tae-su! Do you come to this kind of place often?"

"Me? I'm qualified enough. I've got two balls all right."

He was quite drunk. Misuk poked my side and flushed deeply.

"You can leave if you're that uncomfortable."

"Is that really all right?" she asked, visibly relieved, before fleeing.

Tae-su drank another bowl of milky white rice wine and stared at me with his dilated eyes. His eyes, once filled with youthful longing, were now bloodshot. They revealed nothing. He handed the bowl to me.

"Well, drink!"

Obeying his command, I gulped down the rice wine. It was sour, but all the same, it eased my tension.

"Have some food," he said, tearing off a piece of cold cake and pushing it toward my mouth as if he were going to stuff it in. I obediently ate it.

Then there was nothing to do. He didn't seem to enjoy drinking much. He didn't ask for more wine but simply watched me without blinking. Perhaps he was not inebriated at all.

"I never dreamed I'd run into you in a place like this," he said in a composed voice.

"What do you think a mirage is made of?" I asked calmly.

He lifted the corner of his lip in a smirk but ignored my question.

"Is it something like vapor?" I mumbled to myself.

I was so embarrassed by his staring that I unclasped my laced hands and offered him one over the tin barrel.

"You don't want to touch me?"

"What for?"

"Don't you want to see whether I'm made of vapor or flesh and bone?"

He squeezed my hand until it hurt. His grip grew stronger. I suppressed a scream and looked in his eyes with satisfaction as their dullness gradually turned to longing.

I was grateful to him for the first time for having a tangible desire for me. I wanted to experience more painful sensations than his grip would allow, the various forms of pain that people experienced because they had bodies. Through him I was confirming that I was a human being with a body and that it was a joy to have a body.

"You're so stubborn," he said, releasing my hand when I didn't cry out, even when he had squeezed it with all his might.

"Was that all the pain you can inflict on me?"

"I could have crushed you, but how can I . . ."

"Well, coward!"

I began to caress his hand. It was just the right size, large and trustworthy. What a blessing it was that humans had bodies!

"Do you still dream of a home where a boy with red cheeks lives?"

"What's wrong with that? A boy with red cheeks, a good wife, a fireplace with a simmering stew pot, a window with a curtain. Well, those things are so ordinary that you wouldn't be interested."

"My interest is piquing. Gradually."

"Gradually?"

"Yes, like they are being painted right in front of my eyes. Everything that's not a dream, everything that's not a vapor. I don't want to dream or be anyone's dream ever again. Never." I spoke forcefully and shut my eyes, leaning against him.

"Are you drunk after just one bowl of rice wine? Let's go. Everyone is staring at us."

"Yes, let's go."

I staggered up. I crossed the small tavern slowly, feeling the eyes on me, the eyes that seemed to note of what a scandalous scene this was for a girl to make. In reality, I was not drunk at all. How could anyone get drunk on one bowl of rice wine? But still it was fun to pretend to be. I shifted my weight to Tae-su, staggering wildly and walking in a curvy line when I could have easily walked straight. It was fun to watch Tae-su at his wits' end.

And so I staggered to the entrance of Kyae-dong. Then I straightened up and collected myself.

"Are you all right? I'm sorry. How could I have forced you to drink? I must have been drunk myself."

"What is it like to be drunk?"

"You don't know when you've just experienced it? A little dizzy and a little happy."

"Then it must be like going round and round where you stand."

"Could be."

"You go round and round when you're small and you learn to drink when you're grown up. People must be born with an innate inability to stand the boredom and tedium of being in a world that doesn't spin."

"Here we are. Can I come in?"

"What for?"

"How about offering me a cup of tea?"

"Is that all? Is that all you want?"

"Then are you going to offer me a meal or something?"

"Won't you hurt me? I mean, my body? Like you squeezed my hand a while back? Make it more painful this time. How about leaving a deep mark, so my body won't be floating around in a vapor any longer?"

I invited Tae-su into my room, into my home that was cozy, secret, and warm. He embraced me after I closed both the outer window and intricately latticed window. I was his.

Seventeen

It was a refreshing autumn morning. I silently brought coffee and the morning paper to my husband, who was still sleeping in our bedroom on the second floor. I drew the curtain, revealing the jade-green sky, and the bright light poured into the bedroom. It was deep autumn.

In the yard yellow ginkgo leaves were falling one by one. A wind must have been passing through, for small branches trembled suddenly, and the leaves fell in a dazzling array. It was as if the trees let out the cold wail of "ususu." I couldn't hear the sound because of the thick window pane. I wanted to hear it. It was like an uncontrollable thirst. I pushed back the steel security bars that covered the window and twisted and released the levers to open up the window wide.

The air outside was a bit colder, but the wind had already died down. I listened to the cold wail. Perhaps it was not coming from any tree but was an echo from deep inside of me. Another me that my husband Tae-su could not possess or inflict pain upon. Another me that he could not warm, no matter how hard he tried. Suddenly a heavy pain throbbed in a far corner of my heart.

"Close the window! I might catch a cold."

I pretended not to hear his irritated voice and waited for the wind to pass again. The trees shook and dropped their glittering gold pieces to the earth. Soft yet bristling, comforting yet sorrowful. The feeling of the carpet came back so vividly.

"I said shut the window!" he shouted, after he sneezed.

Was I too old to roll on that carpet now? Or was it that I had too many obligations weighing me down? A yellow scrap fluttered into the room. I finally shut the window and turned.

My husband shook off the ginkgo leaf that had landed like dust on his newspaper and glanced up at me.

That lusterless hair and those tired eyes. This thoroughly middle-aged man was such a stranger that I wanted to hide my face behind my palms.

"I can't believe you! Do you have to wake me up like this? Sunday is the only day that I get to sleep late."

"You're right." I smiled awkwardly and mumbled, "Yes, it's already Sunday," sitting down next to him.

"I'd like to have a nice rest, but Hoon will probably make a fuss if we don't take him somewhere."

He slowly drew me back to the level of the commonplace, the orbit of a wife. I picked up the ginkgo leaf and brought it to my nose, then glanced at the newspaper over his shoulder. In the cultural section, I caught the title, "Posthumous Show of the Works of the Late Ock Hui-do at S Gallery." In my youth, which seemed so long ago, I had wanted to place a fragrant crown on the name Ock Hui-do, but now it wore the crown "the late."

The part of me that had been throbbing heavily now felt a sharp pang. Nothing, no moans or groans, could be uttered or shared with anyone. It was a bitter sorrow of my own. I reminisced about the painful days, holding my breath, enduring the jabbing pain. I hadn't felt such pain since . . . It must have been the day the old house was torn down.

As soon as the wedding was over, my husband had insisted on tearing down the old house. His idea was that the dreary building was an incongruous structure in the vast space, with all its useless rooms that were beyond repair. He wanted to get rid of the old house and sell half the lot to raise the money to build a useful, sturdy Western-style house. It was a rational thing to do. There was no reason to disagree.

The demolition of the house was accomplished quickly. I watched the demolition with an unendurable pain. The elegant eaves and the high ridges were broken down to nothing more than old tiles, and the lofty crossbeams, well-worn beams, and shiny square wooden floor boards ended up in disorderly piles of wood scraps. The lattice windows, which had concealed numerous joys and sorrows, were loaded recklessly onto the wagons of wood-frame peddlers.

My clever husband struck sharp deals with the peddlers, shouting and wagging his finger over trifling amounts of money. Madam-In-Law, who was now my elder sister-in-law, patted me on the back, her teeth protruding as always, and said I was lucky to have found such a sensible husband.

Thus my old house was demolished and reduced to a handful of coins. The house that my father and brothers had dearly loved, the house to which my mother had clung until the day of her death, was torn asunder at the hand of a stranger whom they had never met.

But now that I think of it, perhaps the demolition had really begun on the day the hole was blasted in the servants' quarters, and once begun, had to be finished by someone. Still, I hated to think that I would never see the solemn old house wearing frost on its tiled roof in the morning sun.

I bravely endured that pain, even though it felt like my own body was being demolished. Perhaps I, too, wanted to be demolished and rebuilt.

Just as my husband designed a new house to contain our new life together, I wanted to demolish the "me" that didn't feel comfortable being his wife and create a "me" that would be.

A useful and sturdy, yet vulgar and boxlike house emerged from my husband's design. It all turned out as he intended, a bright, cozy house equipped with a modern kitchen and a garden that even had a lawn and small fountain.

I had insisted on leaving the ginkgo trees in the back yard. The huge trees hardly suited the new garden, but they provided cool shade, even if they threw a gloomy shadow over the new house.

At times I needed their light, their whispers, and their cries. In fact, maybe there was a secret corner somewhere inside me that hadn't been demolished.

"They are holding a posthumous show of Mr. Ock Hui-do's work."

My husband was reading that article. "What's the use of a posthumous show? He couldn't even get a one-man show when he was alive."

I sat in silence.

"Ha! I heard his paintings are very popular among foreigners, for some reason I don't understand."

Maybe he's getting paid back for painting all those damn mongrels, I thought.

"There's nothing more pathetic than praising someone after he dies. It must be the scheme of some art critic."

Figures you'd think up something like that.

"Well, I don't know. What's the use of art and things like that, anyway? The best thing is eat well and live comfortably while you're alive."

Of course, you can't understand. How could the likes of you understand? How could someone like you know that he had to live that way?

My husband dropped the newspaper and stretched languidly. Staring at his nostrils that looked like caves and at the hairs that appeared to fill them when he tilted his head back, I felt contempt and a momentary disgust.

"Daddy, are you up?" Hoon opened the door a crack and peeked in. When he saw his father sitting on the bed with his legs swinging, he ran up and threw himself into his arms. He didn't have an apple in his hand, but he had red cheeks. We not only had a boy with red cheeks, but also a girl with pretty eyes.

"Is your sister still sleeping?"

"She got up and washed her face. And she told me to go and see if you're awake."

"Why are you so curious about when I get up?"

"Well, you said you would take us to somewhere nice on Sunday."

"Did I say that?"

"You did, but now you're going to break your promise."

They made a nice picture. Father and son.

Sitting quietly, I sniffed the ginkgo leaf for a fragrance that wasn't there.

"Honey, it looks like we'll have to take the kids somewhere to save face. Where do you think we should go?"

"Well . . ."

Gazing at the quivering trees through the window, I thought I could hear "ususu."

"We can decide on a place later. How about getting ready first? Let's pack some lunch."

"Yes, yes, Mom. Make seaweed rolled rice, okay?" Hoon moved to my lap, perhaps disappointed at my sitting there with a bored expression. He bounced his chubby bottom up and down.

"Well, yes. I'll make delicious seaweed rice rolls, so you can have a good time with your father and sister."

"Honey, you mean you're not coming?"

"Well . . . no. I don't think so."

"You mean you want me to go alone with the kids like a widower? Nonsense!" His face said it was unthinkable.

"I have somewhere to go by myself."

"Where?"

"To Mr. Ock's art show."

My tone was firmer than necessary and Hoon's whining stopped. He shrank from the silence he couldn't fathom. For a moment, an awkward silence weighed over us.

But then, Hoon started bouncing his bottom up and down more vigorously on my lap.

"It's not fair! It's not fair! You messed up everything, Mom. It's not fair. Not fair!"

The healthy activity in my lap was refreshing. Hugging Hoon impulsively, I felt a surge of maternal love. However, I couldn't help it. I couldn't help my longing.

"Hoon, come here," my husband said in a low voice, yanking him onto his lap.

"I'll play with you today. We'll do lots of things. I'll do whatever you want."

My husband soothed the whimpering Hoon. I observed my husband's self-control in silence and went downstairs.

Breakfast was a quiet and sullen affair. I didn't know how my husband had placated them, but the children didn't say anything.

I paced under the ginkgo trees wearing the cobalt blue silk coat that I had recently had made. I felt sure that my bright outfit went perfectly with the yellow ginkgo leaves. The alley, once filled with old houses, was now bright and clean with newly built Western-style homes.

"I thought I'd go with you." My husband appeared beside me, an embarrassed expression on his face.

"What about the children?"

"I convinced them. They're good. They take after me, you know."

I wanted to be alone, but I was not cruel enough to shake him off now.

"What's wrong with watching the kids for a day?"

"I want to see his pictures, too."

"Is that all?"

"You look pretty today. It would be my pleasure to accompany you."

"Thank you."

S Gallery was on the third floor. We climbed up the stairs and were breathless by the time we got to the entrance to the gallery. I spotted one big naked tree through the door.

Without a glance at any other pictures, I walked directly to it, as if being sucked into it. There were two women under the tree, one standing with a baby on her back and the other striding along with a bundle on her head.

The old tree had seemed to be standing in the midst of a dry spell then, but now it was a naked tree. The old tree and the naked tree. They were similar and yet so different.

A naked tree trembling in the wind during the winter *kimchi* season, a naked tree that had just shed its last leaf. The spring was far, far away, but you could see the tree's feverish yearning for it, a yearning that could bring tears to people who gazed upon it.

The naked tree, standing bravely without a whimper, creating a perfect harmony with its numerous branches. The women passing by the tree in the chilly winter. The women saw only winter before their eyes, but the tree believed in spring, even if it was still far away.

The belief in spring. It was the belief in spring that made the tree look so brave. Suddenly I realized that Ock Hui-do himself was the naked tree. During the time when he was unfortunate, during those dark days when the whole population of his country was joyless, he lived like that tree.

I also realized that I was only a woman who had passed the naked tree, a woman who had paced around it, foolishly waiting for the green leaves that might soothe my tired body and soul.

"Tree and Women."

The picture already belonged to a foreigner.

I didn't know what to do after we left the Gallery S. I was rescued from my daze by my husband's presence. Or was I rescued from the exhaustion or disappointment you felt when you stepped off into a strange railroad station after a long journey?

"How about having a cup of tea somewhere and resting a bit?"

"How about over there?" I gestured to Toksu Palace right in front us. The ginkgo trees in the palace grounds were even more magnificent than ours at home. We sat on a bench under the ginkgo and surrendered ourselves to golden splashes. Children ran, lovers strolled, the bright autumn light streaming down on the faded grass seemed even warmer than in the spring.

"We should have brought the kids along."

My husband dragged me back to the world of common sense. A girl cried in fits and starts over a lost balloon. The red balloon flew far, far away into the cloudless sky. I finally lost the red speck and the sky was so dazzlingly blue that my eyes stung and tears welled up.

My husband must have been following the balloon with his eyes because his eyes were filled with the sky on his tilted face.

However, that was all. His eyes didn't have the youthful longing they used to have ten years before. That was not all. His eyes were devoid of any ambition or torment, save the worldly desire of possessing a woman and raising a family. He was a stranger to me once more, with a few strands of dry hair hanging over his furrowed brow.

In the distance high school students played badminton. The sound of the shuttle cock on the rackets was as sensual as a smack of the young couple's kiss.

Impulsively I showered my husband's furrowed brow with kisses, because I couldn't stand his being a stranger. Because I couldn't stand his being a stranger.

The shadows of the trees lengthened and the wind cried "ususu." The young trees around the fountain had shed their leaves and trembled pitifully now, rubbing each other's branches. But try as they might, they couldn't narrow the distance between them. They just stood quivering even after the wind had passed.

CORNELL EAST ASIA SERIES

To order, please contact the Cornell East Asia Series, East Asia Program, Cornell University, 140 Uris Hall, Ithaca, NY 14853-7601, USA; phone (607) 255-6222, fax (607) 255-1388, internet: kks3@cornell.edu.

The Naked Tree

A coming-of-age novel set during the Korean War, by Pak Wan-so, one of Korea's leading contemporary authors. The award-winning author of more than twenty novels, and numerous short stories and essays, Pak often deals with the themes of Korean War tragedies, middle class values, and women's issues. The novel is rich with scenes of cultural clashes, racial prejudices, and the kinds of misunderstandings that many American soldiers and Koreans experienced during the war years.

YU YOUNG-NAN has translated many English books into Korean and some Korean short stories and novels into English. She received the Korea Modern Literature Translation Award in 1991 and 1992.

12-95/.5M paper/.2M cloth/TS